The Lying Game

Tess Stimson

W F HOWES LTD

This large print edition published in 2013 by
W F Howes Ltd
Unit 4, Rearsby Business Park, Gaddesby Lane,
Rearsby, Leicester LE7 4YH

1 3 5 7 9 10 8 6 4 2

First published in the United Kingdom in 2013
by Pan Books

A CIP catalogue record for this book is available
from the British Library

ISBN 978 1 47123 965 6

Typeset by Palimpsest Book Production Limited,
Falkirk, Stirlingshire
Printed and bound by
CPI Group (UK) Ltd, Croydon, CR0 4YY

For my husband,

Erik.

You're still the one I run to.

THE TIMES

BIRTHS

LOCKWOOD
On 3rd February 1998, at the
Princess Eugenie Hospital, London,
to Harriet (née Morgan) and Oliver,
a beautiful daughter,
Florence Louise May.

CHAPTER 1

HARRIET

If my mother could see me now, Harriet thought wryly as she reached the top of the hillside and bent to cup her knees, panting. For the first twenty-six years of her life she had, like her parents and three younger sisters, been a sophisticated London urbanite: taxi-hailers and latte drinkers all, they'd had the shortcuts of the city inscribed on their hearts and considered the world beyond the M25 as alien and impenetrable as the Amazon jungle.

And then she'd met Oliver Lockwood and her life had been transformed in a way she never could have anticipated.

She straightened now and shaded her eyes to take in the spectacular view. The spring foliage hadn't yet started to come in, so she could see right through the bare trees to the valley below. On a distant slope opposite, ski trails poured down from the mountain summit like rivers of white paint. She couldn't believe how quiet it was, even for rural Vermont, a state one-fifth the size of England with a population of barely six hundred and fifty thousand. Up here, there was no thrum of traffic, no sirens, no planes passing overhead; just the faint whisper of the wind in the trees. Ironic that she'd moved four thousand miles across the ocean to New England and discovered an old England that hadn't existed since before she was born.

Tugging off her thick sheepskin gloves, she pulled out her phone and checked the time. No reception here, she noticed, slightly anxiously; not even one bar. Well, she wasn't going to be long. She'd seen what she needed to see. She'd be home soon, no harm done.

Nonetheless, she picked up her pace as she turned east along the ridgeline. She really shouldn't have come this far from home, not with Oliver a hundred miles away in Connecticut, where he was scouting out a possible location for their latest restaurant, leaving Harriet the parent on call. This wasn't just a nominal responsibility in the Lockwood household, given that their fifteen-year-old daughter Florence had had juvenile diabetes since she was six, and Charlie, at five the youngest of their three boys, had chronic asthma. Either she or Oliver found themselves being called out to one of their expensive private schools to deal with a medical crisis at least twice a month.

She turned at an orange flag marking the boundary of the eleven-acre property for sale and headed back downhill, picking her way carefully through a spider's web of transparent tubing that snaked from one sugar maple to another: there were miles of it

2

– literally two or three miles – weaving back and forth from tree to tree like a giant cat's cradle. It was March, so the tubes were full of maple sap. The clear liquid flowed down the mountain to the holding vats she'd seen earlier behind the small wooden sugar house at the foot of the hill, where it would be boiled off and turned into the familiar amber syrup.

Sugar house. How could Florence not be tempted by that? Even thinking the word made her mouth water. The first time she'd stood in a hot, steaming sugar shack twelve years ago, at the end of their first long, bitter Vermont winter, inhaling the mist of maple syrup as it rose from the evaporators, she thought she'd died and gone to heaven. There was nothing quite as sinfully delicious as the treat Vermonters called sugar-on-snow: hot maple syrup drizzled like lace onto a cup of fresh snow.

She ducked under a maple tube, careful not to dislodge it from the tree. Was it too much to hope that the sugar house would – she smiled inwardly at the pun – sweeten the pill for Florence? Maple syrup was her daughter's one weakness; perhaps the only preference the two of them shared. And lately they'd managed to get her diabetes under control, more or less. Enough for the odd cup of sugar-on-snow, anyway.

She sighed as she zipped her fleece higher against the chill wind coming off the mountain. Florence remained adamantly opposed to the idea of a weekend cabin – 'It's bad enough,' she'd said furiously, 'having to live in Hicksville when I could be in London, without being dragged off to some stupid cabin in the middle of nowhere with three disgusting brothers every weekend' – and Harriet knew that no amount of maple syrup was going to change her daughter's mind.

Sometimes she couldn't help feeling a little cheated. Four children and only one girl, a daughter so unlike herself it was hard to believe they were related. 'I know the feeling,' her mother Sophie had told her briskly when she'd ventured to raise the topic during her visit home to London the previous summer. 'If you hadn't been born at home, I'd have thought they'd switched you at the hospital. Look at your sisters – two in fashion and one in broadcasting, not a car between them, not one of them further away from us than SW6. And then there's you. Half a world away, only happy when you're sorting out somebody's crisis. I swear the only time I ever saw you smile as a child was when we took you to Glastonbury and the tent collapsed and we all had to sleep out in the open in the middle of a muddy field.'

Florence didn't even look like Harriet. She took after Oliver, all glowing caramel skin and blonde health and vitality with the same vivid blue eyes, whereas Harriet and the boys were pale and dark and slender. Harriet found it impossible to hold a meaningful conversation with her daughter; they simply didn't know what to say to each other. And it had nothing to do with her being a teenager, despite what Oliver said. Of course she took it personally! What mother wouldn't? The truth was, Harriet had *never* known what to say to her.

In the beginning, when Florence, her first child, was born and she'd struggled with the shock of motherhood and this tiny, screaming, red-faced package of demands, she'd thought her discomfort was just a question of it all being so *new*, so different, so completely unlike anything she'd done before. Even though Oliver had been just as new to it all and yet seemed able to tell the difference between a hungry cry and a tired one as easily as separating apples from oranges.

Then she'd got the hang of things and developed an efficient routine, telling herself anxiously that it was just as commendable to be a good mother as a natural one, whatever *that* was – but Florence had still looked at her with the distant, quizzical blue gaze of a stranger, clearly waiting for something Harriet simply hadn't known how to give.

She loved her daughter; there was no question of *that*. She'd have walked over hot coals for Florence from the second she heard her first cry. But there was never any real connection between them. Right from the beginning, they were almost painfully polite with one another. Harriet would crouch down on the floor to play with the blocks Florence was building, and the little girl would simply stop what she was doing and wait patiently for her mother to finish before resuming on her own.

But when Florence played with her father, she giggled and knocked over his tower and handed him bricks. Which meant that the problem must be *her* fault. She obviously lacked some crucial maternal instinct. She'd failed at the most important thing she'd ever attempted, and she'd had no idea what to do to put it right.

So she'd retreated into what she *did* know how to do. While Oliver had stayed at home and brainstormed ideas for Play-Doh and finger foods, she'd thrown herself back into work, using her PR skills to take their fledgling sandwich business so far so fast that America had quickly become their logical next step.

And then she'd found herself pregnant again. It hadn't been planned, of course; Oliver had been very keen to have a second child, but privately she'd been terrified of the idea, thinking it akin to throwing good money after bad. How-ever, things couldn't have been more different this time around. The bond between her and baby Samuel had been instant and profound, and for the first time she'd realized exactly what she and Florence were missing. It had been the same with George four years later, and Charlie three years after that. She'd found mothering her sons as easy as breathing. It was only with her daughter that she'd failed.

Slipping slightly in the slushy snow, Harriet reached the bottom of the hill and took a few more photos on her phone for Oliver. She already knew this piece of land was perfect: just an hour away from Burlington, it was rural enough to feed into his rose-tinted need for the full New England experience, but sufficiently proximate to town-maintained roads and electricity pylons to make building a cabin financially viable. It was Oliver's dream, really, the cabin, not hers, but over the years she'd learned that if she left things to him, they would never happen. He specialized in dreams; she was the one who made them reality.

In some ways, it made them the perfect team. She didn't have an ounce of flair or vision herself, but she'd always known exactly how to make the most of his, turning his off-the-grid idea for a green fast-food chain into a successful international business. She could forgive him a little hopeless dreaminess; these days, it was even part of why she loved him.

She knew how lucky she was to have such a good marriage, such a *happy* marriage. Among her half-dozen closest girlfriends, she was the only one without a divorce under her belt. She trusted Oliver implicitly. Even after sixteen years together and four children, he was still her lover, her rock and her best friend − the person she turned to first thing in the morning and last thing at night. With him, she knew what it was to be cherished. He brought her tea in bed in the morning, he rubbed her feet when she was tired, he got up in the night to look after Charlie if he had one of his asthma attacks because he knew how much she needed her sleep. These were the things that mattered, not flowers on their anniversary or expensive jewellery at Christmas – though Oliver gave her those things too. Her mother reminded her frequently that she was blessed, but really Harriet didn't need to be told.

She was just climbing into her ancient Land Cruiser when her phone rang. With a slight sigh, Harriet tugged off her gloves again and answered it.

'This is Denise at Fletcher Allen Hospital,' the woman said. 'Is that Mrs Lockwood?' Harriet chilled. *Not Charlie*, she begged instinctively. *Not again*. Their last trip to the ER, a week before Christmas, had frightened her so badly she hadn't slept for a week afterwards. She didn't think there was anything worse than watching your child literally fighting for every breath. Florence's diabetic lows she'd learned to cope with. A juice box, some glucose tablets, and she was usually fine. She had cross-country practice today; knowing Florence, she'd probably forgotten to load up on carbs first and her sugar had dipped. Going on past experience, by the time Harriet reached the hospital, she'd be up and about and itching to get back to her friends.

She loved all her children equally, of course, but if she had to choose, if she really *had* to choose, it was better that Florence had a crisis than Charlie.

Instantly, she felt guilty. *Only because Charlie is so much sicker*, she amended quickly. She could never actually *choose* between her children. She might not understand Florence the way she understood the boys, but she'd loved her for fifteen years – loved her passionately – and nothing would ever change that.

She took a deep breath. 'Harriet Lockwood here,' she said, and waited.

CHAPTER 2

FLORENCE

Florence's day hadn't started well. It rarely did, since Mom insisted on eating breakfast with her (her mother was somehow convinced eating breakfast together would stop her from getting pregnant or smoking or becoming a Republican or whatever it was her mother was so scared of) and then silently begrudged her every tiny morsel she put in her mouth. It wasn't Florence's fault she was fat. Not everyone could be a perfect size zero like her mother.

They sat in silence at the breakfast table, since Dad had already left to take the boys to their school, and she chomped her way through her second bagel, watching her mother try hard not to notice.

'I thought I'd come and watch you run this afternoon,' Mom said suddenly.

She looked up, alarmed. 'It's only a practice,' she said. 'Not a meet.'

'I know. But it's been ages since I came to cheer you on, and one of my suppliers cancelled on me, so I've got a couple of hours spare later.' She smiled brightly. 'I thought it would be nice if we spent some time together.'

Sometimes Florence wished her mother would just stop *trying*. It would be so much easier on both of them.

She ducked her head again, her ash-blonde hair tumbling across her face. It wasn't that she didn't like talking to her mother, exactly. As parents went, Mom was OK: she didn't stick her with tons of chores or demand to know where she was every minute of the day. But Mom was always worrying about her diabetes, checking up on her, asking her questions, making such a big deal about it all, and sometimes she just wanted to *forget*. She never knew how to respond to Mom's earnest attempts to be her friend. She never had. Mom always seemed to be looking for something *more* from her, though she had no idea what that might be. So, as usual when she didn't know what to say to her mother, she said nothing.

'I don't have to come if you don't want me to,' Mom said finally in a tone that made Florence squirm with guilt. 'It was just an idea.'

'I told you,' she muttered, flushing. 'There's no point. It's just a practice.'

'Yes, of course.' She stood and briskly started to stack the dishwasher. 'Maybe I'll go check out some land instead.'

Florence scowled. What*ever*. Bad enough that she was stuck in this boring little town in this boring dead-end state without spending her week-ends trapped in a stupid cabin a million miles from anywhere. She still didn't see why her parents couldn't have stayed in London. At least then she might have had a *life*.

Normally she'd have dumped her woes on her best friend Amy when she got to school and felt a whole lot better, but last week they'd fallen out over Matt Shaw (who Amy hadn't even noticed till Florence told her she liked him), and the cherry on the cake? Her period had just started. So she wasn't exactly in the mood for algebra and Spanish, and even less in the mood for a cross-country run. Which meant that when it came to it that afternoon, she found herself dawdling alone in a corner of the changing room, hanging back till everyone else had left.

She wasn't much of a runner at the best of times. Or a swimmer, or a basketball player, or a skier. She took after Dad: she was built for comfort, not speed, as her grandmother had once put it bluntly. There was no euphemism for 'fat' Florence hadn't heard: *big-boned, statuesque, Amazonian.* Mom kept saying she'd grow into herself, whatever that meant, but frankly, at five-foot-ten in her bare (size nine) feet, her breasts spilling from their D-cups, she'd grown quite enough already, thank you very much. Next to Mom, petite and boyish and elegantly flat-chested, she felt like an elephant. Poor Mom. Three boys and one daughter, and it had to be the girl who was built like a quarterback.

She caught up with the rest of the class, already streaming across the playing fields to the woods at the rear of the school, and fell into a steady pace around the middle of the pack where no one would notice her. She usually managed to just about hold her own. Vermont, liberal and hippy and green in every sense of the word, was a state where everyone was active and sporty, where no one drove if they could cycle, or cycled if they could walk. She'd long since realized that if you couldn't beat them you might as well join them, at least if you wanted to have friends, so she'd picked the lesser of many evils and opted to make cross-country running her *thing*, so she could at least go at her own pace and stop for a rest if she had to.

Even she had to admit it was a beautiful day to be in the woods. The air was crisp and cold, the sky so bright a blue it hurt. Beneath the trees, purple and white crocuses spiked through thinning patches of snow. She wasn't puffing as much as usual, either, and for once she didn't have a stitch. Maybe Mom was right; perhaps she *was* fitter than she thought.

'Left,' a male voice said behind her.

Automatically, Florence moved out of the runner's way. Matt Shaw strode easily to the front of the field – he must've been late to class or he'd have headed the pack to begin with – and she watched him casually fall into step beside Amy and Olivia, her heart twisting with misery. Florence was only too aware he didn't even know she existed. But she could dream.

She didn't see the patch of ice until it was too late.

She'd tripped and fallen loads of times on cross-country runs. Everybody did; it went with the territory. If you didn't want the rest of the team to think you were totally lame, you just picked yourself up and kept going. Last year, Matt had fallen and actually broken his wrist, but he'd got up and kept running and never said anything about how much it had hurt till the end of the cross-country meet, after their team had won. Half the girls in her class had a crush on him after that.

One moment she was running, and the next the ground had gone from under her. She landed hard and awkwardly on her butt, a sharp, stabbing pain radiating down her left leg. For a moment, as she lay winded on the narrow path, she didn't think she was hurt. Even when she pushed herself up on her elbows and looked down, and saw the blood spreading wetly between her thighs, she simply assumed it was her period, that her pad had leaked: *Oh, God,* she panicked, *everyone – Matt – will see!*

But almost immediately she realized that of course it couldn't be that – the pain was far too intense, there was way too much blood. And then suddenly everything started to blur. It was if she was at the bottom of a swimming pool, looking up through the water at a shimmer of white faces. Their mouths were moving, but all she heard was a distant rumble; she could only guess at the words. *Tourniquet,* she thought she heard, and *broken glass* and then, frighteningly, *femoral artery.* Mrs Caisse, the cross-country coach, pulled the cord from her tracksuit pants, and she watched, too shocked to speak, as her teacher struggled to tie it around Florence's thigh. Something – yes, broken glass – had sliced straight through her thick grey winter jogging bottoms; a bright geyser of crimson blood spurted from her leg, soaking her clothes and the ground and Mrs Caisse. She couldn't quite believe she had so much blood in her. So much blood coming *out* of her, and yet she was still alive.

She started to shiver, suddenly colder than she'd ever been in her life. Mrs Caisse told her she'd called 911, she just had to hang on in there, she was going to be fine. Florence could tell by the fear in her eyes she was lying.

The other girls – and even some of the boys – were crying. Several of them had thrown up in the bushes. Amy and Matt were holding hands, and she felt a flash of irritation that her drama had brought them together. *This is ridiculous*, she thought. *No one ever dies cross-country running.*

And then: *I want my Mom.*

And then nothing.

CHAPTER 3

HARRIET

I *didn't mean it*, Harriet begged, her hands shaking on the wheel. *I didn't mean to choose Florence, I didn't mean it. Oh God, please let her be all right.*

She fought the impulse to jump the red light in front of her and cut across three lanes of traffic into the hospital forecourt. She'd never performed an illegal U-turn or gone more than five miles over the speed limit in her life, but she'd just made the fifty-five minute journey back to Burlington in forty minutes and was beginning to regard red lights as decorative rather than functional.

Change, goddammit!

The second she had a green light, she swung right. Not bothering to park, she simply abandoned the car at a forty-five-degree angle outside the ER, hammering frantically on the automatic glass doors even as they were opening.

'My daughter's been in an accident!' she cried, bursting into the lobby. 'Florence Lockwood?'

'Just a moment,' the receptionist said calmly, reaching for her keyboard.

Harriet strained across the counter, trying to see

16

the woman's screen. 'She goes to Rice High School. She was in some sort of cross-country accident—'

'Florence Lockwood, yes. If you wouldn't mind waiting, someone will be out to see you.'

'Is she all right?'

'Ma'am? Ma'am, if you'd just calm down—'

'I need to be with her! For heaven's sake, she's only fifteen!'

'Absolutely. Someone will be right out.'

With a supreme effort, Harriet reined in her frustration, anxiously clipping and unclipping her hair from its plastic slide as she paced the lobby. *A serious accident*, the nurse had said on the phone. What kind of serious accident could happen to your child on a cross-country run, for God's sake? A broken ankle, yes, a twisted knee or sprained wrist. Concussion, even, if she fell and hit her head on a rock. But none of those scenarios could be classified as a serious accident, could they? Why couldn't they just *tell* her what had happened? Why all this eggshell-treading circumspection? Unless she was . . . unless she was . . .

No. Don't even go there.

'Mrs Lockwood?'

She spun round as a nurse with tired eyes and a patient smile called her name. 'Can I see Florence now?' she demanded.

Harriet had no way of knowing it, but when she was anxious or upset, her cool English accent became even more clipped and patrician. To those who didn't know her, it could be mistaken for arrogance.

The nurse glanced at her clipboard. 'Would you just mind confirming Florence's date of birth for me?'

'Two, three, ninety-eight. Now can—'

'Thank you. If you'd like to come with me, Mrs Lockwood.'

She caught at the woman's arm as she pushed open a pair of flapping plastic doors. 'Please. Can you just tell me if she's OK?'

'I'm sorry, Mrs Lockwood,' the nurse said, gently freeing herself. 'Doctor Murray will be with you in just a moment.'

The woman showed her into a small waiting room decorated in soft shades of taupe and teal. Harriet's anxiety intensified. She'd been to the ER often enough to know they only took relatives to private waiting rooms when it was bad. Very bad.

'Oh God,' Harriet gasped. Suddenly she couldn't feel her legs. 'She's dead, isn't she?'

'No, Mrs Lockwood, of course she's not dead,' the nurse said quickly.

'But it's bad?'

'The doctor is with her now. He'll be able to give you all the details as soon as he's done. I really can't tell you any more than that. I'm so sorry.'

Harriet nodded mutely as she sank onto the sofa. Her mind was whirling with so many what-ifs she was dizzy. She literally couldn't focus – the bland pictures on the wall swam in and out of her vision. By the time the doctor appeared less than five minutes later, she was on the verge of vomiting with fear.

'Stephen Murray,' he said, extending a bony wrist too long for his white coat. 'Please, no need to get up.'

'Can you just spit it out? I'm sorry, but no one has told me anything, and I don't think I can stand it much longer.'

'Of course. Well, the good news is that Florence is stable now.'

Harriet burst into tears.

Without missing a beat, the doctor handed her a box of tissues and perched on the arm of the sofa, displaying two inches of pale, hairy shin between his sock and the hem of his grey wool trousers. 'She's a lucky girl, Mrs Lockwood. Given the nature of her injury, things could have been a great deal more serious. As it is, I'm afraid she's still quite traumatized—'

'What *is* the nature of her injury?'

'I'm sorry?'

'No one,' Harriet said through gritted teeth, 'has actually told me what happened.'

'I'm sorry. I thought someone had explained. Your daughter slipped when she was out running and fell onto some broken glass – a beer bottle, I think – which cut deep into her inner thigh, slicing through her femoral artery. One of those freak, million-to-one accidents. Fortunately, her teacher was able to administer a very effective tourniquet that most certainly saved her life.'

Her mouth was suddenly so dry she could barely swallow. *Saved her life*. Florence had nearly died today. Her daughter had nearly *died*.

'I don't understand,' she said blankly.

He took her confusion literally. 'The body has two femoral arteries that branch off from about mid-abdomen into each thigh.' He sketched a quick diagram on the back of his folder. 'They're among the body's biggest vessels, about the diameter of my pinkie finger in the groin and upper thigh. Stopping blood loss in that region is extremely challenging if the wound is close to the groin, as it's hard to put a tourniquet around it. Without one, there's quick, massive blood loss: you can lose all the blood in your whole body in around five minutes.'

Harriet put her head on her knees, fighting the urge to be sick again.

'Mrs Lockwood, your daughter was very lucky,' the doctor said firmly. 'The cut was low enough that her coach was able to administer a tourniquet before her blood pressure fell too low. She sustained significant blood loss, but neither her brain nor her body organs have been in any way compromised.'

Relief flooded her body like a warm bath. 'She's going to be OK?'

'She should make a full recovery. Obviously she's going to be tired and weak for a while. We had to give her a significant amount of blood, and then there's the shock, of course. I see from her file she's diabetic – we'll have to keep a close eye on her sugar levels. But she's young and strong, and of course we've given her a tetanus booster. She'll be up and about in no time.'

'Can I see her now?'

'Of course. She may seem a bit confused or sleepy, but that's just the pain meds. They'll wear off within the next four to six hours. I'll take you to her now.'

Florence was sleeping when the doctor showed Harriet into a small private room. A nurse looked up from her position at the end of Florence's bed, where she was writing something in her chart.

'It looks worse than it is.' She smiled.

Harriet carefully took her daughter's hand, mindful of the wires and drips connecting her to various monitors and IVs. The sheets were tented over her left leg, which was propped up on several pillows, making her look strangely small in the hospital bed. She was suddenly reminded of the first time she sat vigil by her daughter's bed, a few weeks after Florence's sixth birthday. The morning of that day, she'd seemed a little tired and peaky, and Harriet had taken her to the doctor, expecting to be sent home with antibiotics and instructions to make sure Florence drank plenty of fluids. The next thing she knew, her daughter had been rushed to the paediatric intensive care unit in the midst of what turned out to be a full-blown diabetic crisis.

Even though the doctors had repeatedly told them there was no way of knowing why some children developed juvenile diabetes, that science still couldn't say whether it was triggered by hereditary or environmental factors or a mixture of both, Harriet hadn't been able to help but feel responsible. Florence had *her* genes, after all. She knew deep down that somehow it must be her fault.

Instead of bringing them closer, Florence's diabetes had driven yet another wedge between them. She knew her daughter hated it when she made a fuss, but how could she *not* worry? She fretted over every carb Florence ate, not because she gave a damn about her weight – Florence was perfect as she was, beautiful, a Fifties pin-up in the making – but because she was terrified the diabetes would spin out of control, become unmanageable and brittle. The doctors had warned her what could happen if they didn't keep her sugar levels in check: blindness, kidney failure, nerve damage, even death. But she couldn't tell Florence that, of course. Part of her job as a mother was protecting her daughter from the truth. She just wished she didn't have to pay such a high price for her silence.

'Here,' the nurse said, moving a plastic chair towards her. 'You look like you need to sit down.'

Harriet gazed at her child, suffused not just with love and tenderness, but by a familiar feeling, a feeling unique to her relationship with Florence: guilt.

She hadn't wished this on her daughter. Of course not. Never in a million years would she have wanted something like this to happen.

But.

But. In her heart, she'd put Charlie first. Hadn't she?

Florence stirred suddenly and opened her eyes. 'Sorry,' she said, through thick, dry lips. She licked them and tried again, louder this time. 'Sorry, Mom.'

'You've got nothing to be sorry for,' Harriet said fiercely.

'I wish you'd been here,' Florence murmured sleepily.

Guilt again, thick and treacherous. 'I wish I had been, too.'

'Did you call Daddy?'

'Of course. He's on his way back from Hartford now. He should be here any minute. He sends his love.' She squeezed Florence's hand, but her daughter didn't respond, and, after a moment, she released her. 'There's no need to worry, darling. Everything's going to be fine.'

She heard the fake cheerleader note in her voice and knew Florence could too.

'How are you feeling?' she asked helplessly.

'Bit tired.'

'Of course.'

The silence between them filled the room. If

it were little Charlie in the bed, or George or Sam, she'd have known what to do, what to say. She'd have scooped them up in her arms, regardless of all those wires, and held close what she'd almost lost.

But with Florence, she was at a loss. They were two strangers thrown together by genes and happenstance.

'Flo-Mo! Baby, how're you doing?' Oliver crossed the room in two strides and enveloped his daughter in a tight hug. 'You had me worried witless, you know that?'

'Daddy!'

He parked himself on the bed. 'Jesus, will you take a look at all this,' he said, taking in the bank of monitors. 'It's like the bloody Starship Enterprise.'

Already the colour was coming back into Florence's cheeks. Oliver had this effect on every woman he met, from his daughter to the checkout girls at the supermarket. He simply lit up a room. It wasn't that he was particularly good-looking; a rumpled, crumpled bear of a man with two-day-old greying stubble and overlong dark blond hair, he was more Gerard Depardieu than Robert Redford, though he'd always melted Harriet's knees, from the first moment she'd walked into the cupboard that had passed for his office and explained how she was going to transform his nascent business into an international empire. It was the twinkle in his creased blue eyes, the boyish charm in his wide, uneven smile. He made you feel like the most important person in the world when he was talking to you because, for that moment, to him you were.

'So, Flo-Mo. What's up?' Oliver asked.

'I nearly *died*,' Florence said.

'So I hear.' He rumpled her hair and she grimaced, but didn't pull away. 'Cross-country running as a dangerous sport? Flo-Mo, what are you like?'

Florence tossed her head to clear her fringe from her eyes. It was a gesture she'd inherited from her father; moments later, Oliver did exactly the same thing.

'They had to give me three pints of blood,' she told him, a faint note of pride entering her voice. 'The doctor said I was, like, bleeding out or something. They had to do a blood test to see which type I am, which is A-plus, and—'

'A-*positive*,' Harriet corrected automatically, then kicked herself.

Florence ignored her. 'And I got to go in an ambulance and they put the sirens on, and we totally went down Main Street the wrong way. The boys will be so jealous.'

Oliver laughed. 'You're not kidding. *I'm* jealous.'

Watching them together, father and daughter, heads touching, reflecting an identical smile back at one another, Harriet felt a familiar sense of exclusion. She was the one who'd carried Florence inside her for nine months, who'd literally made her from scratch; and yet it was Oliver to whom Florence turned, Oliver who shared a bond that went beyond flesh and blood. It wasn't that she resented the closeness between her husband and her daughter; far from it. It warmed her heart. She just wished that, for once, she could share it.

'The doctor said if we're lucky, it won't scar too badly,' Harriet murmured, drawing Oliver to one side. 'The cut wasn't terribly long, but it was deep. He's giving her some kind of cosmetic tape to put over the stitches once they come out, the kind the plastic surgeons use to try to prevent scars becoming keloid.'

'Special tape, huh?' Oliver said, turning to tweak Florence's good toes.

'The doctor said I'd be in a bikini by Spring Break,' Florence said lightly. Only the slight tremor in her voice gave her away. 'He reckons you'll hardly be able to see it in a year.'

'That's my girl.' He dropped a kiss on her forehead. 'I know you're upset to be off the cross-country team, but you'll be back up and about before you know it. No real harm done in the end, eh?'

Florence shook her head. Harriet saw how close she was to tears. No wonder, after all she'd been through today.

She pulled her into a hug, and for once Florence didn't seem to mind. 'It's going to be fine,' she soothed, stroking her daughter's fair hair. 'Shhh. It's all going to be fine.'

She'd move heaven and earth to make sure it was.

Subject: Our daughter
Date: 09/02/1998 11:58:36 P.M.
From: sandfairy@gmail.com
To: Patrick.James@INN.com

Patrick – I thought you should know you have a baby daughter. She was born on 3rd February at 2 a.m., weighing 8lbs exactly. I've called her Nell, after my mother.

I know you said you didn't want to know anything about her, but I'm sure once you see her, you'll feel differently. She looks so like you! She's still a bit red and crumpled (I remember you once said all babies look like Churchill) but you can already see how beautiful she's going to be. She has such long dark lashes! You can't see it in the photo, but her eyes are grey right now, like mine. Maybe they'll turn brown like yours when she gets a bit older.

I wish you'd been there when she was born. I won't bore you with the gruesome details, but I had to have an emergency Caesarean, which meant she spent her first day with strangers. But the nurses said she didn't cry at all, which is more than you can say for me when I finally came round. I only got out of hospital this morning.

I'm so sorry about what I said. I didn't mean it. I never would've told your wife, you know that. I was just upset about you not wanting the baby, that's all. Please, can't we put the past behind us and at least try to be friends, for Nell's sake?

Before you ask, this has nothing to do with money. I don't want anything. I've given up my studio in Camden and moved into the flat above Born-Again Vintage, so I can look after

Nell and work in the shop at the same time. We'll be fine. I just want you to be a part of her life, even if it's only a small part. Doesn't she deserve a daddy, too?

I can't put you on her birth certificate unless you come with me to register her. I know you're in Bosnia now, but we've still got five weeks. Please, can't you do that for her, at least?

My mobile number hasn't changed, and you can always reach me by email. I wish you'd get back in touch, even if it's just as friends.

Always yours

Zoey xxx

CHAPTER 4

ZOEY

There was a *reason* no one wrote about London in the spring, Zoey thought as she dashed through the rain from one dripping shop awning to another. There was absolutely nothing romantic about damp shoes and wet hair, especially when you already had the beginnings of a cold. Perhaps if she'd been gazing at a blurry view of the Eiffel Tower through the steamy window of a warm café, her chapped hands wrapped round a *chocolat chaud*, she might feel differently. Islington had an undoubted charm in the summer, when the sun was out and Camden Passage was crammed with market stalls selling everything from Bakelite telephones to amber bangles, and the pavements outside every bistro and café were crowded with chairs and tables. But in the grey of winter, or on a damp, dull spring day like this, north London had *nothing* to recommend it. Oh, what she wouldn't give to be in Paris right now, the hot buttery flakes of a fresh croissant melting like snowflakes on her tongue; or maybe a *croque monsieur* (which always sounded so much more tempting than 'hot ham-and-cheese sandwich'), with butter and melted Emmental oozing down its sides – oh yes, she could almost *taste* it. Clearly she should never have gone without breakfast, not when she always seemed to forget lunch; she was *ravenous* now. But it was hard to feel hungry at seven o'clock in the morning when all you'd done was get out of bed and stumble downstairs. It wasn't as if she had to *walk* to work . . .

'Mum!'

Zoey started. 'Nell! Darling! Where did you spring from?'

'I came looking for *you*,' Nell said crossly, shaking out her purple umbrella. 'I knew you'd get lost.'

'I'm not lost,' Zoey protested. 'Look, there's the library. I know where I am. Why would you think I was lost?'

'You're going the wrong way, for a start.' She tucked her arm into her mother's. 'Come on, we don't want to be the last ones there or we'll get stuck at the back where you can't see Angel, and then you won't be able to follow his moves.'

'Who's Angel?'

'Mu-um! I told you before. He's the Zumba instructor. He's Brazilian,' she added, a little too carelessly.

Zoey might be vague in many respects, but when it came to her fifteen-year-old daughter, she didn't miss a thing. 'Cute, is he?' she asked, nudging Nell with a smile.

'Maybe,' Nell said, blushing furiously.

'I can't think why I agreed to this,' Zoey complained as they dashed back out into the rain, huddling together under Nell's umbrella.

'Because you're thirty-nine, not eighty-nine, and it's time you got out a bit more and had some fun,' Nell retorted. 'Anyway, if you and Richard are going to France on that cycling holiday this summer, you need to get fit.'

She had a point, Zoey thought ruefully. In her current shape, she couldn't cycle to the end of the road, never mind around Provence. Quite how she'd allowed Richard to talk her into this madness she couldn't imagine. Her recipe for the perfect holiday involved a sunlounger by a pool somewhere hot, with a cocktail in one hand and the latest Joanna Trollope in the other. But this year Nell had pleaded to be allowed to go to Cornwall with her best friend Teri and her family, and Richard had really wanted to try something different, something *grown-up*, he'd said, since they didn't have to put themselves through yet another child-friendly trip to Florida or the Costa Brava. France, he'd suggested, or Italy. Zoey had agreed, envisioning something romantic and perhaps a little cultural involving good food and crusty bread and fine wine. A tour of the French vineyards, perhaps, or a trip to Rome. But a *cycling* holiday? Honestly, after eight years together you'd have thought he knew her a little better.

Exercise had never been her strongest suit. On the odd occasion she'd tried working out, she'd run out of puff before the instructor had even finished the warm-up. The last time she'd run more than ten metres was back at school, and even then she'd spent more time tying her shoelaces than on the track. She liked to tell herself men preferred pillowy curves to jutting hip bones, but deep down she wasn't convinced. Especially when her jeans didn't button up and she had to size up *again*.

'Come *on*, Mum,' Nell teased now as Zoey hovered reluctantly at the threshold of the changing rooms. 'You never know, you might actually *enjoy* it.'

She scuttled to the darkest corner she could find and changed into a shapeless old T-shirt of Richard's and a pair of Nell's baggy jogging bottoms, wishing she'd noticed before that they had 'booty' written in large pink letters on the rear. Yanking down the back of her T-shirt with both hands, she sidled after her daughter into the huge mirrored gym, eyeing the lithe, toned bodies all around her in horror. Who *were* these people with their pedometers and heart-rate monitors and water bottles and bizarre five-toed rubber shoes? More to the point, what was *she* doing in the same room?

'You'll be fine,' Nell whispered, trying not to laugh as she propelled her mother from the back of the gym. 'Just stay close to me and copy what I do.'

By design, Zoey hadn't properly seen herself in the mirror for years. She got dressed in the dark without opening the curtains, and put on make-up using a dim fifteen-watt bulb (resisting Nell's pressure to go green and buy CFLs – their harsh light was even less forgiving than that of a plane toilet). She was always the one behind the camera, taking pictures of Nell or Richard, so it had been years since she'd even seen a photograph of herself. But there was no escape from the floor-to-ceiling horror show reflected back at her now. She looked like a cross between a bag lady and a bouncy castle, she thought in dismay, all breasts and bottom. Her fine blonde hair had escaped from its twist and was frizzing unbecomingly around her face, her cheeks were flushed from rushing to the gym, and even beneath the loose T-shirt she could see how lumpy and bumpy her tummy was these days. She didn't look old, exactly; more the subject of benign neglect. Like a once elegant house that had been allowed to fall into disrepair and could use a lick of paint and some repointing.

In the mirror beside her, a limber stranger dipped gracefully to touch her toes. It took Zoey a moment to realize it was her daughter. In contrast to her, Nell seemed the epitome of cool, willowy beauty. She was so poised and . . . *put together*, Zoey thought suddenly. Slim as a quill, and not a hair out of place. You'd never have guessed the two of them were even related, apart from their eyes, which were identical and marked them out instantly as mother and daughter: large and grey and ringed with thick black lashes.

As Nell straightened, Zoey realized with a slight pang that her daughter was actually taller than she was now by at least two inches. Her baby was growing up. In a few short years she'd be leaving home and going off to university. She'd miss her more than she wanted to think about.

It had been tough raising Nell alone, but she'd never for an instant regretted her decision to have her baby by herself. When Patrick had left her, she'd had no one to turn to. The only child of two only children, she'd been born to parents already in their forties by the time she'd made her surprise appearance. Her father had been a handyman at a local school on the outskirts of Oxford, her mother a seamstress at a small dry-cleaner's in town. When Zoey was eight, her father had collapsed in agony from a perforated bowel as he sat in the school boiler room eating his lunch – Ploughman's and pickled onions, the same as every other working day of his life – and had died two days later without ever regaining consciousness. Her mother's death ten years afterwards had been more lingering. It had taken her eighteen months to succumb to leukaemia – eighteen months of blood tests and chemo and vomiting and sheer, unrelenting misery. When she'd finally died in her daughter's arms, Zoey had simply been relieved that it was over. There had been no aunts or uncles, no cousins – no support network to call on. At just eighteen, she'd been on her own.

It was her art teacher at school who'd suggested

she apply to Saint Martins to study fashion. Brought up to make-do-and-mend, and deft with a needle thanks to her mother, Zoey had showcased her creative flair and instinctive understanding of design during her A-level fashion show. With nothing to lose, she'd done as her teacher suggested; and to her lasting surprise, had been not only accepted, but awarded a full scholarship. Four years later, she'd graduated as one of the stars of her year, a bright future apparently assured.

But winning accolades for your avant-garde college collection was one thing; making a living at it quite another. She'd ended up working in numerous gruelling dead-end jobs as she struggled to get her fledgling fashion career off the ground, often too exhausted by the time she got home to her studio in Camden to even pick up her sketch pad. Two years after graduating, she still hadn't finished her first collection.

She'd met Patrick while waitressing at a wine bar on Fleet Street. She'd known he was married from the start: he'd worn a gold wedding band and made no effort to hide it. Or the fact that he was seriously attracted to her and didn't consider his wedding vows important.

She really hadn't been the sort of girl who dated married men. She wasn't a virgin, but only just – a few brief fumbles with other students at Saint Martins (two of whom turned out to be gay), and a short-lived fling with a doped-up musician were the total sum of her sexual experience. She'd been no match for a player like Patrick James.

Thirty-seven to her twenty-four, a news cameraman with INN, he'd been shot twice (in Beirut and Sarajevo), arrested (in Kuwait and Soweto) and beaten up in London (a pub fight over a married girlfriend; nothing to do with his job). In other words, he was a real man in the macho, gung-ho, alpha male sense of the word. Surrounded by floppy-haired, arty metrosexuals too terrified to open a door for her in case she took it the wrong way, Zoey had found his testosterone-fuelled sex appeal irresistible.

For six blissful, agonizing months, she'd lived in a state of suspended animation, scared to go out in case he called, sobbing into her pillow when he didn't. When she'd missed her period she'd been petrified but at the same time secretly thrilled: he'd *have* to leave his wife now.

The day after she'd got two positive lines on a home pregnancy test, she dressed up in her sexiest underwear, cooked him his favourite shepherd's pie, put Roberta Flack on the CD player and broke the news that she was pregnant. At which point Patrick broke the news that so was his wife.

There was never really any question of her not having the baby, even after Patrick abandoned her without a backward glance. She'd been on her own far too long for that; this tiny new life growing inside her was all the family she had. So she gave up the studio in Camden – and with it the last of her dreams of becoming the new Stella McCartney – took out a crippling business mortgage, and moved into the tiny run-down flat above Born-Again Vintage, a failing second-hand thrift shop where she'd been working afternoons and whose owner was only too happy to sell up, take the money and run.

She had been certain that as soon as he saw Nell, Patrick would come back to her. His wife had given him a son just two months after Zoey had announced her own pregnancy, but weren't men supposed to dote on their little girls? She didn't want to be the one to rip his family apart, but she had her own child to consider now. As far as she was concerned, Nell was just as important as his son, and Patrick just as much her father.

In the end, none of it mattered. Six weeks after Nell was born, Patrick was killed by a stray bullet in Bosnia without ever acknowledging his daughter.

For the first seven years, it had been just Zoey and Nell. She'd sworn off men after Patrick, not quite sure if it was Nell she was protecting or herself. And then eight years ago she'd met Richard – sweet, safe, paper-pushing Richard – in the hallway of her accountant's office. Thoughtful, sensitive Richard, who'd treated her as kindly and patiently as if she were a baby bird, never once trying to push her, waiting for her to come to him. Steadfast, loyal Richard, who adored Nell, and she him; he'd become her father in every sense that mattered. He wanted to marry Zoey – he'd made that clear often enough

– but somehow she'd never quite been able to bring herself to say yes. She loved Richard, but there was no *passion*, never had been; and even though she told herself that passion didn't last, indeed had brought her nothing but grief, she still couldn't quite turn her back on it. Not entirely. Not yet.

She was jolted out of her reverie as a deafening Latin American beat suddenly filled the gym, so loud that the floor actually shook beneath her feet. Giving a final futile tug on the hem of her T-shirt, she took a deep breath as a handsome boy in his early twenties, dressed in baggy olive fatigues and a backward-facing baseball cap, moved to the front of the room, his feet already tracking the beat. She might look fat and ridiculous, but Nell wanted her here, so she'd put up with any amount of public humiliation. It was all about Nell. It always had been.

A skinny girl in hot-pink cargo pants sashayed forward, briefly pushing her out of the way. Instantly Zoey blocked her with a hip swing of her own.

No one ever came between Zoey and her daughter.

CHAPTER 5

NELL

This time, Nell thought crossly, her mother had better say yes. Richard was a nice man, even if he was a tiny bit boring. He had a nice job in the civil service – something to do with historic preservation – and a pension and everything. He drove a nice Honda Civic. He wore nice clothes: *dad* clothes, not the hipster gear sad middle-aged blokes usually wore when they were trying to look younger. And he had a nice house in a really nice tree-lined street in the nice part of Islington, near Waitrose, not a tiny two-bedroom flat over a shop in the dodgiest end of the dodgiest part of the borough. He even had a nice dog.

Most importantly, he was nice to Mum. As far as Nell was concerned, that was worth any amount of boring.

She shifted her backpack to the other shoulder and unlocked the kitchen door, shoving it open against the usual jumble of cardboard boxes that had yet to be sorted into saleable items, donations to the Sally Army, or things heading straight for the bin. Mum never said no to anything, even though most of the stuff people donated was crap you wouldn't send a Turkish earthquake victim. Saggy grey bras, horrible old long-johns, single trainers, shirts that were ripped or stained or missing all their buttons. Who did they think actually *wanted* this shit? Half the time it wasn't even *clean*.

'You have to kiss a lot of toads to find your handsome prince,' Mum said elliptically whenever Nell had had enough of the mess and hit the roof; usually around the same time as the cardboard boxes.

The annoying thing was, she was right. Once in every fifty boxes, she'd find a vintage Chanel tweed suit, or an original Mary Quant dress. Those were the clothes that made it to the shop window, the bait that lured customers in.

But what really kept them coming back to Born-Again Vintage weren't those rare classic finds, gorgeous though they were, but the clothes Mum made, the incredible pieces – and they were *pieces*; the word 'clothes' didn't do them justice – she upcycled from other people's cast-offs. She was like Molly Ringwald in *Pretty in Pink* when she took two old pink party dresses and combined them to create a new knockout outfit to wear to her high-school prom. Only what Mum did was far more beautiful and extraordinary.

As Richard pointed out, Mum's clothes weren't clothes at all, they were *Art*. With a capital A.

A long time ago, before Nell was born, Mum had had her own design studio. If it wasn't for

Nell, she'd probably have a wicked fashion label by now, like Stella McCartney or Vivienne Westwood. Instead, she was turning army greatcoats and worn-out tutus into one-off ball gowns for spoilt fashionistas, and Nell knew damn well she was getting paid a fraction of what they were worth. If only Mum would just *market* herself properly.

She ducked round a half-dressed mannequin at the foot of the narrow stairs and took them two at a time up to her tiny room. Anyone else would have turned the recession-led belt-tightening and sudden fashion for recycling to their advantage; but not Mum. She still saw her stuff as little more than a hobby on the side, when in reality it was the shop's USP, the only thing keeping them afloat these days. If Nell hadn't taken over the books last year and insisted her mother start charging halfway sensible prices, they'd have probably gone broke by now.

Flinging herself on her narrow bed, she folded her arms behind her head and gazed up at the hand-painted celestial ceiling Mum had done for her when she was a baby. It wasn't herself she worried for; she'd be off to uni in three years, striking out on her own. She knew exactly what she wanted to do, too – she'd always known: forensic anthropology. Like in *Bones*. She had a photographic memory, a strong stomach, and had been solving puzzles and riddles since she was old enough to read. She'd never been much good at art or literature, but she'd wired her first plug at six, and html was as familiar to her as English. Mum couldn't even work the TV remote control.

Frowning, she chewed the inside of her cheek. She had to get Mum settled before she left home. Mum had never been what you'd call practical, and she was getting dippier by the year. She'd never cope without someone to sort out her computer when it crashed or remind her to pay the council tax.

Mum had met Richard when she was seven, and until then Nell hadn't realized how much she'd been missing. She loved Richard; she always had. She totally thought of him as her dad, but even after all these years, Mum still held him at arm's length, refusing to marry him or even allow him to move into their flat, terrified of pushing Nell out. Nell *wanted* to be pushed out. How could she live her own life if she was always worrying about Mum?

This summer's trip to France, for example, and her own holiday in Cornwall with her best friend Teri and her family. She'd set the whole thing up for one reason and one reason only: Mum and Richard needed to spend time on their own without her playing gooseberry if they were ever going to get it together. She just wanted to see Mum married so she could relax.

'Nell?' Mum called up the stairs. 'Is that you?'

She swung her feet onto the floor. 'No. Just a burglar having a nap.'

A moment later, Mum stuck her head round the bedroom door. She had a habit of wearing her failed creations – those too avant-garde or just plain weird to sell – and today was no exception. Her skirt had once been a pair of jeans and a sequined dress; instead of a jumper, she was wearing an ex-apron embellished with pieces of a feather boa, and on her feet were a pair of patchwork gladiator boots she'd practically lived in all winter.

'It's Zumba tonight, isn't it?' Mum asked brightly.

Nell winced. To her total disbelief – and embarrassment – her mother had turned out to be a pretty good dancer. Very good, in fact. Ten minutes into the class last week and she'd been swinging her hips all over the shop like a Lebanese belly dancer. When Nell had called her on it, she'd smiled mysteriously and said something about a misspent youth and dancing being like learning to ride a bike. Angel hadn't been able to take his eyes off her, even though Mum was twice his age and was wearing those awful Juicy Couture jogging bottoms Nell had tried to throw out twice. If it were anyone but her mother, Nell would've wanted to rip her eyes out.

'Mum!' she exclaimed now, sitting up sharply. 'You're going out for dinner with Richard, remember? Your anniversary?'

Mum waved her hand dismissively. 'Never mind that. It's not a real one, just eight years since we met. We can go out another time. Richard won't mind.'

'Of course he will! He's gone to a lot of trouble. He's booked that new Italian you wanted to try and everything.' She brushed a few stray purple boa feathers from her mother's shoulders. 'And you might kind of want to tone down the hippie thing tonight. Just a bit. Maybe you could wear that jersey dress Richard likes? You know, the long grey one with the silver belt? And perhaps some different shoes?'

'I smell a rat,' her mother said lightly.

'Mum. Be nice.'

'He's going to ask me to marry him again, isn't he?'

'Would it really be so bad if he did?'

'I like things the way they are,' Mum said stubbornly.

Nell rolled her eyes. 'You can't keep saying no, Mum. Richard's got the patience of a saint but he won't wait around for ever. And he's so *nice*. I don't understand why you haven't said yes already. He loves you. And you love him. Don't you?'

'I suppose so. No, that's not fair. I *do* love him, yes.' She sighed. 'But *nice* isn't always enough, darling girl.'

'But Mum, you're practically living together as it is. I don't know what the big deal is about making it official.'

'If it's not a big deal, why do you keep pushing it?'

'Because it would be nice to have the thing *settled*,' Nell said. 'Please, if he asks you again, can't you just say yes? You need him.'

I need him, she thought. She loved spending weekends at Richard's big, airy house, or curling up with him and Mum on the sofa in front of *Britain's Got Talent*. Like a *normal* family.

'Sweetie, if we're going to continue this conversation, I think I'm going to need one of your cigarettes.'

'Mum!'

'Come on, darling. You can't be the only fifteen-year-old in London without a secret supply of Silk Cut.'

'Marlboros, actually,' Nell said sheepishly.

'I don't need to tell you these are for emergency use only,' Mum warned, opening the tiny bedroom window beside Nell's bed. 'This is a very bad habit to get into.'

'I'll bear that in mind.'

'Your father used to smoke Marlboros,' Mum said unexpectedly. 'Only brand he ever liked.'

Nell went very still. Mum hardly ever mentioned her father. Nell hadn't even known his full name until she was ten, when Richard had persuaded her mother to share the basic facts with her. Over the years since then, Mum had let slip rare nuggets of information when she was in a nostalgic mood, leaving her to stitch together a shadowy sense of the man whose genes she shared. She knew her father was dead, that many of her questions would always remain unanswered; but recently her longing to know more about him had started to gnaw at her. It wasn't just that she needed to know who her father was; she needed to know who *she* was.

Just before Christmas, she'd finally plucked up the courage to look up her father online. It had been weird to read so much about this man to whom she was biologically connected and yet didn't know at all. She'd stared at his photo for ages, searching his face for her own features. He was dark-haired like her – turning a bit salt-and-pepper actually – but apart from that, she hadn't recognized anything of herself in him. He might as well have been a perfect stranger. Which, after all, was what he was.

'He used to blow smoke rings,' Mum mused now, more to herself than to her. 'He could make them go through each other. I used to call him Gandalf. God, he was sexy. There was just something about him. When he was in a room, you couldn't see anyone else.' She smiled wistfully. 'You know the first thing he said to me? "As soon as I saw you, I knew we'd be friends or lovers. And now you've smiled, I know it'll be both." You probably think that's terribly cheesy, but I'd never met anyone like him. He literally swept me off my feet.'

Nell held her breath. Her mother had never opened up like this. 'Did you know he was married?' she asked hesitantly. 'I mean, right at the beginning?'

'Oh yes. He never tried to hide it. But I couldn't stay away from him. I didn't *want* to. He was like a drug. I couldn't get enough of him.'

Mum shivered, as if a ghost had walked over her grave. 'I suppose I'd better go and get dressed, then,' she said, stubbing her cigarette out on the brick window sill. 'Seeing as how I have to tone down "that hippie thing" before I go out.'

Nell stared into space for a long time after her mother had left. She adored Richard; he was the one who'd taught her to ride a bicycle, helped her with her maths homework, sneaked her onto the roller coaster at Thorpe Park after Mum had forbidden it and didn't rat her out when it had made her sick. She was sad she'd never get to meet her birth dad, of course, but in some ways it made things easier; it would have felt disloyal seeking him out when Richard was, to all intents and purposes, her father.

But that didn't mean she couldn't get to know who Patrick had been.

Suddenly decisive, she flipped open her laptop and pulled up her Facebook page. She scrolled through her messages until she found the one she was looking for. Normally she replied to emails instantly, but this one had been sitting unanswered in her inbox for weeks. The one from Ryan James. Her brother.

She was ready to talk to him now.

Subject: Florence Lockwood
Date: 19/07/2000 3:21:36 P.M.
From: bkennedy@kennedyrhinehart.co.uk
To: dcarter@princesseugenie.co.uk

Dannah,

Wondered if you'd had a chance to follow up on Florence Lockwood, per my referral last month. Curious one. The mother came to me clearly very anxious about her lack of rapport with her daughter, but in my view there's absolutely nothing wrong with the child re her language skills and social development. However, she seems oddly reluctant to talk in front of her mother. Be interested to know what you make of it.

Ben

Subject: re: Florence Lockwood
Date: 19/07/2000 5:41:02 P.M.
From: dcarter@princesseugenie.co.uk
To: bkennedy@kennedyrhinehart.co.uk

Ben,

Good timing. Harriet Lockwood brought her daughter in today for assessment. I'll be writing up a full report later this week, but I'm with you: the child met all developmental milestones during our time alone, but when Mum is present, she does indeed shut down. However, she doesn't appear afraid of her mother, and there are no other signs that there is a problem at home. Florence is lively, animated and affectionate towards Harriet, who is clearly a caring and concerned parent. The family is about to relocate to America, and Harriet is also pregnant with her second child, so there may be some additional stresses at home, but I don't think this is the underlying cause of the lack of rapport. Rather, the issue seems to stem from a fundamental inability for the two to communicate on a meaningful level.

By Harriet's own admission, she found the adjustment to motherhood difficult. I suspect that this anxiety has transmitted itself to the child, who is reflecting Mum's own nervousness when around her. The long-term implications for Florence's development are minimal, but the potential impact on the mother–daughter relationship does give me some concern. Given the family's upcoming relocation, however, all I can do is recommend that Harriet pursue the idea of family therapy in the States.

I will, of course, forward my full report to you later in the week, but I see no need for a follow-up this end unless requested by Mrs Lockwood.

Dannah

CHAPTER 6

HARRIET

Once the idea had entered Harriet's head, it took root. She tried to ignore it, but it was like an aching tooth she couldn't leave alone.

What if Oliver wasn't Florence's father?

The notion would be unthinkable to anyone who knew her now, but she hadn't always been this sensible, uptight (yes, she knew what people thought of her) wife and mother. She might seem the definition of virtue and restraint today, but her past – her pre-Oliver past – had been a very different matter. She'd had a wild side Oliver knew nothing about, and which had been buried so long that even Harriet had started to forget it had existed. For sixteen years she'd been able to draw a firm line under that part of her life, separating it from the life she had now, the life that had started the day she married Oliver. But suddenly she could no longer be sure – not *absolutely* – that those two very distinct phases of her life hadn't slightly overlapped.

You'd think you'd know, wouldn't you, if you'd been unfaithful to your husband? But clearly it wasn't always quite so cut and dried. Sometimes, under certain circumstances – the kind of circumstances facilitated by alcohol – there might be room for doubt. Until last week, it had never occurred to her Oliver might not be Florence's father. But she couldn't argue with the facts: Florence's blood group was A-positive. And she and Oliver were both O.

As Holmes would say: *When you have eliminated the impossible, whatever remains, however improbable, must be the truth.*

Reluctant as she was to believe it was true, her school biology lessons weren't so long ago that she'd forgotten everything. When both parents were blood group O – by far the most common blood group in the world – their children could only be group O too. A hundred online searches had confirmed what she'd suspected from the moment Florence had raised the whole wretched subject. It was scientifically impossible for Harriet and Oliver to have a child whose blood type was A. Which meant that Florence could not, *could not*, be Oliver's daughter.

She'd checked with Florence's doctor, of course, hoping against hope that her daughter had made a mistake, misheard, muddled things up. But no, the doctor had said Florence was indeed A-positive. It had been in her records since she she'd first been diagnosed with diabetes nine years ago, and they'd tested her again before giving her the transfusion after her accident, of course, just to be sure. The hospital hadn't made a mistake. She was the one who'd done that, sixteen years ago.

Harriet put her head down on her desk and sobbed. If only she could remember!

The truth was, there were rather a lot of things from her rackety pre-Oliver days she couldn't quite remember. It wasn't that she'd had a *problem* with alcohol, exactly. She hadn't got drunk every day, or even every other day. She hadn't reached for a bottle as soon as she'd got home from work, as so many of her friends did. But at weekends, or at a party, or a wedding (or, indeed, a funeral), she'd occasionally had more than was good for her.

Sometimes considerably more.

As a child and adolescent, she'd been painfully uncertain. Fearsomely bright, worryingly thin, the ugly duckling in a family of confident, attractive swans, she'd had few friends and little in the way of a social life. As for boys, by the time she'd left for Oxford, she still hadn't been kissed.

But she'd known university was a time for re-invention. She'd taken herself in hand with her usual thoroughness, and by the end of that first Michaelmas term, she'd effected an astonishing transformation. Gone were the pie-crust blouses and sensible knee-length corduroy skirts; the glasses had been traded for contacts, and the long, centre-parted mousey hair for a glossy chestnut bob. When she'd arrived home for Christmas, her parents hadn't recognized her.

But what had enabled her to carry it off was the

discovery of her personal Philosopher's Stone, the magic ingredient that turned her from shy wallflower into belle of the ball: alcohol.

It had astonished her how just a few drinks made her sparkle. Suddenly she was witty and entertaining, confident in her ability to amuse and allure. Belief in yourself, she'd quickly discovered, was far sexier than a perfect nose or a D-cup chest. A couple of gin and tonics, two or three glasses of wine and she could flirt and dance and tease with the best of them. Within a week of the start of Hilary term, she'd lost her virginity to a first-year history student at Corpus; by the time Trinity term had ended and she'd gone down for the summer, she and Ben had been happily going steady.

They'd dated throughout their second and final years. After graduation (both of them obtaining a respectable 2:1), Harriet had joined a PR firm as a junior accounts manager (aka dogsbody), and Ben had become 'something in the City'. For the time being, Harriet had commuted to central London from her parents' home in Kensington while Ben had moved in with his older brother in Putney, but it had been understood by both that this was just a temporary arrangement. Once they had a bit of money put by (which Ben had been quick to assure her wouldn't be long, given the ridiculous amount he was now being paid), they'd find a flat and put things on a 'more formal footing', as he quaintly phrased it. Harriet's mother had already been to Peter Jones and picked out their wedding china.

But just weeks after starting her new job, she'd met Dylan Poland, an advertising executive ten years her senior, and fallen violently in love. Within days, she'd broken off their unofficial engagement. Ben had been broken-hearted, and Harriet had been wracked with guilt but too much in love to care.

The affair had lasted three months, at which point Dylan had left her for a twenty-year-old company intern. It had been Harriet's turn to nurse a broken heart, and it had taken five years for it to truly mend. But in the meantime she'd had sex. Lots of sex. With lots of men. Quite often, she'd woken up in a strange bed with a man she didn't recognize, forced to piece together the events of the night before from the quantity of used condoms on the floor. She hadn't liked herself very much, but had consoled herself with the thought that at least she'd always used protection.

And then she'd met Oliver.

She was twenty-six by this time, an associate director for a boutique PR firm who'd headhunted her eighteen months earlier. Her company had been approached by the new young CEO of a new young sandwich company that had been riding high on the back of the green eco wave and now needed their help to take it to the next level. Harriet had done more than that. As Oliver often joked, she'd liked the new young CEO so much, she'd married him.

The attraction between them had been immediate and mutual. At the end of their first business meeting, he'd invited her out to dinner. At the end of their first date, she'd invited him home to bed.

To her surprise, he'd politely but firmly turned her down. 'I'm holding out for what you're *not* prepared to give,' he'd told her.

For the first time, she'd looked at him properly. Like all the men who'd spun through the revolving door of her bedroom over the past five years, Oliver Lockwood had been charming and good-looking, albeit in a crumpled, rugby-prop-forward kind of way. But unlike all the other men, he had a calm certainty about him, as if he knew exactly who he was and what he was about, and therefore had nothing to prove – in the bedroom or out of it. Intrigued, she'd accepted his offer of a second date. Which had ended exactly the same way. As did a third, and then a fourth.

'Is it me?' she'd asked finally. 'Don't you *want* to go to bed with me?'

'More than you can imagine,' Oliver said feelingly. 'But I don't want to be another notch on your bedpost. I'm in this for the long haul.'

So, it turned out, was Harriet. Love crept up on her unawares, quietly stealing into her heart and putting down roots while she was looking the other way. What she felt for Oliver was nothing like the incendiary passion she'd had for Dylan Poland, nor the security blanket of her cosy relationship with Ben. This was *love*, the kind of love Shakespeare had written about, the ever-fixed mark that looks on tempests and is never shaken. And when they had finally slept together, two months after they'd met, she'd understood at last why Oliver had waited.

He'd proposed the next morning, and she'd accepted without hesitation. *When I saw you I fell in love, and you smiled because you knew.*

The week before their wedding, she'd been shopping for a going-away outfit in South Molton Street when she'd unexpectedly run into Ben. Over the past few years they'd become friends, meeting up a couple of times a year for a drink; although, if she was honest, guilt was always a lingering factor in their friendship.

'I gather congratulations are in order,' Ben had said, kissing her on the cheek.

She'd glanced awkwardly at the small princess-cut diamond on her left hand. 'Oh. Yes. You remember Oliver, don't you?'

'He's a lucky guy,' Ben said. 'You know I'm getting married myself in a few months?'

'Oh, Ben, that's wonderful,' Harriet said warmly. 'I'm so pleased for you. Katy, isn't it?'

He'd laughed. 'Actually, no. That ended a while back. Her name's Julia, and we only met a couple of months ago. It's a long story.' He'd hesitated. 'Look, I don't suppose you want to go for a quick drink? I know a great little wine bar just round the corner. If you've got time, it would be great to catch up properly.'

It had seemed churlish to say no. One quick drink had turned into two; two drinks had turned into two bottles. She'd forgotten what good company Ben could be. They'd been together for three years, after all – they shared a lot of history. And Ben was part of the life she was about to leave behind for ever; it had seemed fitting to close out the chapter with him.

When they'd finally stumbled outside several hours later, she'd been surprised to find it was already dark.

'Hey!' Ben had exclaimed, catching her arm as she'd lurched sideways. 'We'd better get some coffee into you. You can't go home like this.'

She'd been in no position to argue. Still struggling to stand upright, she'd let Ben hail a taxi and help her into it. Resting her head against his shoulder, she'd closed her eyes as the world spun. She hadn't been this drunk for ages. She couldn't let Oliver see her like this.

When the taxi had dropped them off, she'd realized she was outside Ben's flat.

'Ben, are you sure this is a good idea?' she'd said doubtfully. 'Won't Julia mind?'

'She's at her parents' this weekend. Come on. A cup of strong coffee, and we'll pour you into a cab home.'

His apartment had hardly changed. Still the same sofa they'd once made out on, though it now sported scatter cushions – his fiancée's influence, she supposed – and the same vintage movie posters on the walls. She'd picked up a photo of a pretty dark-haired girl in a silver frame. *This must be Julia.* It had been a little disconcerting to realize how much like Harriet she looked.

'Kettle's on,' Ben had said, coming out of the kitchen. 'But there's something I want you to try first.'

He'd handed her a glass full of amber liquid, and she'd laughed. 'Ben, I can't. I'm going to have a monster hangover tomorrow as it is.'

'Forty-year-old single malt. You'll regret it for ever if you don't.'

Except it hadn't been the whisky she'd ended up regretting, of course. Waking up naked in Ben's bed the next morning, Harriet had never been more ashamed in her life. No matter that she hadn't been able to remember anything after her second glass of Glenmorangie (which had gone down like velvet – she did remember *that*); she'd cheated on Oliver, and they weren't even married yet.

Ben had found her huddled in the bathroom crying her eyes out.

'Harry, darling, please stop,' he'd said, crouching on the floor beside her. 'There's no need to cry. Nothing happened, I promise.'

'But I'm *naked*!' Harriet had sobbed, pulling the bathroom towel tighter around her chest.

He'd looked abashed. 'Well. You, um, you were

a bit sick. Quite a lot, actually. All over your clothes. And the sofa—'

'You undressed me?'

'I had to,' he'd protested. 'You'd kind of passed out at that point. I put everything in the machine, I hope that's OK. It's just drying now.'

She'd closed her eyes and moaned.

'Look, it's nothing I haven't seen before,' he'd said awkwardly. 'Honestly, Harry. You don't have to worry. No one's ever going to know.'

The problem, Harriet thought despairingly now, sixteen years later, raising her head from her desk and blowing her nose, was that even *she* didn't know what had really happened. Maybe Ben had just been trying to be kind and spare her feelings. Or perhaps he'd regretted it as much as she had. After all, he'd had just as much to lose. The last thing he'd needed was the complication of an ex-girlfriend on the scene.

She paced towards the window. Charlie and George were building a huge snowman in the back garden, while Sam directed proceedings from his position on the lowest branch of a maple tree. There was no sign of Florence, naturally. She'd be holed up in her room until May, plugged into her iPad.

Florence. Their honeymoon baby, named after the city in Italy where they'd stayed. Born exactly eight months and three weeks after the wedding.

Nine months after that night with Ben.

Harriet pressed the heels of her hands into her

eyes. If Oliver wasn't Florence's father, it could only be Ben. *Oh God, what the hell was she going to do?*

Harriet was puritanically truthful. She told salesgirls if they gave her too much change, and pointed out mistakes in her favour on restaurant receipts. Once, when she'd discovered that a 'fake' Tiffany lamp she'd picked up at a car boot sale was in fact genuine, she'd spent days tracking down its former owner so that she could pay a fair price. On her wedding day, she'd made a promise to herself that what happened that night with Ben would be the only lie between them, that she would never lie to Oliver again, either by word or omission, and it was one she'd kept.

But how could she tell him about this? He'd be devastated. And Florence, too, if she ever found out. Yet how could she *not* tell him? Keeping it secret would destroy the essence of their marriage – turn it into an empty sham, a lie.

The screensaver on her laptop changed to a photograph of Oliver and Florence in the garden, arms round each other, laughing. They were so alike in every way, far more so than she and Florence. How could it be that she wasn't his? *How?*

Suddenly she made up her mind. She wasn't going to make a decision that would change their entire lives without being *absolutely sure* of her facts.

Running upstairs, she collected Florence's

toothbrush from her bathroom, and then her own and Oliver's from their ensuite down the hall. DNA testing was the only way to be certain. Once she *knew*, she could decide what to do.

She wasn't a religious woman, but for the first time in years she found herself praying.

CHAPTER 7

OLIVER

Oliver had had to cancel several important meetings to be home in time to take Florence to her Spring Prom, but there was no way in hell he was going to miss it. He wanted to vet what she was wearing, for a start. She might think she was all grown up, but at fifteen was still a child as far as he was concerned.

He needn't have worried. As he stood in the hall, stamping snow from his boots and unwinding his scarf, his daughter floated down the stairs in a cloud of delicate grey chiffon and beaded velvet. Oliver froze for a moment, his breath catching in his throat. Her long blonde hair was parted simply to one side, and she was wearing a plain silver cross at her neck and the pretty pearl studs Harriet's mother had given her for Christmas in her ears. He could see she had make-up on – a little silvery eye-shadow and a light sheen of lip gloss – but it was subtle enough that he didn't mind. She looked exactly as a fifteen-year-old girl *should* look – beautiful and fresh and innocent.

She did a little twirl, and the sequined handkerchief

points of her skirt whispered around her legs. 'What d'you think?'

'You look beautiful,' he said softly. He caught her hands in his and held them wide. 'The belle of the ball.'

'My dress is all right?' Florence asked anxiously. 'You don't think it's a bit babyish?'

'Darling, you look perfect. Very grown-up.'

'Really?'

'Absolutely.'

This was why he'd moved his family to Vermont, he thought as she shrugged happily into her warm grey wool coat. So that his fifteen-year-old daughter could grow up in a world of chaperoned school dances and pretty dresses that accentuated her youthful beauty without sexualizing her in any way. So that his twelve-year-old son could cycle down to the corner shop for a pint of milk without being abducted by some kind of pervert. Florence complained they lived in a backwater, but if by that she meant a town where you could still leave your back door unlocked all day, where teenage boys shovelled snow from pensioners' driveways and thought 'hell' was a swear word, then yes, he was happy to hold his hands up. His brother's daughter was a year younger than Florence, but when they'd visited London last summer, the girl had slouched into the room in a cropped top and denim hot pants with her arse hanging out, and had only opened her mouth to swear. All the girls dressed like that these days, his brother had said weakly. Oliver had seen it himself every time he got on a tube – girls of thirteen and fourteen in tight skirts and high heels, drinking and swearing and flashing their knickers. There was no way he was having *his* daughter grow up like that.

He dropped Florence at her high school, where the dance was being held, supervised by teachers and parent volunteers. No doubt savvy, streetwise London teenagers like his niece would laugh at the demure dresses the Vermont girls were wearing, with their corsages and pretty headbands and flat ballet pumps; but he'd take a bet their fathers wouldn't.

Harriet was home from work by the time he got back, holed up in her study.

'You missed Florence,' Oliver said, sticking his head round her door. 'It was her prom tonight.'

'I hadn't forgotten,' she said irritably. 'I was working.'

He raised an eyebrow in surprise at her tone. 'I didn't say you had. I think she'd have liked you to take her to her first prom, that's all.'

'Of course she wouldn't. She'd much rather have you.'

There was nothing he could say to this, because they both knew it was true. Harriet was a good mother to all four of their children, but she'd never managed to connect with her daughter the way she had with the boys. Florence had always gravitated towards her father, something that he knew grieved Harriet intensely. It had only got worse over the years, especially after she'd been diagnosed with diabetes; for some reason she'd made her mother the scapegoat, resisting Harriet's attempts to manage the illness, resenting every reminder of it. There were times when Oliver wondered if Florence actually blamed her mother for the fact that she had it, however illogical that seemed.

'D'you fancy going to Flatbread Pizza for dinner?' he asked his wife now, trying to lighten the mood. 'I forgot to take anything out of the freezer, and you know how much the boys like it there.'

'I don't have time,' she said without looking up. 'You go if you want.'

'You need to eat, Harriet.'

'I'll grab a sandwich or something later. I've got to get this finished tonight.'

He hesitated, then clicked the door shut behind him and crouched down beside her chair. 'What is it, Harry?' he asked gently. 'I know you're worried about the business, but there's more to it than that, isn't there? I haven't seen you smile for weeks. Are you not feeling well? Is something wrong?'

She gestured towards the spreadsheet on the screen in front of her. 'We're weathering this recession better than most, but we're getting to the point where we've got to start making some tough decisions. I'm not happy about what's going on in Manchester. I keep asking the North of England office to send me the accounts, and they keep stalling. And I don't think now is the time to expand into Connecticut—'

'C'mon, Harriet,' Oliver interrupted. 'This is me you're talking to. You're not addressing the board. If you want to talk more about Manchester or Connecticut, we can, but that's not the problem here, is it?'

It was his gift, to be able to read people like an open book; no one more than his wife.

Harriet looked directly at him for the first time. She seemed tired and anxious, as she so often was these days since the recession had hit; but there was something new in her dark eyes, something it took him a moment to identify. *Guilt.*

She took a deep breath and he braced himself to deal with whatever she was about to throw his way. The business was going down the tubes. She'd put the house up as collateral. Whatever it was, he knew they could deal with it. Together.

But then she glanced away, turned back to her computer, and he knew that whatever she'd been about to say, the moment had passed.

'It's been a tough month,' she said, clicking on her keyboard. 'Even with insurance covering eighty per cent of Florence's hospital costs, we're still out of pocket by several thousand dollars.'

'We'll find it,' Oliver said automatically.

He leaned in to kiss her. She tilted her cheek sideways towards him, but didn't take her eyes from her screen. Oliver inhaled the coconut scent of her hair, the smell of her skin, warm beneath his lips, and suddenly, instantly, he was hard.

Gently, he lifted her fine brown hair from the nape of her neck and kissed it. She didn't respond, but her fingers had stopped moving across the keyboard. His lips moved down the knobs of her vertebrae from her hairline to the edge of her cashmere sweater, and he sensed, rather than felt, a tiny shiver ripple through her. Slowly his kisses moved along her shoulder, his teeth edging her sweater away to expose her skin. Still she hadn't turned towards him, but her head tilted slightly back against his chest; not an invitation, but not rejection either.

He stroked the outside of her arms as he continued to kiss her shoulders, the tips of his fingers brushing lightly against the swell of her small, high breasts. He repeated the motion, this time his hands moving fractionally inwards, finding her breasts more surely. Again they passed across her body, and this time, her nipples hardened beneath his touch and he heard her breath hitch.

'Oliver,' she murmured, stopping his hand with her own.

'Relax,' he whispered in her ear.

His palms swept across her belly – flatter than ever, even after four children – and then down over her toned thighs, feeling the warmth of her whippet-slim body through her jeans.

'Oliver, I'm in the middle of something,' she protested.

He smiled. 'So am I.'

He stroked the inside of her thighs. She pressed her legs together, and he didn't force the issue, merely continuing to stroke her from her knees to her groin with the tips of his fingers, gently, back and forth, back and forth, all the time kissing her neck, nuzzling her shoulder, and after a few moments her legs relaxed and parted again, enough for him to stroke upwards to the centre of her.

Again, the catch of breath in her throat, the signal that she wanted him as much as he wanted her. He swivelled her office chair towards him and sank to his knees in front of her. She started to tangle her hands in his thick blond hair, to pull him upright towards her, wanting to kiss him properly, but gently he pressed her arms back against the chair. He eased her sweater upwards and buried his face in her belly. Her skin was even softer than the cashmere sweater, scented with the subtle perfume of the gardenia body lotion she favoured. His erection pressed uncomfortably against his zip as he slipped his fingers beneath her cotton bra, thumbing her right nipple, his breath warm against her belly as he kissed her there.

'Please, Oliver. Not . . . not now. I can't.'

'Tell me you want me to stop.'

He'd found the waistband of her jeans now, was deftly unbuckling the exquisite Mexican belt he'd bought her for her last birthday, finding his way beneath the harsh denim to the velvety skin beneath.

'There are things we need to talk about . . .'

'I still don't hear you telling me to stop.'

His fingers had worked beneath her cotton knickers now, probing through the whorls of silky dark hair to the moist acorn of her clitoris. She gasped, her back arching, and this time when she twined her hands in his hair, he let her.

'The boys . . .' she breathed.

'Will be fine.'

'They might come in.'

'Not until they've learned to pick the lock.'

His erection was painful now, and he stood to unbuckle his own belt, kicking off his shoes and tugging off his socks before letting his trousers fall to the floor. He tugged at his wife's jeans, lifting her bottom off the chair so that he could pull them down her legs, taking her driving shoes with them.

'Oliver – really – there's something we have to . . . ohhh.'

For he had hooked his thumbs into the sides of her knickers, peeling them away, and buried his tongue in the slippery wet warmth of her, parting her labia with his fingers and teasing her with quick, darting licks. She tasted slightly tangy, as she always did, his favourite taste in the world. Her clitoris swelled beneath his attention, and he gentled his tongue, barely feathering across it. Her breath was coming faster now, and he raised his head, kneeling so that he could reach her breasts, pulling off her sweater and unfastening her bra with the ease of long practice. His hand had replaced his tongue between her legs, two fingers sliding either side of her clitoris without actually touching it, driving her ever closer to orgasm.

As he felt her start to shudder, he stood and picked her up, carrying her to the thick plaited rug in front of her study fireplace. Shedding the last of his clothes, he covered her naked body with his own, his erection digging into her belly.

She squirmed away from him. 'I can't, Oliver. Not until we talk.'

He pulled her back towards him. 'We are talking,' he breathed. 'This is how we talk.'

She was so wet for him, so warm and welcoming. He slithered back between her thighs, his mouth once more on her clitoris, his arms reaching upwards so that he could thumb her nipples again, knowing what she needed, what she wanted. Her response was instant. He tasted her arousal, felt her bucking beneath him. It was true, what he'd said: this was how they talked. It always had been.

He had no idea how many lovers she'd had before they met, and he'd never asked. His own experience was modest by most standards, he knew; his tally had stood at just four when he met Harriet, even though he'd been twenty-seven years old. The elder of two boys, brought up by loving parents in comfortable middle-class affluence, he'd never felt it necessary to prove himself by his conquests. Women weren't trophies to him. None of the four women who'd preceded Harriet had been serious contenders for the post of Mrs Lockwood, but he'd treated each relationship with respect; it said much for his charm and good nature that even after gently easing himself out of the various romances – for he had been the instigator in all four break-ups – he'd still remained on good terms with them all.

But the instant Harriet had walked into his office, all nervous energy and huge grey eyes and fierce determination, he'd known that here, finally, was a woman with whom he could spend the rest of his life.

He'd also realized very quickly that it was going to be hard to breach the defensive walls she'd erected around herself; very hard indeed.

Their first date had proved him right. She'd thrown up more barricades than the Kremlin during the Cold War. Outwardly confident and – after a few drinks – more than a little sexually aggressive, she'd kept her feelings walled off, unreachable. He'd known that if he was to win her, he was going to have to box very clever indeed. Which was why, even though he had a hard-on the size of Nelson's Column, he'd turned down her invitation back to her flat at the end of that first night.

And again the second.

And the third.

It had taken all his resolve and self-control (and he practically had blisters on his right hand); but when on their fourth date she'd rather plaintively asked him 'Don't you *want* to go to bed with me?', he'd known his strategy was working.

And when they did finally sleep together, more than two months after they'd met, she'd given herself to him body *and* soul. The sex had been extraordinary, beyond anything either of them had ever experienced. It was as if each knew what the other wanted before they themselves knew. He'd asked her to marry him the next morning, but really it had almost seemed redundant. How could you find the person who completed you so utterly and *not* marry them?

Even now, after sixteen years and four children, the bedroom was where they restored themselves to each other. It was how they communicated, made up, healed and soothed one another. The one place where they could never lie.

He pushed himself up on his forearms now and looked at his wife, more beautiful to him than she had ever been. His erection probed firmly between her thighs, slick with her arousal. He'd never known a woman to ejaculate when she came before, but Harriet did, and it drove him crazy with lust. He coated himself in her juices, sliding his cock either side of her clitoris, describing lazy figures-of-eight, holding back from entering her as long as he was able.

Finally he could stand it no more and thrust his length inside her. But for once, her legs didn't open in warm welcome. Instead, she clamped her thighs together, forcing him out of her.

He hesitated, confused. She wanted him; he knew it, he could feel it, *smell* it. If she was trying to prolong his pleasure, it wasn't going to work; he was so hard, he knew he couldn't last much longer. Gently, he eased himself back into her, but again she pulled away, forcing him out.

'Harry, please,' he breathed. 'Don't make me wait any longer.'

Suddenly she wriggled backwards and sat up. 'No,' she panted.

'*No?*'

'I told you, I *can't*.'

For a moment he stared at her, trying to work out if this was some kind of game. She groped for her sweater and held it against her breasts, and he realized she was serious.

Leaping to his feet, he grabbed his trousers and furiously started to stumble into them.

'What the fuck, Harriet?' he exclaimed, his voice bitter with frustration. 'You let me halfway inside you and *then* you decide to change your mind?'

'Oliver,' Harriet said, and her voice was very calm suddenly. Very certain. 'I tried to tell you. I did try. I *told* you we had to talk.'

My Mummy
by Nell Sands aged 6¾

I love my Mummy becase she is specill because she will always love me no matter what. Also she is specil because she cooks me pizza. she buys me things. She also cooks for me. I love her because she takes me to school and we are always late. And even when I'm bad she will always love me. She lets me watch t.v. and She takes me to the movies and ice skating and she likes too play with me. My Mummy doesent have a job she makes things. Somtimes she lets me help her and we have fun. Also she buys food like colliflower, corn, peas, carrots and potatows and she gives me ice creem. She likes to nap. My Mummy is always kind and she has a shiny smooth face and a very big heart. She is the best Mummy in the world. That is why I love my Mummy.

CHAPTER 8

ZOEY

Zoey liked waking up next to Richard. She loved the comforting bulk of his heavy body in the bed next to her, and the warmth of him radiating beneath the covers. It was a bit of a squash for the two of them, admittedly; they were neither of them exactly thin, and she still had the same small double bed with the pale green wicker headboard she'd bought just before Nell was born. But it was cosy and comfy and she *much* preferred it to Richard's sleek black California King bed, which was far too wide and lonely. She liked the feeling of Richard's body pressed against hers during the night, his belly warm and reassuring against her back. She'd spent too many years sleeping on her own; she wanted to *know* he was there.

She liked sex with Richard, too. It was, well, *comfortable*. That might not seem a very exciting way of putting it to someone Nell's age, but she was done with passion. Passion wasn't comfortable; was, in fact, the very antithesis of comfortable, with all its nail-biting drama and tension and roller-coaster emotion. As for the practicalities of sex itself, she didn't want to do it on the kitchen table (cold and rather unhygienic, she always thought) or swing from the chandeliers (assuming, of course, she could find one to take her weight); she liked the missionary position, it was satisfying and pleasurable, and when she was lying down, her breasts didn't sag and her tummy didn't gather in rolls where her waist should be. It was nice to have an orgasm, of course, and it did sometimes happen, but she really didn't mind if it didn't. She'd never been very good at them, and thankfully Richard wasn't one of those men who felt he had to prove himself by making her come five times before breakfast. Frankly, sex was nice, but – talking of breakfast – given the choice she'd much rather have a chocolate croissant.

She reached out now from beneath the covers and groped for her bathrobe, then squirmed out of bed and quickly pulled it on before Richard could wake up and catch her naked. He loved her curves – he often told her she would look even lovelier if she put on a few more pounds (not exactly a challenge, that, Zoey thought ruefully, knotting the belt around her ever-expanding middle) – but loving her curves by the forgiving light of a fifteen-watt bulb was one thing, and loving them in the bright April sunshine of a Saturday morning quite another.

Downstairs, she put the kettle on to boil and rummaged among the dirty crockery in the sink to wash out a couple of mugs, absent-mindedly munching on a crumbling digestive biscuit she'd just found in her dressing-gown pocket. She couldn't wait for Nell to come home so she could tell her the news. Her daughter had stayed last night with Teri, a friend of hers from school, but she'd promised to be home in time to go with Zoey to Camden Passage market. She could go by herself, of course, or even with Richard, though he wasn't a very good shopping buddy as he loathed browsing – he was far too goal-orientated – but Camden Passage was *their* thing, hers and Nell's. They'd spent most Saturday mornings there since Nell was a baby, sifting through amber cameos and silver buttons and tiny Victorian button boots. She knew the day was fast approaching when Nell wouldn't have time to spend Saturday mornings with her, or indeed any other mornings. She'd be off living her own life, as, of course, she should be. But in the meantime, Zoey intended to savour every moment.

She sighed as she poured boiling water into the mugs. Nell was spending more and more time at Teri's these days. Her daughter was trying to be tactful so she could have time with Richard, of course; but she knew it wasn't just that. Teri was one of five children, four of whom still lived at home, along with two elderly grandparents. Zoey had been to their house, which was quite literally bursting at the seams. Teri's father had erected a sort of permanent tent affair at the side of the kitchen, in which two of the older boys slept. He and his wife both worked two jobs to support their family, and all but the youngest child had paper rounds and part-time jobs. Their cramped house was crowded, noisy, chaotic, filled with the laughter and bickering of family life – and she knew Nell loved every second she was there.

She'd never been able to give her daughter the extended family she craved, the brothers and sisters, the grandparents, the aunts and uncles and cousins. But by finally agreeing to marry Richard, maybe Nell could at least have the family of her own she'd always longed for.

It was the right decision, she thought firmly, picking up their mugs and turning towards the steep stairs. Of course it was. Richard was a good man. He loved her. She could see herself growing old with him. Wasn't that what marriage was all about?

She'd just reached the landing when Richard came charging out of the bedroom as if the Devil was after him, shoes in one hand, shirt unbuttoned. Tea slopped over her hands, scalding them, and she quickly put the mugs down on the hall stand.

'Richard! What's going on?'

'The hospital just called. My mother's had another fall. A neighbour found her. They think she's broken her hip.'

'Oh, darling, I'm so sorry. Is she going to be OK?'

'She's eighty-four,' he sighed, shoving his bare feet into his shoes. 'She shouldn't be living alone.

This is the third time she's fallen. But she won't hear of moving into a home. I keep telling her she should come and live with me, but she says she doesn't want to be a burden.' He ran a hand through his thinning hair. 'Frankly, she'd be less of a burden if I didn't have to worry about her all the time.'

She felt dreadfully sorry for Richard, of course, but in truth her sympathy was more with his mother, whom Zoey admired tremendously. Alice Quinn had raised four sons single-handedly after Richard's father died from a heart attack aged just fifty, and had already buried two of them for the same reason. She was proud and fiercely independent, and she still had all her marbles very firmly in place. Of *course* she couldn't stomach the thought of having to be grateful to her own son for the roof over her head! She was afraid he'd end up resenting her, and that would break her heart.

Zoey had a feeling she knew where this was going, even if Richard didn't. Alice was practically Nell's grandmother. Family stuck together. It was obvious: Alice had to come and live with her. How she'd juggle running the shop and looking after a sick old lady, she had no idea, but she'd find a way.

'Will you call me later?' Zoey asked anxiously as she followed him down the stairs. 'Let me know how she's doing?'

'Of course. Look, darling, I'm sorry about this. Of all the weekends for this to happen—'

'Don't be silly. As if it matters. We'll celebrate another time.' She kissed his cheek. 'Now go, and try not to worry. Alice is a fighter. She'll pull through.'

They both turned at the sound of a key in the back door. 'Darling!' Zoey exclaimed as Nell shoved the door open against the usual clutter of boxes and junk cluttering the hallway. 'You're home early!'

Nell bent to pick up the post trapped under the door and handed it to her mother. 'I brought Teri back with me,' she said redundantly as her friend followed her into the hall. 'Mum! It's nearly ten o'clock and you're not even dressed!'

Zoey glanced down as if surprised to find herself still in her bathrobe. 'Sorry, darling. I got a bit side-tracked.'

Richard pulled on his jacket. 'Sorry to run, girls, but I have to go.'

'Alice has had a fall,' Zoey explained. 'Richard's got to get to the hospital.'

Nell looked stricken. 'Oh no! Is she going to be OK?'

'Let's hope so,' he said heavily. 'Look, I'm sorry, sweetheart, but I really do have to go. I know I promised I'd take you and Mum to dinner tonight, and there was something we wanted to tell you, but—'

Nell threw her arms round him in a warm hug, cutting him off. 'Richard! Just give Alice a kiss from me, OK? Tell her she has to get better soon. She promised to teach me how to make brownies.'

As soon as the door closed behind him, she gave her mother a little push towards the stairs. 'Come on, Mum. Go and put something on. We need to buy Alice a get-well present. Old people need to feel valued – it helps them get better quicker. We did it in social studies.'

Zoey quickly dumped the junk mail in the bin and shoved the brown envelopes and a formal-looking white letter postmarked from the Princess Eugenie Hospital – the results of her Pap smear, at a guess – into an overflowing kitchen drawer and rammed it shut. Nothing that couldn't wait.

She puffed up the stairs again and opened her wardrobe, sifting through the packed rails. Alice's accident was awful, of course, and she was terribly worried about her, but she couldn't help feeling a tiny bit relieved at her own reprieve. Nell would be delighted she'd finally agreed to marry Richard – there was no question of *that*. But frankly she could do with another few hours to get used to the idea herself before they broke the news. After all, she'd only said yes last night, and it was going to mean big changes to all their lives. They'd have to move in with Richard, for a start; they could hardly expect him to live here.

She knew Nell loved it when they stayed at Richard's house – the bedroom he'd given her was twice the size of her own, and even had an ensuite – but he lived well outside the catchment area for her comprehensive. Maybe they could wangle something, get post sent to the old address, but even if the school didn't find out they'd moved, it would still be a long commute for Nell every day. Hanging out with her friends and after-school activities would be more difficult to arrange. And if the school *did* find out they'd moved out of the area, Nell could find herself forced to start somewhere entirely new just in time for her A-levels.

But what really gnawed at her, beyond logistics and practicalities, was that it would no longer be just the two of them – Nell and Zoey, an unbeatable team. Even though Richard had been part of their family for eight years, was Nell's father in every way that mattered, marriage would change things. There'd be no going back after this.

She gave herself a mental shake. Nell was right: it was just a piece of paper. Nothing that really mattered would change. Marrying Richard was a *good* thing.

The girls had tidied up the kitchen and were waiting impatiently by the back door when she finally came downstairs in an ankle-length pink skirt scattered with mirrors, and a loose orange linen tunic belted around the hips. She'd paired the outfit with boots (it *was* only April) and a battered leather messenger bag she'd had for twenty years, long before they'd become trendy.

'You look really cool, Mrs Sands,' Teri said admiringly.

'Oh, please don't call me that! It was never Mrs, and anyway, it makes me feel so old. I keep telling you, darling, call me Zoey.'

'Sorry, Mrs – I mean Zoey.'

'Now then,' Zoey said, 'where shall we go first?'

Teri giggled. She really was a pretty girl, Zoey thought, with her white-blonde hair, bright blue eyes and curvaceous figure. Beside Nell's pale, dark-haired beauty, they certainly made a striking pair.

It took them twenty minutes to walk to Upper Street, the two girls giggling and whispering arm-in-arm a couple of paces ahead of her. She didn't mind; Nell and Teri were like sisters, and Zoey didn't begrudge them their secrets and girlish confidences. It would have been so lovely if she could've given Nell a *real* sister. If Patrick had lived. If he'd left his wife for her and Nell . . .

'Mum! Hey, Mum, what d'you think of this?'

Nell had stopped by a market stall at the entrance to the Pierrepont Arcade and was plucking an aquamarine T-shirt from a rail. She held it out. 'Isn't this a gorgeous colour?'

'Oh, darling. It's lovely. And with your hair—'

'Mum! Not for me. For *you*.'

She looked doubtful. 'Nell, I couldn't – it's far too clingy for me.'

'Mum, it *so* isn't. It's totally cool.' She held it against Zoey. 'Teri, doesn't it make her eyes look, like, amazing?'

'Darling, you don't think it's a little . . . well . . . low-cut for me?'

'Mum, you're not even forty! Stop being so paranoid. It'll make your boobs look fantastic, trust me. Richard'll love it.'

Zoey found herself being hustled into a small cubicle curtained off at the back of the arcade, the T-shirt clutched to her chest. Nell was right, she thought with some surprise as she put the shirt on and studied her reflection in the small mirror pinned to the curtain: it *did* bring out the colour of her eyes, and her boobs looked . . . well, yes, fantastic. Somehow the T-shirt managed to cling to them but then skim lightly over her tummy, immediately knocking ten pounds off her. Well, six, at least.

'I *told* you,' Nell said smugly as Zoey paid for it.

'You've got a really good eye,' she heard Teri say as the girls traipsed into the arcade and stopped to admire some Victorian cameos. 'You should go to fashion college or something. You'd be brilliant.'

'Fashion's not really my thing,' Nell shrugged. 'Anyway, Mum's the one with the real talent. She was a way cool designer when she was young. She could've been totally famous if she hadn't had me.'

Zoey felt a warm tingle spread to her toes. So many of her friends bemoaned the fact that their teenage daughters never spoke to them except to demand transport and clean laundry, and would rather poke out their own eyes than willingly spend time with them. She had no idea what she'd done to deserve a daughter like Nell, but at this moment she knew she was the luckiest woman in the world.

She'd completely forgotten about the white envelope on top of the pile of letters she'd shoved into the kitchen drawer.

CHAPTER 9

HARRIET

'I wish you'd never told me!' Oliver yelled.

'How could I keep something like this to myself?' Harriet shouted back.

They'd been having the same argument for three weeks. Three weeks of going round and round the same subject, having the same fight, rehashing the same facts – and getting nowhere.

It had taken twenty-seven days for the DNA results to come through. For twenty-seven days Harriet hadn't slept, had hardly eaten, had spent her days in a waking nightmare and her turbulent nights drenched in sweat. When Oliver had asked her what was wrong, she'd blamed it on worry over the shock of suddenly learning her father had to have bladder surgery – to remove a tumour the doctors had assured them was benign – and then felt intensely guilty both for using her father's illness in such a selfish way and because Oliver made a point of asking after him often and treating her with exceptionally understanding sweetness.

When she'd finally seen the white envelope in the mailbox and recognized its embossed logo, she'd pleaded a headache and begged Oliver to do the school run, then fled upstairs and locked herself in the bathroom, her body trembling with nerves, her mouth dry with fear. Downstairs, the usual morning chaos – 'Where are my soccer boots? Mom! Dad! I can't find my boots!' 'Who finished the Cheerios? Sam, that's *so* not cool, you know I don't like Cornflakes!' 'I can't find my homework! I left it *right here*!' – peaked in a crescendo of running feet and slammed doors, and was then replaced with terrifying, empty silence.

She had waited five minutes, ten, needing to be certain nothing had been forgotten, no packed lunches left behind. When she was quite sure no one was coming back, she closed the lavatory seat, sat down and stared at the envelope in her hands.

Was Oliver Florence's father? Or was it Ben?

It had to be Oliver. She couldn't imagine the consequences if . . .

Was Oliver Florence's father?

It all came down to this. A few sentences on a piece of paper.

She had ripped open the envelope, tearing the contents in her haste. She'd pulled out four pages of charts and closely typed writing stapled together, and a covering letter. Her hands were shaking so much, she couldn't even bring the words into focus. In the end, she'd had to flatten the letter on her lap so she could read it. *Paternal subject: Oliver Peter Lockwood . . . Maternal subject: Harriet Jane Lockwood . . . Minor subject: Florence May Lockwood . . .*

Then the usual legal disclaimers about chain of custody, *not to be relied on in court* − yes, yes.

And then the words that changed everything.

It took her three attempts simply to comprehend what the letter was saying. She read it through a fourth time, to be absolutely sure she hadn't made a mistake. Then she turned to the accompanying pages of charts and scientific analysis, looking for a way out, a loophole. It could have been written in Mandarin for all the sense it made.

She had turned back to the letter and read it a fifth and final time. Then she had flipped open the lid of the lavatory and vomited and vomited into it until her throat and mouth burned with acid.

She'd spent all afternoon obsessively reading about similar cases online. It didn't happen very often, of course, especially these days when there was such tight security at hospitals, identity bracelets were put on mother and child, prints of tiny hands and feet were carefully taken and filed with the baby's medical notes. Most of the stories she'd found of babies carelessly muddled up had taken place in small village hospitals and dated back to the Fifties. Some mistakes had been quickly rectified; others hadn't been discovered for years. Two girls switched at birth in 1951 in a small town in Wisconsin hadn't discovered the truth until they were forty-three years old. But mistakes like this did still happen, even now. Only three years ago, two Russian women had discovered they'd been given the wrong daughters twelve years before. A few years before that, two newborn Czech girls had been muddled up, and the mistake hadn't come to light for nine months. And it wasn't just Eastern Europe. In 2008, two mothers in Illinois had been given the wrong baby boys after they'd been taken to be circumcised, and their bracelets had come off and been accidentally swapped. It happened. She couldn't think how it had happened in London in 1998, but it had. The DNA results were unequivocal. Florence May Lockwood was not related in any way to Oliver Peter Lockwood or to Harriet Jane Lockwood. She was not their biological child.

It was unthinkable. Unbelievable. But Florence was not their daughter.

She had entirely forgotten it was Florence's prom that night until Oliver came into her study and found her still obsessively scouring the Internet. She'd quickly pulled up a work spreadsheet so he wouldn't see what she was doing as he chattered on and on about taking the kids to Flatbread Pizza. She had to tell him. But how? How could you tell the man you loved something that would break his heart? Did he really need to know?

But then he'd kissed her neck, stroked her shoulders, touched her in the way only he knew how, and she'd realized she couldn't do it, couldn't keep this lie from him. It would always be there between them, eating away at their marriage. They'd always been honest with each other. It was a fundamental pillar of their relationship. Even as her body responded to him, as he'd stripped her naked and moved inside her, she'd known she couldn't keep her secret any longer and pushed him away.

As he'd yanked on his trousers, furious and hurt, she'd laid it all out before him: the terrible, creeping doubt that had consumed her after Florence's accident, about sending off their toothbrushes, secretly, without consulting him, without asking him.

And Ben. She'd had to tell him about Ben, since that was the starting point of all this.

At first, that hadn't seemed to matter. All he could focus on was Florence.

'*How?*' he'd demanded when he'd finally understood what she was saying to him, when he'd read the letter three, four, five times, as she had, and thrown it back at her. 'How can this have happened? I was with you when she was born! I held her, I even cut the cord! I watched them put the bracelet on her, I saw them bath her and wash her, I was with her every second! How could there have been a mistake? Jesus Christ, that damn hospital identity bracelet is stuck in your bloody baby book! Mistakes like that just don't happen these days!'

'They do,' she'd said wearily. 'You weren't with Florence every second of every day. She went off to the nursery with all the other babies, remember? She was there for three days. It could have happened at any time.'

'But you *breastfed* her, Harriet! She came back to you every few hours! For God's sake, wouldn't you have *noticed* if you'd had the wrong baby?'

You were her mother. What kind of mother doesn't know her own child?

He hadn't said that, of course. He hadn't needed to.

'It was all so *new*,' she'd pleaded, knowing how weak it sounded. 'It took me a while to get to know her. Everyone kept saying how much she looked like you when we took her home, even you! Why *would* I think she wasn't ours? How could I have known?'

'Remember the stork-bite?' he'd said suddenly. 'That pink birthmark on the back of her neck?'

'Of course—'

'And how quickly it faded?'

'The midwife said it would. It wasn't a proper birthmark, it was just from the delivery.'

'Yes, but to fade *completely* in twenty-four hours?'

Oh God! How had she not remembered this? He was right. They'd both remarked on it at the time, how quickly the birthmark had vanished. Overnight, in fact. And then they'd forgotten about it, too caught up in the chaos of new parenthood to give it another thought.

Somewhere out there was a little girl who *had* gone home with a birthmark. *Their daughter.*

'The first night in the hospital,' she'd said, piecing it together. 'You'd gone home to sleep. The fire alarm went off. Florence was in the nursery. I tried to go to her, but the nurses said it was just a false alarm, told us all to go back to bed. But they were all running around, no one knew what was happening—'

'Florence is our daughter,' he'd interrupted as if she hadn't spoken. 'We've loved her and raised her for fifteen years. I'm her father. You're her mother. That's all that matters.'

'Our *child* is out there!' she'd cried then. 'The baby I carried inside me for nine months! We can't just ignore that!'

'Yes we can.'

She'd stared at him incredulously. 'Oliver, we can't just pretend this hasn't happened! We can't just abandon her! She's our daughter!'

'No! *Florence* is our daughter!'

'Of course she is! I love her as much as you do. Nothing's going to change that. But we have another daughter somewhere out there, a child who's *part* of us.' The tears were falling now, fast and hot on her hands. 'We've got no idea where she is, Oliver, how she is, what kind of family she's with—'

'Precisely.' His tone had softened. 'Harriet, we have no idea what kind of family she's with, or what they might make of all of this. Have you thought through what might happen if we try to find her? Suppose we track down the people who have our biological child – and that's a big *if* right there. People move, women marry, change their names . . . it wouldn't be easy. But OK, suppose we found her. What do you think the other family might do?'

'They'd be shocked, like we are, but then—'

'Then what? Suppose they decided they wanted their daughter – *our* daughter, Florence – back? Suppose they decided to sue for custody?'

'They couldn't do that!'

'We don't know that. Right now, we don't know anything. I've got no idea of the legal ramifications of this, and nor have you. God knows which court would have jurisdiction or what they might decide. All I know is that if we leave well alone, we'll never have to find out.'

He wasn't listening to her. He'd made up his mind. All he cared about was making this go away.

'Please, Oliver. *Please*. We can't just forget about it. Forget about *her*. I can't, I *can't*, not now I know.'

'You're the one who opened Pandora's box!' His voice had cracked. 'Why couldn't you have just left it alone?'

'I told you,' she'd whispered. 'I had to *know*.'

'*I* didn't have to know!' he'd cried furiously. 'Don't you realize what you've done? We have to keep this from Florence for the rest of her life! I'm going to have to lie to my daughter again and again, look her in the eye and *lie* to her, just because *you* needed to know!'

'What else could I do?' she'd said helplessly.

'Nothing,' Oliver had shot back. 'You could have done *nothing*.'

The room had shrunk to the four feet between them, a distance that suddenly seemed unbridgeable.

He'd crossed his arms, literally barring her from getting close. 'Tell me, Harriet. All those stories you looked up online. How many of them had a happy ending?'

She'd stared wretchedly at her hands, tears blurring her vision. The Czech babies: at nine months old, when the switch had been discovered, the authorities had decided it was in the best interests of the children to be switched back. Nine months old! A baby knew you by then, reached out for you, smiled at you. Your love for it was part of the warp and weft of your very being. How could you be expected to swap your baby for another as if you were exchanging a handbag?

Oliver was right. What if the other family *did* sue for custody? There had been several cases right here in America where that had happened, with confused children forced to shuttle between the parents who'd raised them and their biological parents like the children of divorce, only a hundred times worse. Was that really what she wanted for Florence? It would scar her irreparably. And what if – like some of the children she'd read about – Florence decided she wanted to live with her birth parents instead?

If she looked for her baby, the child she'd carried and nurtured and given birth to, she risked losing Florence, the daughter she'd raised and loved for so long.

How could she choose? How could anyone expect a mother to *choose*?

'I know it hurts,' Oliver had said painfully. 'It's the same for me. But we have to forget about this. We have to put it behind us for ever.'

'And . . . if I can't?'

'You have to.' His expression had hardened. 'I swear to God, Harriet – if you don't let this go, if you do anything to risk this family, *anything*, I will never forgive you.'

That hadn't been the end of it, of course. For the past three weeks, they'd returned to the subject again and again, rehashing the same arguments, hitting the same roadblocks and resolving nothing. Oliver was adamant: she was to do nothing, say nothing, forget she'd ever opened that letter. He refused to discuss it or tell her how he really felt, as if burying his head in the sand would change anything. For the first time in sixteen years of marriage, she had no idea what was really going on in his head, and it frightened her. They'd disagreed about important things before – whether to have a second child, for instance – but nothing had ever left them implacably polarized like this. The gulf between them yawned wider every day. She'd once read that the death of a child caused ninety per cent of marriages to collapse as each parent retreated into their own grief. They hadn't lost Florence, of course, and yet in some ways it was almost as if they *had* been bereaved.

She did her best to treat Florence the same as always, as if nothing had happened. If anything, she was more attentive than usual, fussing over her, double-checking her sugar levels, driving her to school instead of letting her walk, as if determined to prove to Oliver – to prove to *herself* – that she loved Florence as much as she ever had. But she couldn't look at her without thinking of her *other* daughter, the child whose name she didn't even know, and wondering if the mother looking after her could possibly love her as much.

Some of what Oliver said made sense – she knew that. If she pursued this and tried to find their biological daughter, she'd be taking them all into uncharted territory. But she couldn't just forget about it, even if Oliver could. It had happened. They had to face it. She had to find her child.

She just prayed that one day Oliver would understand.

CHAPTER 10

FLORENCE

Florence despised her diabetes. She hated the shots every time she ate, the finger pricks to test her sugar levels, the maths nightmare involved in working out the carb content of every-thing she consumed and the consequent amount of insulin she had to inject, the fact that she always had to be aware of the terrifying sugar lows which could kill her in hours, and the insidious sugar highs which could slowly destroy her kidneys, her nerve endings, her sight.

But what she hated most, what drove her beyond insane, was the way it had turned her mother into a suffocating nightmare. Helicopter parent? She was like a one-woman Black Hawk squadron.

She *never* stopped checking up on her. She pressed glucose tabs into her hand in front of her friends every time she went out. Phoned the school nurse practically every day to ask whether she'd eaten all her lunch, had taken her insulin, wasn't running low – as if she was still in kindergarten, not fifteen! And her mother's constant *guilt*, as if it was Mom's fault Florence had diabetes in the first place. She didn't blame Mom, but she knew

Mom thought she did. Every time she took Florence to the specialist, she acted guilty, and that just made her feel guilty too; and she was *so* over feeling guilty about Mom.

At first, when she'd been newly diagnosed, it hadn't been so bad. She'd only been six, and hadn't minded – too much – being looked after and fussed over. But as she'd gotten older and learned to manage her diabetes herself, Mom hadn't grown up with her. If anything, she'd gotten worse. She hadn't been allowed to go to a sleepover until she was thirteen, and even then Mom had totally embarrassed her by calling every hour to check she was all right. She hadn't tried it again. It wasn't worth it.

'Did you remember your diabetes pack?' her mother asked now as they entered the hospital waiting room.

'Yes.'

'And your insulin monitor? They have to enter that in their computer—'

'Yes, Mom, I *know*. We've come here every three months for, like, *years*. You don't even need to be here. I can do it myself.'

'Don't be silly, Florence. I'm your mother.'

'Don't I know it,' she muttered beneath her breath.

Mom marched up to the receptionist. 'We're here to see Dr Magda Lancaster. My daughter is Florence Lockwood. She has diabetes.'

'They know that,' she hissed furiously. 'Everyone here does. It's a freaking *diabetes* clinic.'

She stormed to the far corner of the waiting room and, so that her mother couldn't sit next to her, deliberately chose a single chair between two other patients, both girls not much older than she was. Neither of *them* had their mothers with them, she noticed bitterly.

Her mother frowned and then took a seat on the other side of one of the girls. 'I hope your A1C number is better than last time,' she said fretfully across her. 'Your sugar's been running high lately. And you know what Dr Lancaster said last time. If we don't manage it properly you'll end up with kidney damage or—'

'Mom,' she snapped. 'I get it.'

She grabbed a magazine from the table and pointedly buried her head in it. Her mother subsided, but she could feel the angst radiating from her. She knew her mother worried, she did *get* it, but sometimes all that worrying seemed to be about her diabetes, her schoolwork, her college chances – and none of it about Florence herself. When was the last time Mom had asked her how she felt about anything?

In the last few weeks, things at home had moved to a whole new level. Her mother was just being plain *weird*. She kept catching Mom staring at her when she thought she wasn't looking, like she was doing right now. She held the magazine closer to her face. One minute Mom was hugging her in the hallway like she was five years old – something she hadn't done since she *was* five – and the next she was gazing at her like she'd never seen her before. And what was this weird new obsession with all their old photo albums? She'd been poring over them practically every night. In the end, Dad had grabbed them away from her and locked them in his study. He wasn't himself, either. She'd heard them arguing at night, when they thought she was asleep, and during the day they barely talked to each other. God, she hoped they weren't going to get divorced. If they were, there was no way she was going to live with Mom.

'Florence Lockwood?'

A nurse in teddy-bear scrubs stood at the entrance to the doctor's office, clipboard in hand.

'Come on, Florence,' her mother beckoned, leaping to her feet.

'Mom, you don't have to come in.'

'I need to hear what Dr Lancaster has to say. Please, Florence, I don't know why you're being so *difficult*.'

She threw down the magazine and slouched after her mother, arms folded over her baggy school sweatshirt, cheeks burning. They went through the usual routine: blood pressure, height, weight – 'Sweetheart, it's *normal* to put on a bit of weight, you're still growing!' – and a pinprick sugar test, and then followed the nurse into an examination room with brightly coloured parrots and monkeys painted all over the walls. She couldn't wait till she was eighteen and could be treated in the adult diabetes clinic. This was just humiliating.

They sat in strained silence on the uncomfortable plastic chairs, Florence tapping an impatient beat on the floor with one of her trainers.

'Florence, please. Stop that.'

She stopped for a few moments, and then deliberately started up again. Her mother sighed and stood up to peer out of the window. Three floors below them, workmen manoeuvred earth-movers and cranes. A new hospital wing, or maybe an extension of the ever-expanding parking lot. Screw the environment, right?

The door opened. 'Hey, Florence,' Dr Lancaster said, leaning casually against the exam counter and folding her arms. 'How are things today?'

She liked that the doctor talked to *her*, looked at *her*, not her mother. 'Same old. I like your necklace,' she added diffidently.

'My husband gave it to me on our anniversary last year. He says it's called steampunk. Is that right? Victorian Gothic. It's made from an old watch fob and chain from England.'

Florence's face lit up. 'I love steampunk. It's so *Twilight*. I've tried making a few things from old jewellery and watch gears, but it's so hard to get the right pieces in this country. I saw this amazing necklace online the other day – it'd been made from a tiny glass globe compass that'd been set in a—'

'Darling, don't let's waste the doctor's time,' Mom interrupted. 'How's her A1C? Her sugar's been really hard to control this past couple of months. Of course, it doesn't help when she snacks and doesn't cover it with insulin . . .'

'It's higher than we'd like,' the doctor admitted. 'I'm a little worried, Florence, looking at your numbers—'

'We've tried cutting down on carbs, but it's not easy,' Mom said quickly. 'I've even been baking my own bread, and I try to make sure she has a protein frittata for breakfast, but I don't have any control over what she eats at school, and I'm sure that's a large part of the problem.'

Teacher's pet, Florence thought sourly. *It's not my fault, doctor. Florence is the one who let the team down.*

She zoned out as they pored over her chart, talking numbers, ratios, correction factors. She was sick of it, sick of the monitoring and calculations and the damn shots. OK, yes, she cheated sometimes. Now and again she had half a can of a friend's soda or some popcorn at the movies, and she didn't cover it with insulin. So what? Mom should try walking in her shoes for five minutes before she started bitching about being *irresponsible*.

'Do you think we should consider the pump again?' Mom asked the doctor. 'You said it might control her sugar better once she hit puberty.'

Her head snapped up. If she heard the word *period*, she swore to God she was out of here.

'That has to be Florence's decision, Mrs Lockwood.'

'No pump,' she said flatly.

'I don't know why you won't even *consider* it,' her mother sighed. 'It would give you so much more freedom. The pump would do all the maths for you. You wouldn't have to have a shot every time you wanted a glass of orange juice—'

'I don't want to be attached to a stupid pump like there's something *wrong* with me!' she exploded. 'At least with the shots, they're over and done with and I can get on with my life! You think I want to walk around with a stupid lump under my clothes reminding everyone I'm a freak? I just have diabetes, Mom! It's not who I *am*!'

'I'm just thinking about what's best for you—'

'No you're not! You're thinking about what's best for *you*!'

There was a brief silence.

'Mrs Lockwood,' the doctor said gently, opening the door. 'Why don't you go and grab a coffee while Florence and I have a chat?'

Her mother hesitated. Florence scowled at her trainers. Maybe she had gone a bit far with that last dig, but she wasn't going to give Mom a break. Not this time.

'The machine is just down the hall,' the doctor added. 'I'll come update you when we're done.'

Why does it have to be this hard? Florence thought unhappily as the door closed behind her mother. She'd seen her friends' mothers bickering with them, laying down rules, vetoing short skirts and parties; but she'd also seen them shopping together, gossiping about boys, being *friends*. She and Mom were like total strangers. She couldn't imagine going to her mother with a problem, or asking her advice. She'd as soon stop some random woman in the street.

She'd expected the third degree the minute she came back to the waiting room, but to her surprise, Mom said nothing. They collected the car from the parking lot and drove home in silence. Florence shot her several sidelong glances, waiting for the other shoe to drop, but Mom seemed lost in her own thoughts. See, *weird*. Normally she'd have torn her a new one over the way she'd sassed her in front of the doctor, but it was like Mom had forgotten about it already. Like somehow in the grand scheme of things, it didn't even matter.

As soon as they unlocked the back door and stepped into the mudroom, Dad came through from the kitchen as if he'd been waiting for them. Florence went to give him a hug, but he waved her away without looking at her, his gaze boring straight into her mother. She'd never seen the expression on his face before: an icy, blanched anger, his blue eyes slate-grey with fury, a muscle working at the base of his jaw as he struggled to rein in his temper. She had no idea what had made him this angry with her mother, but it had to be really, *really* bad.

Florence quailed in the doorway as he stepped forward and thrust an open letter at Mom, forcing her to take it. When he spoke, his voice was as cold and unforgiving as his expression.

'Harriet,' he hissed between clenched teeth, *'what have you done?'*

CHAPTER 11

ZOEY

Zoey simply didn't believe it. It was so ridiculous, she wanted to laugh. So *out there*, as Nell would say, she'd have thought it was an April Fool's joke, except that it was now May.

She tucked the letter into the pocket of her sloppy purple cardigan and filled the kettle with water. If it really wasn't a joke – and surely no one would take a joke this far, with embossed headed notepaper and tests at the *hospital*, for heaven's sake – then it was clearly a mistake. Given that the Princess Eugenie had sent two women home with the wrong babies, as they were suggesting they had, then obviously they were more than capable of muddling up a couple of letters and sending them out to the wrong people.

She edged past the teetering pile of cardboard boxes in the hallway – she really must get round to sorting them out before Nell had kittens – and took two mugs of tea into the tiny sitting room.

'Can I see the letter again?' Richard said as she handed him his mug.

She pulled it out of her pocket. 'You'd think they could at least get *this* right,' she said cheerfully, kicking off her shoes and curling up next to him on the sofa. 'Some poor woman out there has been told everything's fine, while I've obviously got the letter meant for her. Can you imagine how she's going to feel when she finds out?'

'Zoey,' he said, frowning. 'I think we need to talk about this.'

She laughed. 'I can't see why. I'll just call the hospital, tell them they've screwed up, and leave them to sort it out.'

'Where's the first letter?'

She stood up and rummaged through a heap of papers on her writing bureau. It had taken her ten days to get round to opening the first letter, the one she'd shoved in her kitchen drawer. It hadn't been her Pap smear results after all; instead, she'd been surprised to find a request from the Princess Eugenie Hospital that she and Nell – and Nell's father, though obviously that wasn't going to happen – come in to 'clarify some confusion' with regard to Nell's medical records. It had all sounded so routine, it hadn't occurred to her to be concerned. She hadn't even mentioned it to Richard. The hospital had given them an appointment for the following week, and she had, without questioning, taken Nell to it. Zoey trusted authority, believed in it. People who ran things had to know better than she did; she relied on it.

The two of them had been in and out of the surgery in ten minutes. A simple cheek swab each and they were done.

Thinking back now, maybe it *was* a little odd that they'd been seen so quickly; she'd taken her new Maeve Binchy for the waiting room and hadn't even had time to get it out of her bag. But why should she have been suspicious? This was a *hospital*, for goodness' sake. They knew what they were doing. Didn't they?

'It's obviously a mistake,' she said again as Richard reread both letters. 'I'll just let them know and—'

'Zoey,' he said, 'Zoey, what if it's not?'

'Oh, don't be silly! Nell's the spitting image of Patrick! You only have to *look* at her. No, this is ridiculous. Some pen-pusher's got his wires crossed and made an almighty cock-up, that's all this is.'

'The hospital seems fairly sure of the facts.'

She leaned over his shoulder and pointed at the second letter. 'A *discrepancy*. That's what it says. Look. They're just saying there's a discrepancy in the results. They haven't been able to test her father, obviously, so that probably messed everything up. It's a big hospital – dozens of babies must have been born the same day as Nell. They've just asked us to come back for more tests, which means even the doctors can't tell their left hands from their right.'

'Or they're trying to soften the blow until you come in, so they can tell you the full story in person.' He took her hand. 'Look, darling. I'm not trying to upset you. But you need to face this. What if the hospital is *right*?'

She stared at him. Richard was the steadiest, safest, most conservative man she knew. He never leapt to conclusions or took anything for granted until he had it before him written out in triplicate, and preferably notarized. If he was taking this seriously, if he thought it might be true . . .

No. There was no way this could be true. *How* could the hospital be right? She was Nell's mother! She'd loved her fiercely with every fibre of her being for fifteen years. When Nell hurt, *she* hurt. When Nell smiled, *she* smiled. She'd fed and changed and bathed her, she knew every freckle and scar, she'd kissed every scraped knee and taught her to roller skate and plait her hair. She saw herself reflected in her daughter every day; not physically, though they'd always shared those great grey eyes, but in the way she thought, in her mannerisms and quirks. How could Nell be any *more* hers?

A devil of doubt on her shoulder prodded her. *Quirks and mannerisms could be learned.* She'd raised her alone for years; of course Nell reflected her. Even the grey eyes – was that just wishful thinking?

'I'm not going for any more tests,' she said firmly. 'They can't *make* me, can they?'

'I don't know,' he admitted. 'I'm not a lawyer. Maybe. Look, Zoey, the important thing is no one can take Nell from you, not now. She's not a baby – she's fifteen years old. They're not about to switch her back. But if she isn't your biological daughter – wait, I'm only saying *if* – that means somewhere out there is a child who *is*.'

She felt as if she'd been punched in the stomach. *Her daughter; Patrick's daughter.* The sudden, atavistic need to find and protect her was overwhelming.

No. Nell was her daughter. In every way that counted.

'If this turns out to be true,' he said quietly, 'do you think you have a right to keep it from her?'

'What good will it do her to know?' she cried. 'She's happy. You and I are getting married. Why complicate things?'

'She may have brothers and sisters, Zoey. Grandparents. Aunts and uncles . . .'

She caught her breath. *Brothers and sisters.* The family Nell had longed for all her life. How could she keep that from her?

To protect her. 'Brothers and sisters she's never even *met*.'

'She may also have a father.'

'You're her father,' Zoey said staunchly. 'You have been for eight years. You're all the father she's ever needed.'

'That's sweet of you to say so. But we both know it's not really true.'

For a long moment she said nothing.

'You think the hospital's right, don't you?' she asked finally.

She could see him choosing his words with care. 'I think they must be fairly sure of their facts this time round, for legal reasons if nothing else. If they've made a mistake, they're already liable for millions. They'd hardly want to make that worse.'

'I don't care about *money*!'

'I know that. But you have to understand this is bigger than you and Nell now. This other woman, the other mother, clearly isn't going to let it drop, not now she's forced the hospital to track you down. This is going to take on a life of its own.'

Her hand trembled as she raised her mug to her lips. Her tea had long gone cold, but she drank it anyway. Her mouth was so dry she could hardly swallow.

'I think you need to prepare Nell,' he said gently. 'She needs to hear it from you.'

'She doesn't need to hear it at all. *We're* her family, Richard. *We're* all she needs.'

They both turned at the sound of a key in the back door. Moments later, Nell erupted into the sitting room, dumping her backpack on the floor. She looked excited but tense, bouncing lightly on the balls of her feet as if she was about to bolt from the room. Zoey recognized the look on her face: she'd seen it when Nell had confessed to breaking her sewing machine running up an outfit for design class that had come top of the year, and when she'd admitted to bunking off school to see the Stones in concert a year or two ago. Pride and guilt in equal measure.

'Go on then,' she sighed. 'Today can hardly get any worse.'

'Mum,' Nell said, her eyes brilliant. 'Mum, I've just met my brother.'

'*Patrick's* son?' Zoey said. 'How? Why? *How?*' she said again.

Nell grinned with triumph. 'OK. So I knew he had a son called Ryan – it mentioned him in an article I read online. It took me a while to find the right Ryan James on Facebook – it would have been a whole lot easier if he was called something like Bretzina – but in the end I tracked him down. We've been texting and stuff for a couple of months now. We thought it would be cool to take the afternoon off and meet up for real. It's OK, Mum. You don't have to worry. Ryan's cool.'

'But why?' she said, bewildered. '*Why* would you want to meet him?'

'He's her brother,' Richard said quietly.

She was stunned. That Nell should seek out Patrick's son was the last thing she'd ever expected. All this time, and she'd never said a word about wanting to find her father's family. And then to find out about it today of all days. When Ryan might not be Nell's brother after all.

She buried her face in her hands, not knowing whether to laugh or cry.

'Mum? Mum, you are OK with this, right?'

'I – yes – it's just a shock, that's all.' She straightened up and forced a smile. 'Does his mother know you're in touch?'

Nell looked uncomfortable. 'I don't think so.

She's never mentioned me to Ryan. I'm guessing my dad never told her?'

Zoey shook her head.

'Ryan was really cool about it,' Nell said, perching on the sofa next to Richard. 'He was a bit surprised to discover I existed at first, especially when he found out he was only a couple of months older than me, so our dad must've . . . you know. Been a bit of a player, was how Ryan put it.' She grinned. 'But I think he kind of likes that, in a weird way. His mum got married again, and she never talks about his dad. He said it was kind of cool to meet me. Sort of like getting a little piece of his dad back.'

'He . . . sounds very . . . cool,' Zoey managed. 'Very . . . like Patrick.'

'You think so? Would you like to see a picture of him? I took one on my phone—'

'Nell, your mum's had a long day,' Richard said calmly. 'Why don't you give her a bit of time to catch up with all this, and we can talk about it at dinner?'

'Mum? You don't mind, do you? I'm not trying to diss you or Richard.'

'It's OK,' he said. 'Neither of us thought you were. It's only natural you'd want to know about Patrick and his family. Of course we don't mind.'

She threw her arms round him. 'I knew you'd understand. No one could ever be my dad but you.'

Richard pinked with pleasure as she kissed the top of his balding head. 'Get on with you, Nell.'

'Patrick's *son*?' Zoey repeated softly as Nell disappeared upstairs. 'What was she *thinking*?'

'That she wanted to reach out to her family.'

'But I don't understand where this has come from. She hardly ever even talks about Patrick.'

'She doesn't, or you don't?'

She hesitated. 'You're right. I should've told her she had a half-brother, not left her to find him by herself. We should've done it together. I just didn't think . . . I didn't realize.'

'None of this means she loves you any less. I think she's just curious. She just wants to know who she is. It's understandable, isn't it?'

She stared down at her hands. 'I have to tell her, don't I? About the – the mix-up.'

'I think you do. Yes.'

'Will you come with me to the hospital?'

'Oh, Zo.' He pulled her into his arms and she buried her head in the soft flannel of his shirt. 'I'll be with you every step of the way.'

She gripped Richard's hand as hard as if she was giving birth again as they sat in the ornate office of the hospital director two days later, listening to a stranger explain that the daughter she'd loved and looked after for fifteen years was not the child she'd carried inside her, was in fact someone else's child, a cuckoo baby. She didn't cry. She didn't get angry. She should have known this beautiful, smart, willowy girl who'd amazed and delighted her all these years didn't really belong to her. Was far more than she'd ever deserved.

She let Richard ask the questions, let the apologies and explanations wash over her. What did any of it matter now, how it had happened or why. *The fire alarm . . . only possible theory . . . thorough review of procedures, could never happen again . . . Prepared to make a very generous settlement . . . total confidentiality . . . counselling will be made available . . . anything we can do to facilitate reintegration between the two families . . . naturally, given they live in America . . .*

'America?' she said sharply, looking up. 'What do you mean, *America?*'

'Ms Sands, as I've been trying to explain. The Lockwoods relocated to Vermont twelve years ago. Of course we realize this is an added complication in enabling contact between the two families, which is why our lawyers are prepared to agree a most generous—'

'It doesn't make things any more complicated at all,' she said abruptly, standing and gathering her coat. 'You said the Lockwoods are a very nice family. They have a comfortable life, my child is happy and healthy. That's all I need to know.'

'Zoey—'

'No, Richard. When I feel the time is right, I'll tell Nell. She'll be eighteen in a few years, able to decide for herself what she wants to do. But I don't want to meet . . . the other child. I *can't.*'

'Florence,' he said quietly. 'She's called Florence.'

117

She struggled with that for a moment. *Florence.* Giving her a name suddenly made her real. She could see the girl's face in her mind's eye, a version of Zoey herself when she was younger, as Nell had never been.

She forced the vision away. The baby she'd once carried had grown up into a teenager she didn't know. *Nell* was her daughter in the only way that mattered, and she'd fight tooth and nail to protect her.

'Mrs Lockwood is very anxious to have contact with her biological child,' the director said nervously. 'I was hoping we could all come to some arrangement . . .'

She pulled on her coat. 'I'm sorry, but the answer is *no*. I understand that's hard for Mrs Lockwood, but I have to put Nell first.'

'You realize it's not going to end here,' Richard murmured once they had left the director's office and were taking the lift down to the hospital car park. 'This woman seems very keen to make contact with Nell. I'm not actually sure we'll be able to prevent her, in the end.'

'Then I'll just have to do my level best to try.'

'She may decide to take this to court. Is that really what you want?'

Zoey slammed her bag on top of the car. '*None* of this is what I want! But if that woman insists on access to *my* child, she'll have to come through me first! Courts move slowly, Richard, you know that, especially when you're dealing with two

118

separate legal systems in different countries. There are ways to drag this out. Every month I can protect Nell from this, I intend to. With any luck we can spin it out long enough for her to be able to make her own decisions when the time comes.'

Time. That's all she wanted. Time to find a way to prepare Nell for this, if such a thing was even possible. She knew she couldn't keep it from her for ever, but Nell was still only fifteen. Zoey wanted to protect her just a little bit longer. Was that really too much to ask?

Her question was answered ten days later when she answered the kitchen door and came face to face with a woman who could only be Nell's mother.

LAW OFFICES

TOPOLESKI, WILLIAMS & OUIMETTE, P.L.L.C.

100 MAIN STREET

P.O. BOX 1100

BURLINGTON, VERMONT 05402-1100

JERROLD M. TOPOLESKI   **JENNIFER HARRIS, PARALEGAL**

KAREN A. WILLIAMS   **BENJAMIN GREEN, PARALEGAL**

MICHEL OUIMETTE

TELEPHONE: (802) 881 6768

FACSIMILE: (802) 881 6769

OF COUNSEL:

TERESA P. FLETCHER (802) 881 6767

May 7, 2013

Harriet Lockwood

260 Maple Street

Burlington

VT 05401

Dear Mrs Lockwood,

Enclosed please find confirmation of receipt of funds from the proceeds of sale from your shares in Lockwood Ltd, in the amount of $150,000.00. The funds will be held in our company accounts as requested. Should you require us to wire the funds in whole or in part to your bank in London, England, please provide us with a minimum of forty-eight hours' notice to ensure availability when required.

Sincerely,

Jerry Topoleski

Enclosure

CHAPTER 12

HARRIET

In sixteen years, Harriet could count on the fingers of one hand the times she and Oliver had fought – really *fought*. When she'd cancelled a skiing holiday because she refused to leave Florence – newly diagnosed with diabetes – with his parents and he'd castigated her as overprotective. When he'd taken out a new loan for the business without telling her, using their home as collateral; although by the time she'd found out, he'd already paid it back with interest.

Now it seemed fighting was all they did.

'You want to *abandon* your own daughter?' she cried. 'We know who she is, where she is, and you don't even want to *see* her?'

'I've always known who and where she is,' he said shortly. 'About ten feet along the hall.'

'Be serious, Oliver.'

He stepped out of the shower and snapped a towel around his waist. 'I've never been more serious. *Florence* is my daughter. How many times do I have to tell you that?'

'But she *isn't*! When are you going to face up to that? You can't keep burying your head in the sand!'

'I'm not burying my head in the sand. I'm trying to protect Florence!'

'And letting her live a lie for the rest of her life is protecting her, is it?'

'Damn straight!' he shouted. 'Do you have any idea what you've done, Harriet? You started this thing, sending off those bloody toothbrushes to ease your guilty conscience, and then you contacted the hospital behind my back after I begged you not to. When will you realize this isn't just about you? It's about all of us: you, me, Florence, the boys – and another family who are being put through hell right now because of you! God alone knows how those poor people are feeling! How is this helping anyone?'

'I was thinking of our daughter,' she protested tearfully. 'I had to know she was all right!'

'*Our* daughter is safe at home, here with us, where she's always been! You weren't thinking of anyone but yourself!'

'That's not true—'

'Isn't it? You've made a mess of things with Florence, and you thought this would finally get you off the hook. Give you a brand-new dream daughter to get it right with. Well, I've got news for you. *You're* the one who screwed up your relationship with Florence. It has nothing to do with whether she has our genes or not.'

She reeled. He'd never spoken to her like this, *never*. No matter how bad things had got, even in their worst fights when they'd reduced each other to tears, he'd never gone for her soft under-belly, her Achilles' heel. He'd always fought fairly. In their relationship, she was the one who stormed and yelled, and he was the voice of reason, even if that reason caused him to be furious at times.

She'd thought he would understand, would forgive her, once she'd actually found their birth daughter. He'd want to see Nell – their daughter was called Nell – and that would make everything she'd done to bring it about all right.

She'd never imagined he'd look at her the way he was looking at her now, as if he didn't even know her. As if he didn't *want* to know her.

'I love Florence. This has nothing to do with how I feel about her,' she pleaded. 'I just couldn't let Nell go, not now, not without—'

'You keep telling yourself that,' he said coldly, flinging his towel on the bed. 'Maybe a part of it's even true. But ask yourself this, Harriet. If it were Sam or George or Charlie, would you still feel this way?'

She'd asked herself that same question many times over the past few weeks, and in the dead of night, when she stared up at the ceiling and forced herself to face the truth of who and what she was, she'd known the answer was no. The ache and sense of loss would still have been there, of course, if it had been Sam or George or Charlie who'd been mixed up. But it wouldn't have been coloured by an emotion so shameful she found it hard to admit even to herself. It wouldn't have been shot through with *relief*.

All those times she'd asked herself what was wrong with her because she couldn't feel the same bond with Florence she felt with her boys. All the times she'd looked at her daughter and seen the eyes of a stranger looking back. The guilt and the doubt and the self-recrimination – none of it need ever have existed. She and Florence lacked the natural connection of mother and child because they *weren't*.

She loved Florence, there was no question of that. She'd step in front of a speeding train to save her. But there was a *reason* they weren't close. There was a *reason* Florence had always felt like a cuckoo in the nest.

She followed Oliver as he stormed into his dressing room, automatically picking up his wet towel from the bed and putting it neatly in the laundry basket. 'You're not being fair,' she said, struggling to keep her emotions in check. 'What was I supposed to do? Don't you think Florence deserves to know the truth?'

'Yes, maybe. When she's older, when she's more able to deal with it.' He yanked on a pair of trousers and grimly buckled his belt. 'We could have prepared her, found a way to help her through it. We'd have been in control. But thanks to you, it's out of our hands now. You've lit the fucking touch-paper and there's no going back now. God alone knows what you've brought down on our heads.'

'It doesn't have to be like that,' she said eagerly, following him as he stalked back to the bathroom. 'There's no reason everything has to change, not really. Once we've all got used to the idea and the dust has settled—'

'What planet are you living on?' He turned to her, his expression incredulous. 'What do you think is going to happen? We'll swap daughters for a few weeks every now and then like they're a couple of exchange students? All go on holiday together like some big happy family? How exactly d'you think this is going to work?'

'Divorced families manage it,' she protested. 'I know this isn't the same, but if we all work together—'

'We have no idea how this other family is going to respond. We know nothing about them. How do you know what they're going to want?'

'Why can't you just try to be supportive? Is that too much to ask?'

'I can't support you, Harriet! Not on this!'

'This is because of what I told you about Ben, isn't it? I've said I'm sorry – I don't know what more I can do. Nothing happened! It was only the blood group thing that made me ever think it had! Ben's out of the picture, the DNA test proves that. I've never cheated on you, I swear—'

'This has nothing to do with Ben.' He leaned on the vanity, his head bowed. 'Harriet, I love you,' he said quietly. 'That's not going to change. You're my wife. Whatever you've done, I'm not going anywhere.

126

But I'm struggling very hard to understand how you could have gone behind my back on something this important. Do you think I'm not hurting over this too? Don't you think I care about that little girl out there as well? But this isn't about either of us. It's about Florence.'

'I understand that.'

'Well, you have a strange way of showing it.'

'But if Nell's family want to try to work something out? If they feel the same as I do, what then?'

He sighed. 'We'll cross that bridge when we come to it. Let them make the next move. You've got to give this time, Harriet. Stop pushing it. Promise me you'll leave this alone for now, until we decide – *together* – what comes next. Please. I need you to promise me that.'

'I promise,' she said.

At the time, she meant it.

She stared up at the crumbling Georgian terrace in front of her in dismay. This wasn't what she'd expected. She and Oliver had a restaurant on Islington's Upper Street, neighboured by expensive antique stores and chic clothes shops and stylish French bistros; the homes in the streets nearby cost upward of seven figures and had Audis and BMWs in their 'Residents Only' parking bays. When she'd found out Nell lived in Islington, she'd pictured her sifting through rails of designer jeans or laughing with her friends as she drank cappuccinos at a pavement café. Not . . . *this*.

127

She peered through the grimy window of the shop. 'Born-Again Vintage'. Dear God. She *was* in the right place.

She glanced down the street. How had her child ended up living in a place like this? Rubbish littered the pavement, spilling out of black plastic bags dumped by the side of the road, and more than one window in the row of narrow houses in front of her was boarded up. A lurching derelict pushed a supermarket trolley laden with his scavenges along the other side of the street; two teenagers slouched past her as she lingered, speculatively eyeing her handbag. Quickly, she flicked her diamond engagement ring around so that the stone dug into her palm and was no longer visible. She stuck out like a sore thumb in her court shoes and expensive grey trouser suit. She should have just worn jeans.

She eyed the shop again. A sign in the window said it was open, but she could see neither customers nor staff. Maybe Nell didn't actually *live* here, she thought hopefully. Perhaps this was just the shop address.

She walked to the end of the street and turned right, and then right again, approaching the terraces from the rear. A group of teenagers lounging against a parked car watched her sullenly as she approached, and she studiously ignored them. For the first time, she wished Oliver were here.

She'd honestly never intended to break her promise to him. She'd been so certain that once Nell's family had got over the initial shock they'd want to reach out to her the way she'd reached out to them. She'd created a legal fund to fight for Nell as a precaution, that's all. She was sure she'd never actually have to use it. Florence was this woman's biological child, for heaven's sake. How could a mother ignore that?

But her lawyer had been very clear. This woman, Zoey Sands, wanted nothing to do with either her or Florence. She'd refused even to consider it. Despite pressure from both Harriet's lawyer and the hospital director – who was desperate to avoid any publicity and wanted to make this go away in any way he could – the woman had refused to budge.

Oliver said she had to let it go. *Give it time,* he kept saying. *Let the girls grow up a bit more, keep their childhood innocence as long as they can.* But she'd already given up fifteen years! How could she bear to miss another day of Nell's life when she'd missed so much already?

So she'd gone behind Oliver's back. She'd found Zoey Sands' address, and she'd told her husband she was going to New York for a few days to celebrate a friend's American book launch. Which, in fairness, she had done. And as soon as it was over, she'd got on a plane to London.

She stopped now outside the rear of number 33.

Once she met Zoey, woman to woman, mother to mother, she knew they'd work this out. Oliver need never know how it had happened, need never even know she'd been here.

Her heart thudded as she knocked on the kitchen door. A grimy net curtain covered the glass, so all she could see as she waited was a vague shadow on the other side. *Florence's mother.* The woman who'd raised Nell as her own.

She stared in disbelief as the door opened.

She'd have recognized Zoey anywhere.

It was as if Florence was staring back at her: the same grey eyes, the same unruly blonde hair, the same full mouth. She was tall, though not as tall as Florence; and she had a round voluptuousness Harriet guessed Florence would inherit in a few more years. If she'd seen Zoey's photograph, there would have been no need for DNA tests. Her genes ran through Florence like the name in a stick of rock.

'I know who you are,' Zoey said faintly. 'You look just like her.'

'You're Florence's mother,' she returned.

'No. I'm *Nell's* mother.'

She nodded. 'Yes. Of course. But—'

'You'd better come in.'

The woman turned without waiting for a response, her strange pink skirt billowing around her bare feet. Harriet followed her down the crowded hall to the kitchen, stepping around towering blocks of cardboard boxes and half-clothed mannequins and hat racks. She had no idea if Zoey was moving house, or if it was always like this.

'Tea?' Zoey said.

'You don't have to go to any trouble—'

'You're here now.'

She sat at the cramped kitchen table, suppressing the urge to wipe the sticky seat first. Her pantry at home was larger than this entire room. Every surface was covered with the detritus of family life: heaps of envelopes and magazines, open boxes of cereal, dirty crockery, a sweatshirt – Nell's? – thrown over the back of a chair. Fabric swatches were strewn like party streamers across the top of everything; beads and buttons and ribbons tangled across the kettle, the stove, even the taps beside the sink. Harriet didn't know how anyone could live in such clutter. At home, her granite surfaces gleamed, their virgin surfaces unblemished by anything beyond a few expensive chrome appliances, most of them bought by Oliver. Even the boys knew better than to dump their backpacks on the worktop the way Nell had.

She searched for something neutral to say. 'Have you lived here long?'

'Since I was pregnant with Nell –'

She broke off abruptly. Harriet smiled sadly. 'It's OK. I know what you meant. I keep doing the same thing.'

'How do you take your tea?'

'Black, no sugar.'

Zoey fished a couple of mugs from the sink and

gave them a quick rinse, threw in the teabags, then added three spoonfuls of sugar to one of the mugs before pouring in the boiling water. No teapot. Harriet tried not to wince.

She handed Harriet her tea, then wrapped the trailing sleeves of her rather grubby purple cardigan around herself and sat down.

'Why are you here?' she asked. Her tone was neither hostile nor friendly. Despite her ditzy appearance and chaotic house, Harriet suddenly realized she wasn't a pushover, nor someone to be taken lightly. Not where Nell was concerned.

'I know how hard this is for you,' she said carefully. 'I'm probably the only person who does. Nell's your daughter, but she's my daughter too. You must see how I couldn't just walk away from that.'

'But it isn't about you, is it?'

She sounded just like Oliver.

Harriet sighed. 'Look, I understand you want to protect Nell. The last thing I'd ever want to do is hurt her, or Florence. But don't you think they need to know the truth about who they are? Nell has a father and three brothers. Grandparents. Cousins. Doesn't she deserve to be allowed to make a choice about knowing them?'

'If you force this on her now, you're taking that choice away from her.'

'She doesn't even know about me. What choice is that?'

'And . . . Florence.' Zoey stumbled slightly saying

her name. 'Are you giving her the same choice? Have you told *her*?'

She flushed. 'Not yet. My husband thought we should wait. But—'

'Your husband sounds like a good man.'

'He is. He's a wonderful father. If Nell just met him . . .'

Zoey's jaw set stubbornly in a way she recognized only too well. 'I'm sorry you came all this way, Harriet, but I'm not going to change my mind. In a few years, when Nell is old enough to understand the implications, perhaps then she'll want to meet you all.' Her voice softened slightly. 'Look, you seem like a nice woman. I'm sure you've done a wonderful job with Florence. I'm sure she's happy and well looked-after. That's all I need to know.'

'You must want to see Florence,' she insisted. 'You're her *mother*!'

'No, Harriet. *You* are.'

Harriet put down her cup and stood up, at a loss for words. Zoey wasn't at all what she'd expected. She'd thought this would be so much easier; that the other woman would be so grateful she'd taken the initiative, so desperate to hear all she could about Florence, that somehow they'd figure out between them what to do next, because they both really wanted the same thing. But she was so . . . so *calm* about it all. As if it didn't really matter; as if it hadn't changed *anything*.

She turned back to Zoey as she reached the

kitchen door. 'Thank you,' she said. 'For at least hearing me out.'

Zoey nodded and Harriet opened the door.

And came face to face with Nell.

CHAPTER 13

NELL

Nell ran a finger over her swollen lips, unable to suppress a secret smile. *Her first kiss.* Her first real one, that is; she'd snogged a few boys under the school stairwell, but they'd been about as erotic as being licked by Richard's Labrador, and nearly as sloppy. Not so much a kiss as a face-bath. Frankly, she'd take the dog any day.

But *this*. She hugged herself, still glowing. That had been a *kiss*. The kind of kiss you read about in books. A Darcy and Elizabeth Bennet kiss. Kate and Leo. The kind of kiss that made her nipples tingle and her body throb. She wanted more. More kisses. More *everything*.

Her Nikes felt like they were hovering three inches above the pavement as she walked home. She shouldn't have bunked off again, but no way could she have sat through double French after that kiss. She just wanted to go home and lie on her bed and stare at the ceiling and relive every amazing second. She'd tell Mum she had her period or something. *Sweet fifteen and she'd been kissed!*

She ran her hand along the railings of the houses she passed, humming to herself. She ought to feel more confused about this, or guilty, or something. But she didn't. She couldn't. It just felt too *right*.

She'd never thought she was into girls. It had never crossed her mind. She had posters of Robert Pattinson on her wall, and she thought the lead singer in McFly was hot. She'd never really looked at the other girls when they changed or showered together, not in that way. She couldn't imagine kissing any of them, even now.

But when Teri kissed her, it was different. It wasn't about Teri being a girl. It was about Teri being *Teri*.

She knew Teri wasn't gay, either. She was sixteen already, in the year above Nell, and she'd been out with quite a few boys at school. She'd lost her virginity to one of them, a really hot black basketball player in Year 12; she'd told her all about it, every last detail, and the two of them had giggled over it together. *It's true*, Teri had said, *what they say about black men*. She'd laughed with her, not really understanding but happy to be included in Teri's confidence.

And Teri was beautiful, there was no question about that. She was one of the school idols, acknowledged as pretty and popular and smart. Everyone knew she was one to watch. It would've been easy to get a crush on her, but Nell never had. They were just friends. Both of them were on all the school sports teams, they ran cross-country and played netball, they had a lot in common. She'd stayed over at Teri's house a thousand times and nothing had ever happened. She'd never even considered it might.

She crossed the road onto her street. She still didn't know how it had started. They'd been practising netball in the gym during break, and then they'd gone outside to sneak a cigarette, perching on the high grass bank behind the school building, out of sight. They'd been sharing a single Marlboro between them, passing it back and forth, huddled together on the grass. And then, somehow, the cigarette was gone and they were kissing. She didn't know who'd initiated it. It'd all happened so naturally. One minute they were talking and laughing and the next . . .

Teri tasted sweet, despite the cigarettes. Like honey, or wine. They'd fallen back on the grass, still kissing, stroking each other's bodies over the T-shirts and gym shorts, and then Teri's hand was somehow beneath her top, slipping into her bra, finding her small pink nipple and making her dizzy with wanting. She'd reached for Teri, too, tentatively at first, seeking out her breast, feeling its weight and softness, the two of them breathing each other in.

After a long moment, they'd broken apart and looked at each other, and laughed in shared, nervous pleasure. They'd kissed again. And she'd known it wasn't just her, Teri felt it too.

Her phone beeped. She smiled when she saw Teri's name on her message screen. **U free tonite?**

Yes, she texted back. **Where?**

Evry1 out. Come over. 7?

C U then. xx

She reached the back of the house and fished around in her bag for her keys, still smiling. A moment later, the kitchen door opened and she nearly ran into one of Mum's customers as she came out.

'Oh, sorry,' Nell said, stepping out of the way. She slid her phone into her jeans and hitched her bag onto her shoulder. 'Mum? I wasn't feeling great, so I came home early. I'm going upstairs for a bit, OK?'

The woman didn't move. She was just *staring*, like she'd seen a ghost.

'Harriet,' Mum said, touching the woman's arm. 'Harriet, *no.*'

There was a note of panic in her voice. Nell had never seen her mother look so upset. And the other woman, you'd think she was about to burst into tears.

'I've wanted to meet you for such a long time,' she said, gazing at Nell intensely. 'I'm Harriet.'

'OK,' Nell said warily. 'Mum? What's going on?'

'Nothing, darling. Harriet's an . . . an old friend. She was just leaving.'

Nell didn't buy that for a minute. She gave the woman a sharp, assessing glance. There was something familiar about her, though she couldn't

138

remember meeting her before. She didn't look like any of Mum's friends, or even a client. She was wearing a stiff grey business suit, her dark hair pulled back in a neat French plait, and she had tiny diamond studs in her ears. She wasn't wearing make-up, but her short nails were polished and well cared for, and there wasn't a single scuff mark on her shoes. Nell adored her mother's funky, eclectic look, but she had to admit there had been times, especially at school events, when she'd wished Mum looked just a little bit more like this woman.

'Do I, like, know you or something?' Nell asked, puzzled.

'Something like that,' the woman said faintly.

'Harriet—'

The woman turned towards Mum. 'Zoey, please. I can't just *leave*.'

'Look, I'm starving,' Nell said, suddenly bored with their adult drama. 'I'm going to make myself a sandwich.'

She politely pushed past them into the hallway. Whatever crazy stuff was going on between Mum and this woman, she didn't want any part of it. She wanted to go upstairs and close her eyes and think about Teri.

She scrabbled around in the kitchen for a clean plate, gave up and settled for one that was at least clean*ish* – she smiled inwardly: *camp clean*, Richard called it when they'd first gone camping a few summers ago – and made herself a peanut-butter sandwich. She could hear Mum and the other woman talking intently in the hallway, though she couldn't make out what they were saying beyond a few disjointed snatches of conversation. *Just want to talk to her . . . promise not to . . . five minutes, that's all . . .*

She heard them move down the hall.

'Nell,' Mum called, sounding tense. 'Can you come in here a minute?'

She wandered into the sitting room, munching her sandwich. 'What?'

'Harriet and I thought you'd like to join us,' Mum said.

'OK,' she said thickly through a mouthful of peanut butter.

'I used to work near here,' the woman said, leaning forward on the sofa. 'My husband and I own the Green Machine on Upper Street.'

Nell leaned against the wall and nodded. 'Yeah. I know it. Cool.'

'We moved to America about twelve years ago,' the woman added. 'We have a daughter the . . . the same age as you, Florence, and three younger boys, Sam, George, and Charlie.' She fumbled in her handbag and thrust a photograph at Nell. 'Here. That's them with my husband, Oliver, when we were at Nantucket last summer.'

She wiped a hand on her jeans and took the photo. She had no idea why a total stranger was showing her pictures of her kids, but whatever. She could play along for five minutes if it meant

Mum not asking questions about why she was home in the middle of the day.

'They look nice,' she said politely, returning the photograph.

'We live in Vermont,' the woman added eagerly. 'They call it the Green Mountain State. It's quite like England, though we get a lot more snow. Have you ever skied, Nell?'

She shrugged. 'Not many mountains round here.'

'I'm sure you'd like it if you tried it. We go snow-shoeing in the winter, and the boys have even tried ice-climbing. Do you like sports?'

'I'm on most of the teams at school.'

'Really?' She sounded as thrilled as if Nell had just said she was an Olympic medalist. 'I used to be on every team at school when I was your age! What d'you like best, Nell?'

'Athletics, I suppose.'

'Me, too!'

Nell took another bite of her sandwich and peered in the mirror on the wall behind her to wipe off a smudge of peanut butter. The woman was sitting directly behind her, her image floating over Nell's shoulder; and suddenly she saw it. She couldn't think how she hadn't twigged before. God, she was an idiot. No wonder the woman looked familiar! Nell saw the same face in the mirror *every day*! The same fine-boned features, the same grey eyes, the same *every*thing.

She whirled round. 'You're not just a friend, are you?'

The woman and Mum sat perfectly still.

'We're related, aren't we?' Nell demanded.

Slowly the woman nodded.

'Are you, like, my dad's sister or something?'

'I'm sorry?'

'My dad,' Nell said impatiently. 'Patrick James. Ryan told you about me, right? So, are you my aunt or what?'

'No,' the woman said faintly. 'No, I'm not related to your dad.'

'Then how come you look so much like me?' Nell turned back to the mirror so she could see their reflections side by side again, and pointed. 'I mean, look at us! You could be, like, my mother!'

'Yes,' the woman said. 'I could.'

'She is,' Mum said quietly.

The woman glanced at Mum, and Nell saw something pass between them, an understanding. 'What?' she demanded.

'Harriet *is* your mother,' Mum said.

She gaped. 'You're kidding me? Like, she was an egg donor or something?'

'No.' Mum sighed. 'Nell, could you sit down?'

'I don't need to sit down. I just need someone to tell me what's going on.'

'The day after you were born,' Mum said, dragging out each word as if it actually hurt her to say them, 'there was a fire alarm at the hospital. It was chaos. Nurses were running round everywhere, not sure if it was a false alarm or not, wondering if they should evacuate everyone. And somehow . . . somehow in all the confusion there was a mistake in the nursery. Two of the babies got mixed up.'

She tried to take this in. 'Am I one of them?' she asked finally.

'Yes. You and Harriet's little girl.'

For a long moment, she couldn't think of anything to say. Teri was never going to believe this. It was like some kind of switched-at-birth made-for-TV movie. *She* didn't believe it, and she was right in the middle of it.

'Is this for real? Are you *sure*?'

'We're sure,' Mum said quietly. 'Those tests at the hospital last month confirmed it.'

'Why didn't you just tell me that's what they were for?

'Sweetheart, I'm so sorry—'

'Never mind. I get it. You didn't want to upset me until you were certain, blah, blah.' She took a deep breath. 'OK, OK. So what you're saying is, I should've gone home with Harriet. She's, like, my birth mother.'

'I know this must be a huge shock,' Mum said desperately. 'But it doesn't change anything. You're still my daughter. I still love you as much as I always have. Nothing's changed, sweetheart, you have to believe that.'

'Hold on. I'm processing here.' She paced to the other side of the sitting room, then came back to the chair and sat down, folding her arms. 'OK then. So I've spent all this time thinking I had a dad who was pretty much just a sperm donor. Patrick did his thing, you got knocked up, and then he checked out. And then later you met Richard, and he's pretty much been my dad ever since.'

'Nell—'

'So the way I see it is this. I survived all this time without a dad. Well, without an actual *biological* dad. Richard's all I've ever needed.'

'He loves you as much as if you were his own.'

'So have you.'

Mum looked at Harriet helplessly.

Honestly, she thought. *How complicated do they all have to make it?*

'I'm sure you're a really nice person,' she told Harriet earnestly. 'I'm sure you're a great mum and everything. But Mum – Zoey – look, she's my *mum*, same as Richard's my dad. I don't want to upset you or anything, but I don't think family's about who you're related to. It's about who you love, right? Mum and Richard have done an amazing job. It's kind of cool to meet you, and it would be nice to meet your family one day, but Mum's right. When you come down to it, nothing's really changed.'

'I'm not trying to take your mum's place,' Harriet said quickly. 'I don't want to change anything. I just want to be part of your life, if you'll let me.'

'Can I ask you something?'

'Anything.'

'What's she like? Your daughter, I mean. I guess she's sort of my twin, in a weird way. Does she look like Mum?'

'Yes,' Harriet said faintly. 'Florence looks just like your Mum.'

'Does she know?'

'Not yet.' Harriet hesitated. 'My husband didn't want to tell her. He thinks it'll upset her too much.'

'Well, I think you should. It's kind of unfair if she's the only one who doesn't know.' Nell shrugged. 'Maybe I could talk to her, if it would help. After all, we're totally in the same boat. She might feel better if she knew somebody who understood what it feels like.'

For a long moment, Harriet didn't speak. 'You're right, Nell,' she said finally. 'Your mum *has* done an amazing job. She must be so proud of you.'

'So, OK then. What happens now?'

Harriet glanced nervously at her mother.

'That rather depends on what you and Zoey want to do. Perhaps . . . perhaps you could come out for a visit. When your mum is ready,' she added hastily. 'I don't mean to rush you or anything.'

'America? Wow. Cool.'

'Nell, I'm not sure that's going to be possible,' Mum said carefully. 'It's very expensive, flying to the States, and there's the shop to think of—'

'If it's a question of money, I'm happy to help.'

'I appreciate that, Harriet. I don't want to be rude, but this has all happened so fast. I'm not sure any of us should be making any plans just yet. Not until we all know a little bit more about where we are.'

Nell stood up. 'Look, if it's OK, I really need to chill for a bit. I'm kind of tired.'

'Are you all right?' Mum asked anxiously. 'If you want to talk . . .'

She smiled. 'It's all right, Mum. I know where you are.'

She picked up her bag and took the stairs two at a time to her room. It was weird – you'd think she'd feel more bothered by this. Maybe it was because she'd never come from a so-called 'normal' family in the first place. Richard wasn't related to her, but she loved him just as much as she loved Mum. If this woman, Harriet, was her biological mother, that was OK; it didn't change how she felt about Mum. The only problem, as far as she could see, was how Mum was going to deal with this.

She lay on her bed and stared at the ceiling. She didn't need more parents – she already had them; though it would be interesting to get to know Harriet and – what was his name? – Oliver. Maybe she'd finally learn where she'd got her knack with plugs. But three brothers. Real brothers, not half-brothers. *Family.*

Now *that* was cool.

Subject: (no subject)
Date: 29/05/2013 10:36:12 A.M.
From: dancarter@princesseugenie.co.uk
To: l.morgan@dailynews.co.uk

Sent from the Internet (details)

Lesley – got a great story for you. Major hospital fuck-up. Heads are going to roll when this breaks, trust me. Fill you in when I see you. Usual finder's fee for the tip, but if you want paperwork, could cost a bit extra. Trust me, your editor's going to want to find the cash for this one.

Dan

CHAPTER 14

OLIVER

Oliver couldn't remember ever wanting to hit his wife before. He'd never hit a woman in his life, and he wasn't about to start now. But two months ago he'd never have thought he'd even feel the impulse, much less have to fight to suppress it. She'd pushed him closer to the edge than he'd believed possible, and for that alone he could scarcely bear to be in the same room with her.

'And you thought this would be OK?' he repeated, his voice shaking with fury. 'What the fuck did I ever say to make you think this would ever be *OK*?'

'But you don't understand,' Harriet protested. 'It's going to work out! It's going to be fine! Isn't that what you wanted?'

'What I *wanted* was for you leave this alone. What I *wanted* was for you to listen to me. But what *I* wanted doesn't seem to have come into it. All that's mattered to you is what *you've* wanted!'

'That's not true! Nell wants to come here, to meet you and the boys, she said so! She—'

'Goddammit, Harriet! What about *Florence*?

What about what *she* wants? How in Christ's name am I going to go downstairs and tell her she's not our daughter, some strange girl on the other side of the world is? What d'you think that's going to do to her? To our family?' He swung towards her, his face inches from her own. 'What in hell made you go chasing off to London to find her? Who the fuck d'you think you *are*?'

'I'm Nell's mother!' Harriet cried.

'You're Florence's mother first!'

They stared at each other, breathless with emotion. He felt as if he was looking at a complete stranger. His *wife* would never have done this. His wife would never have gone behind his back, lied outright to him, broken every rule that had ever sustained their marriage. He didn't know this woman. He didn't *want* to know her.

'What makes you think Florence isn't strong enough to deal with this, Oliver?' Harriet asked finally. 'Nell was. Why would you think our daughter isn't up to the truth?'

'How do you know if Nell was fine with it or not? You have no idea how she really feels, you barely *know* her! You appear out of nowhere, turn her life upside down, and then disappear. How the hell would you know what's really going on inside her head?'

'She called me the day after I went round to Zoey's. She wanted to meet me again. She wanted to know all about you and the boys.'

'So, OK, maybe she *is* fine with it. So what? That

doesn't mean Florence will be!' He shook his head angrily. 'You say you love her, and yet you do this to her. How could you, when you know how much it's going to hurt her?'

'Not if we handle it right! If we sit down and tell her together, make it clear nothing has to change, she's still our daughter—'

'What planet are you living on? You're going to trade her in for a better model, and you think she's going to be OK with that? What the hell is *wrong* with you?'

'Don't be ridiculous! Of course Nell isn't a better model!'

'That's how Florence will see it!'

'I can't just airbrush Nell away!' Harriet cried in anguish. 'You want me to pretend this never happened, but every time I look at Florence, I see Nell! I don't want this huge, awful lie between us. I can barely look my daughter in the eye!' She started to cry again. 'I know you think I should've waited, but it wasn't just about Nell. It was about Florence, too. I need things to be normal with her again. Please, Oliver. Can't you *try* to understand?'

Despite his anger, the raw pain in his wife's eyes moved him. For a moment, he tried to put himself in her shoes. As far as he was concerned, Florence was his daughter; somehow, he'd managed to bury whatever feelings he might have had for Nell, the child he'd lost, and forced himself to think only of Florence. Perhaps it had simply been too much to ask Harriet to do the same. She'd carried Nell

150

inside her for nine months, felt her baby move, nurtured her, given her life. Perhaps the bond between a mother and her child *was* different: a primal, biological tie that he didn't and could never understand.

He tried not to listen to the voice inside his head that told him Harriet had brought all this on herself. She'd sent off those toothbrushes for DNA tests, she'd contacted the hospital in London, she'd got on a plane and flown four thousand miles across the ocean, all without telling him. How was he ever supposed to trust her again?

No. He'd known her for sixteen years, and she'd never let him down before. Surely she'd never have gone behind his back like this if she hadn't been desperate?

And what about that night with Ben? the voice whispered. *What's her excuse for that?*

'You keep saying you're trying to protect Florence,' Harriet said quietly, her hand on his sleeve. 'Are you sure it's not yourself you're trying to protect?'

He hesitated. Deep down, he knew she had a point. He'd fought so hard to make this go away because he couldn't bear to face it. But fighting with Harriet wasn't going to help Florence get through this.

'Whatever happens, we're in this together,' he said wearily. Awkwardly, he put his arms around her, tightening his hold as he tucked her head beneath his chin. 'You're my wife, and I love you. What matters now is holding this family together. We can't fight about this any more. We have to be on the same page, Harriet.'

'I'm sorry,' she whispered into his chest.

'I know you are. I'm sorry too.'

After a long moment, she freed herself and pulled her phone from her pocket. Wiping away her tears, she tabbed through it and handed it to him.

He stared at the picture. A smiling teenage girl with Harriet's neat, dark hair and delicate features gazed back at him. He could see Sam in her, and George; he could see himself. So this was Nell. The daughter he and Harriet had made together, a part of both of them.

He handed the phone back to Harriet. He didn't know what he felt. The girl in the photo was a total stranger, and yet he felt a pull towards her he couldn't explain.

'We'll tell Florence together,' he said.

He knew his daughter better than anyone. He'd watched her grow up; he'd seen her through teething and chickenpox, first-day-at-school jitters, fourth-grade rivalries and teenage angst. He'd known this would cut her to the quick, destroy in an instant the self-esteem he'd spent years trying to shore up, and it broke his heart more than he could bear that he'd been proved right.

'No,' he said as Harriet leaped to her feet to follow Florence upstairs. 'Leave her. I'll go.'

'We should go together.'

'No,' he sighed.

'You can't let her make this all my fault,' she pleaded.

'Harriet, I'm not going to make you the bad guy, but if Florence needs to be angry with you right now, you're just going to have to take it. You opened this box. I won't let her divide and rule us, but she has to know that I'm in her corner. Just let me handle this. Please.'

To his surprise, Florence opened her bedroom door immediately when he knocked. Her eyes were red, but she'd stopped crying.

She curled up in the window seat, wrapping her arms around her legs and pressing her cheek against her knees as if she was five years old. Oliver sat on the bed close enough to be there if she needed him, but far enough away to give her space.

'What do you need to know?' he asked briskly.

She raised her head. Her relief that he wasn't going to smother her with more emotion was evident. In his view, Harriet's apologies and tears and repeated declarations of love had done as much harm as good. Florence didn't need drama. She needed *facts* – solid hard ground to stand on.

'You said I don't have to go and live with this woman,' Florence stated.

'Absolutely not. We're your family. There's no question of you *ever* having to leave.'

'Do I have to meet her when she comes here?'

'No one's going to make you do anything you don't want to do, Flo-Mo.'

'Do you think I should, though?'

He hesitated. He'd promised himself he wouldn't push Florence one way or the other; he would simply present her with options and support whatever she chose to do. But he also knew she needed some sense that she didn't have to shoulder the responsibility of such an important decision on her own.

'I can't give you the right answer, Florence, because there isn't one. But I will tell you there's nothing to be afraid of. If you're not ready to meet Zoey right now, that's fine. If you're never ready, that's fine too. But don't be afraid, Flo-Mo. That doesn't do anyone any good.'

She picked at the chipped polish on her toenails. 'Are you afraid, Daddy?'

'You're my girl, Flo-Mo. Nothing's going to change that.'

'But you must be curious about meeting this – this other girl.'

'A bit. Yes. And a bit nervous, too. Well, quite a lot nervous, if I'm honest.'

'Because you're scared you might not like her?'

'Pretty much.'

'I think Mom already likes her better than me,' Florence muttered, ducking her head again. 'I've never been what she wanted. I can't blame her for wanting her real daughter back.'

He knew better than to argue the point now, when everything was still so raw. Nothing he could say would change Florence's mind. He just prayed to God that when it came to it, Harriet didn't let her down.

'*You're* our real daughter,' he said softly.

'I'm not scared *you'll* love Nell more,' Florence said stoutly. 'Maybe you'll love her differently, but I know you won't love her *more*.'

'Not possible,' Oliver agreed.

For a long time, she said nothing, just fiddled with her bare toes.

'So what is it you're so afraid of, Flo-Mo?' he asked softly.

'The thing is . . .' she said finally, her voice small. 'The thing is, Daddy. What if I like Zoey better than Mom?'

His heart contracted. His sweet girl shouldn't be facing so many complicated, grown-up feelings. *Why hadn't he been able to protect her?*

'Oh, sweetheart,' he sighed, moving next to her. 'It's OK. Whatever you feel is OK. This isn't a competition. We can love different people in different ways. Maybe you'd like Zoey.' He pulled her into a hug. 'Maybe you wouldn't. Perhaps you *would* get on better with her than you do with Mom. It wouldn't make you a bad person, or a bad daughter. At the end of the day, this isn't about Mom, or me, or even Zoey. It's about *you*.'

She took a breath. 'OK then.'

'OK what?'

'I think I'd rather get it over with,' she said, her voice shaking only slightly. 'Call Zoey and Nell and ask them to come.'

155

CHAPTER 15

ZOEY

Zoey tightened her seatbelt across her lap and gripped the armrests, closing her eyes and counting to ten as the plane started to descend. She wasn't a great flyer at the best of times, even on wide-bodied jumbos, and this tiny plane quite terrified her. If she dared open her eyes she could see right over the pilot's shoulder into the cockpit, and before they'd taken off, the co-pilot had had to redistribute the sixteen passengers around the plane to ensure their weight was even. Every small air current tossed them up and down as if they were on a roller coaster. How far away *was* Burlington, anyway, if the only planes that flew there from New York were puddle-jumpers like this?

Nell reached across the narrow aisle and tapped her hand. 'Mum! Look out the window! I think we're over Vermont now. It's so pretty, and so *green*!'

'How nice,' she said faintly, her eyes tightly shut.

'Come on. You can see all the little towns so clearly from up here. Look at the church spires, and the red barns – it's just like a postcard!'

Steeling herself, she peeked out of the window. Nell was right: the landscape spread out below them was almost too perfect to be real, with its farms and barns dotting fields and hills like small toys. In the distance, she could see the mist-covered spine of the Adirondack Mountains and the glittering silver water of Lake Champlain, which ran the length of Vermont right into Canada. It *was* beautiful. She could only imagine how stunning the view would be later in the year when the trees were aflame in the reds, oranges and yellows of autumn.

The plane gave a sudden lurch, and she gasped and closed her eyes again. Next time, she was getting the train from New York. Or hiring a car. Or walking.

The only good thing about being terrified of flying was that it hadn't given her time to think. But in a few minutes they'd be landing in Burlington. She'd be meeting Florence for the first time. Oh God, she felt sick just thinking about it.

Nell seemed to have no such nerves. Before the plane had even finished taxiing down the tiny runway, she'd pulled on her denim jacket and picked up her bag, her hand on the seatbelt clasp ready to release it the moment the aircraft came to a stop. Zoey could see how excited she was. She didn't want to put a damper on Nell's spirits, but she was torn between hoping Nell didn't end up disappointed, and a nasty, selfish fear that everything would go *too* well. She found her daughter's equanimity with the whole situation unnerving. It had been Nell who'd reached out to Harriet in London, going to her hotel, pushing for this trip to the States. What if she fell in love with her new family, her brothers, life in Vermont? What if she decided she wanted to *stay* here?

She gave herself a mental shake. Of course Nell wouldn't want to stay here! She was just curious, that's all. Her real family, her home, Richard, were all in London. She wouldn't want to leave them. Would she?

'It's going to be fine, Mum,' Nell said, linking her arm with Zoey's as they stepped onto the tarmac. 'We're going to have a great week, and then we're going to go home and life will go back to normal. Stop worrying.'

She should never have agreed to come, she thought despairingly. Everything was happening too fast. A week ago, she'd never even met Harriet; now she was being railroaded into spending half-term with the woman. Nell seemed fine with it, though with teenagers how could you know what was really going on in their heads? But Richard said they had to follow Nell's lead, and Nell had really wanted to spend the holidays meeting her birth family. All she could do now was cross her fingers and pray she hadn't made a terrible mistake.

Nell was positively fizzing with excitement as they pushed open a pair of double doors into the airport lobby. They spotted Harriet immediately, clad in carefully pressed jeans and immaculate trainers and a sleeveless mulberry-coloured fleece vest. Zoey was immensely relieved to see she was alone. The thought of meeting Florence for the first time in the public anonymity of an airport had haunted her dreams for weeks.

'Harriet!' Nell called, waving energetically to her. *At least she hadn't run into her arms.*

Zoey hung back as Harriet came towards them with a tentative smile. She gave Nell a quick hug, careful not to let it last too long, and turned awkwardly to Zoey. 'I'm so glad you could come.'

'It's lovely of you to have us,' she said politely.

'Oliver and the boys are waiting for us at home,' the other woman added as they made their way to the baggage carousel. 'We thought it would be easier rather than putting everyone through an emotional scene at the airport.'

Seconds ago she'd been thinking the same thing. Now she bridled. Yet again, Harriet was calling the shots. The woman was like a fierce rip tide, constantly dragging Zoey out of her depth.

'There's my bag!' Nell exclaimed, leaping forward and pulling her suitcase off the carousel. Moments later Zoey's case appeared, and they manhandled the bags onto a trolley then trundled out of the airport towards the car park.

Harriet stopped and clicked her key fob at a monstrous silver 4x4. 'This is yours?' Nell exclaimed. 'It's *massive!*'

'Terrible gas-guzzler,' Harriet said apologetically. 'But with four children, and then skis in the winter, and carpooling the boys' friends to basketball and baseball . . .'

'We don't even have a car, never mind one like this.' They loaded the suitcases into the boot and Nell climbed into the back. 'Hey, why d'you have *two* DVD systems?'

'Florence insisted,' Harriet sighed, handing a couple of dollar bills to the toll attendant as they left the car park. 'She said it wasn't fair her brothers kept outvoting her on what to watch.'

'Well, at least I can even things up a bit now,' Nell grinned.

Florence sounds like a bit of a madam, Zoey thought; then caught herself. It wasn't fair to judge the girl before she'd even met her.

Harriet was clearly more nervous than she was letting on, keeping up a stream of brittle chatter as she drove them into Burlington, pointing out organic cheese stores and alpine shops as if she was a guide for Lonely Planet. Zoey took in barely one word in ten. In a few minutes, she'd meet Florence. She was by turns terrified she wouldn't like her and then equally terrified she'd like her too much. What if she was as cool and intimidating as Harriet? What if she didn't even want to *speak* to Zoey? How did Nell make all this look so *easy*?

The car breasted the top of a steep hill, and suddenly Burlington was spread out before them. An avenue of trees clad in May blossom led down to the sparkling lake, the Adirondacks misty in the far distance. 'Oh, how lovely,' Zoey exclaimed, startled out of her own thoughts.

'The lake's the most beautiful part of living here,' Harriet said, turning left into a street lined with striking Victorian houses, many of which boasted gothic turrets and intricate wrought-iron cupolas. 'It's wonderful in the summer. There are some lovely beaches, and a cycle path round the lake. And in the Fall, of course, the views are simply stunning. I've never seen such colours. Even in winter, it's pretty dramatic, with the lake icing over. It took a bit of getting used to, after growing up in London, but I don't think I could ever live anywhere else now.'

She took another right turn, and the lake was before them again, closer this time. The houses on this leafy street were smaller, a combination of classic clapboard wraparounds and eighteenth-century red-brick homes. They passed a number of sorority and fraternity houses; it was the end of the university year here, and students sunbathed in the gentle May sunshine on the lawn, or lounged in deckchairs on porches, beers in hand, playing music from open windows. Zoey caught the distinct sweet smell of dope as they drove past one house and sighed regretfully. She could use some of that herself right now.

Moments later, Harriet pulled into the steep driveway of an immense three-storey Victorian house overlooking the lake. Zoey took an instant dislike to it. It looked like something out of *The*

Addams Family with its grey granite walls and spooky pointed turret. She couldn't think of anywhere that seemed less like a *home*.

'Wow!' Nell exclaimed. 'Is this yours?'

'It's not as grand as it looks,' Harriet said awkwardly.

Privately, Zoey begged to differ. The wood-panelled entrance hall into which Harriet showed them was larger than her whole house. An immense crystal chandelier hung from its coffered cherrywood ceiling, and soft Persian carpets covered the polished hardwood floors. A sweeping staircase rose from the centre of the hall, curving around what looked suspiciously like Tiffany stained glass in the double-height windows. If Harriet didn't consider *this* grand, she dreaded to think what the woman must've made of Zoey's tiny, cramped house in London.

'Oliver!' Harriet called up the stairs.

There was a thunder of feet from a distant part of the house. Moments later, three dark-haired boys rushed down the staircase and erupted into the hall, pushing and shoving to get to them first.

Oliver followed his sons, his expression tired but welcoming. Zoey's first surprised thought was that Nell didn't look a bit like him. He was a large, bear-like man, with tousled dirty-blond hair and piercing blue eyes. Clearly, like the three boys, Nell had inherited Harriet's looks, not her father's. Zoey found herself instantly warming to him as he fought his way through the noisy tumble of children and held out a huge hand. There was something about him that reminded her of Patrick. His easy charm, perhaps.

'Sorry about the noise,' he yelled above the excited chatter of his sons. '*Boys!* Give it a rest! We can't hear ourselves think!'

'Oliver,' Harriet said gently.

'Come on, let's go through to the kitchen,' Oliver said, shepherding them towards the rear of the house. 'Boys, take it up to the playroom, please. You can come and say hello properly when Nell and Zoey have had a cup of tea and a chance to relax.'

As one, the three boys turned and swarmed back upstairs. Suddenly, the youngest – Charlie, if Zoey remembered correctly – stopped on the half-landing. 'Are you my real sister?' he asked Nell, his clear, piping voice echoing around the hallway.

There was a tense silence. All three adults automatically turned to Nell.

Nell smiled and leaned on the banister to look up at Charlie. 'I wouldn't say *real*,' she said easily. 'I'm just a different sort of sister. I don't think it matters much what kind, do you? I'm just Nell. Is that OK with you?'

'Do you like *Twilight*?' Charlie asked suspiciously.

'Hate it.'

'Have you got a boyfriend?'

'Hate them too,' Nell said cheerfully.

Charlie came down a couple of stairs. 'Have you ever seen a dead body?' he asked in a piercing whisper. '*I* have.'

'Charlie,' Oliver reproved.

'But Dad, I have! That old man on the bench by the lake. Mom was there – she saw him too. Dead as a yoyo, she said so!'

'Dodo,' Harriet said faintly.

'I once saw a man's head lying on the road,' Nell whispered loudly back to Charlie. 'He was in a car crash and it was *cut right off*.'

Charlie's eyes widened. 'Was he still alive? Did his lips move?'

'*Charlie*,' Oliver said firmly, but Zoey could see his lips were twitching with the effort not to laugh. 'Up to the playroom. *Now*.'

'But I want to talk to Nell—'

'How about that cup of tea?' Zoey asked desperately.

'Good idea,' Harriet gasped. 'Lapsang or Darjeeling?'

PG Tips, Zoey wanted to say, but managed to hold her tongue. For some reason, Harriet seemed to bring out the worst in her. She was just so bossy and . . . *schoolmarmish*.

She followed Harriet and Oliver into a kitchen large enough to play cricket in. The shiny double-fronted fridge was only marginally smaller than Zoey's bedroom, and gleaming granite work surfaces and chrome appliances sparkled in every direction. A huge industrial steel hood hung over the eight-burner stove, alongside which were racks of gorgeous copper saucepans, clearly well-used, and rows and rows of exotic spices. Evidently the bloody woman was some kind of Nigella Lawson. Was there anything she couldn't do?

'Where's Florence?' Harriet asked Oliver.

'She'll be down,' he said, carefully relaxed.

Harriet looked fretful. 'She should be here to greet our guests.'

Guests? Zoey thought indignantly. *A little more than that, surely?*

'Oh, please, let her come to me in her own time,' she said quickly. 'I'd hate for her to feel rushed.'

Oliver threw her a grateful look, and Zoey felt a tingle of playground complicity. She liked him already. She just hoped Florence took after him rather than his wife.

'Just give her a little space,' he told Harriet tightly. 'So, Nell. Would you like something to eat, or would you rather go to your room and change first?'

Before Nell could answer, there was a resounding crash from upstairs, followed by a hushed silence then a loud, aggrieved wail.

'Charlie,' Harriet said through gritted teeth. 'I'm so sorry, I'd better go and sort this out. Nell, why don't you come up with me, and I can show you your room at the same time?'

'She means well,' Oliver sighed as his wife disappeared upstairs.

'Yes, of course.'

That wicked twitch around the corners of his mouth again. 'I know she can seem a little full-on, but it's just her way. She feels threatened when

165

she's not organizing something. Sometimes it's better to sit back and let her get on with things.'

'Is that what you did when it came to finding Nell?'

He looked slightly taken aback. 'You don't pull any punches, do you?'

'Sorry. But I get the feeling you weren't exactly on the same page as Harriet about any of this.'

'What gave it away?' he asked dryly. 'Look, Zoey, it's nothing personal. But Florence isn't quite as confident and independent as Nell seems. She's a little more . . . fragile. Emotionally, I mean. I know we couldn't have kept this secret for ever, but fifteen is *so* young. I just wonder if it wouldn't have been better if we'd waited.'

'That's exactly what I told those lawyers at the hospital!' she exclaimed. 'I know Nell seems to be taking this in her stride, but it's still an awful lot for a young girl to get used to. And I can't imagine how Florence is feeling, having us descend on her like this. I know Harriet said she wanted us to come, but the poor girl must be terrified. Heaven knows what she really makes of it all.'

'You're very like her,' Oliver said suddenly. 'You look just like her, of course − I'm sure Harriet's already told you that − but I can see now where she gets her straight-talking from. Not to mention her sweet nature and beautiful smile,' he added, his blue eyes sparkling.

Zoey blushed. 'Is she really like me?'

'More than I'd expected,' he said, his expression

suddenly intense. 'It's strange, but I feel like you and I have known each other for a long time.'

She dropped her eyes, unnerved by the unexpected intimacy of his gaze. But she knew exactly what he meant. Nell might not have inherited his looks, but she could see now where her confidence and charm had come from. Zoey felt oddly at ease with him, as if they'd been friends for years rather than minutes.

The strange moment was broken by the return of Nell and Harriet to the kitchen. 'Come *on*,' Harriet was urging the figure behind her.

Florence scowled as her mother propelled her forward, ducking her head so that her hair fell forward and covered her eyes. *How like Patrick she is*, Zoey thought instantly. *And how very unlike Nell.* Looking at the two girls, it was hard to see how they could ever have been mixed up, though of course all babies looked the same when they were born. Now, they couldn't be more different. Even though they were exactly the same age, Nell seemed years older. It wasn't just her streetwise London style, which made Florence's jeans and T-shirt seem hopelessly unsophisticated. She had a polished self-assurance Florence lacked. Zoey found herself simultaneously proud of the girl she'd raised, and profoundly sorry for Florence, who for all her material privilege was so clearly lost and out of her depth.

'I like your outfit,' Florence said shyly, touching her sleeve. 'Is that top from Carnaby Street or something?'

'Actually, I made it,' Zoey said, smiling warmly. 'I just sort of threw it together. Nell says I look like a bag lady most of the time. I've never been very good at doing *neat*.'

'I really like it,' Florence said again. 'Mom told me you have a shop, and you design your own clothes. I'd love to be able to do that. I was thinking of maybe taking fashion as my major when I go to college—'

'Fashion is a hobby, Florence, not a career,' Harriet interrupted.

'I studied fashion at Saint Martins in London,' Zoey said with a touch of defiance. 'It's where some of the biggest names in fashion started, including Stella McCartney.'

'But so hard to break into,' Harriet said. 'So many would-be designers just end up in shops. What do you want to study at college, Nell?'

'Forensic anthropology,' Nell said instantly. 'I'd love to be like that woman in the TV show *Bones*. Maybe even get a job at somewhere like the Jeffersonian.'

Zoey shuddered. 'She has a cast-iron stomach. I cover my eyes when I'm watching *Casualty*, but she's got a collection of scene-of-crime photos that make my blood run cold.'

'I've had plenty of practice at building up resistance with your cooking,' Nell teased.

'You see how Nell has a plan?' Harriet said, turning to Florence. 'You just need to find a focus.

You can't expect to compete with the best unless you do.'

'Seems to me she does have a focus,' Zoey said lightly. 'There's a lot of things you can do with a degree in fashion. Anyway, if you enjoy what you're doing, isn't that the main thing?'

'The main thing is getting a qualification you can actually *use*,' Harriet said stiffly. 'Jobs aren't exactly thick on the ground these days. If you're paying two hundred thousand dollars for a degree, you need to go into a field where you've actually got a hope of earning it back.'

Zoey felt a flash of maternal protectiveness. Nell had never really needed her to play the mother hen; these days, more often than not, it was the other way round. But poor little Florence could clearly use some help standing up to Harriet. No daughter of Zoey's was going to be told what she could and couldn't do.

'I've heard there are some wonderful thrift stores and second-hand shops in Vermont,' she said to Florence. 'I'd love to check them out while I'm here, and see if I can pick up some bits and pieces for the shop. I don't suppose you'd like to come with me? It would be great to have another eye to help me choose.'

'Sure,' Florence said diffidently, her cheeks pinking with pleasure.

'Diet Coke?' Oliver asked the girls before Harriet could start in again.

'In glasses, please,' Harriet said.

Zoey caught Oliver's eye, and the two of them smothered a smile. She'd be handing round coasters next.

Harriet made tea – no mugs here: a proper teapot, and porcelain cups – and kept up a steady stream of small talk as she set the table. *If only she'd stop trying so hard,* Zoey thought. *Let everyone get to know each other naturally.* She was going to kill them all with kindness if she didn't let up.

Clearly Oliver thought the same thing. 'Why don't I take your cases up to your rooms?' he said, standing up. 'Give you a chance to relax before dinner.'

'Zoey's in the guest room, and I've put Nell in Florence's,' Harriet said. 'Florence, you're sleeping on the futon in Daddy's study. It's only for a week.'

'Sure. Give Nell my room,' Florence said bitterly.

Before Zoey could protest, Nell stepped in.

'I don't suppose Florence and I could share? I mean, if you don't mind, Florence? It would kind of be cool to have a sleepover together. It's not like I've got any sisters or anything, and it'd be much more fun than sleeping on my own.'

Florence shrugged, but Zoey could tell she was mollified. 'Sounds like the perfect solution,' she said firmly.

'Thank God for that,' Oliver sighed. He threw Zoey a quick wink. She couldn't help smiling back.

Maybe this visit wasn't going to be a complete disaster after all.

Subject: We're here!
Date: 30/05/2013 14:21:03 P.M.
From: nellsands@gmail.com
To: tericlarkson@gmail.com

Sent from the Internet (details)

Greetings from the good old US of A! Sorry I couldn't text before but my phone doesn't work here, and it's a total pain to email – they only have one computer in the kitchen as Harriet won't let anyone have one in their bedroom, can you believe it?! (Only one TV too, and they all go to bed at nine!!! If it wasn't for jetlag no way would I be up in time for breakfast at 6.30!) Harriet is kind of intense, she's arranged stuff for us to do every day and she's mega-organized, which def. makes a change! (I can't imagine her forgetting to pay the electric bill and getting cut off like certain people we know!!! LOL.) Yesterday we walked for miles round a lake, and she's booked for us to go zip-lining (I think you hang onto a handle and whizz down a cable!) in the mountains tomorrow, while Mum takes Florence trawling round second-hand shops (yawn). Harriet took me shopping today (I was totally dreading it, you should see what people here wear, it's the Town that Fashion Forgot!! I thought she'd have me in stonewashed denim or a hand-knitted poncho!!) but there's a couple of good shops, she bought me some Hudson jeans! Result!! She said it was nice to shop with someone like me, and then Florence burst into tears and said Harriet meant she was fat, which she totally isn't! *Drama!!* Harriet is so OTT. I haven't seen much of Oliver but he seems really nice. Mum likes him

171

way better than Harriet, though that isn't saying much. The two of them are chalk and cheese, Mum with her crystals and karma and Harriet all sensible shoes and alphabetized DVDs (seriously!). On the first day they had this major debate about whether you should put milk in a cup before or after the tea, and they were being really polite but you could tell they just wanted to kill each other! Mainly I feel sorry for Florence. I like her but she's so shy it's hard to get her to talk about anything. Well I'd better go now, we're all going to Maine for a couple of days to eat lobster (!!) and it's TOTAL chaos trying to get everyone ready! Wish you were here (and for all the wrong reasons!!!). See you next week, don't do anything I wouldn't do,

Nell xoxoxo

CHAPTER 16

FLORENCE

Florence hadn't wanted to like Zoey. Even though Mom clearly wished she could trade her in for a prettier, slimmer model, she still felt a kind of misplaced loyalty towards her. Whenever she found herself responding to Zoey's kindness, she felt guilty and had to force herself to squash her feelings. It was hard, because Zoey was so *nice*. Warm and honest and totally uncritical, exactly the kind of mother she'd always wanted. And would have *had*, except for this awful mix-up. But then if she hadn't had Mom, she wouldn't have had Dad, either. It was all so unfair.

She dug her hands into the pockets of her green Puffa jacket and furiously kicked pebbles as she crunched her way up the beach away from the others. Another of Mom's bright ideas: driving four hours up to Maine so they could all freeze to death boiling crustaceans alive beside the ocean. It might be late May, but the breeze blowing off the grey north Atlantic was damp and ice-cold. And she didn't even *like* lobster.

Everyone else thought it was a wonderful idea, she thought bitterly. Even Nell, with her green save-the-planet routine, was apparently happy to eat the poor boiled lobster. She glanced back down the beach. Dad had gone off to collect driftwood for the fire, and Mom and Nell were busily setting up beach chairs and unpacking the picnic and efficiently arranging enamel plates and bowls on a large flat rock, while the boys yelled and laughed and ran round in circles, waving their arms like windmills. Nell looked so much at home – part of the family already. In her whole life she didn't think she'd ever fitted in like that.

Tears mingled with the salty spray from the ocean as it beat hard against the rocky coast. She didn't want to feel sorry for herself, but it was hard not to. Nell was everything Mom had ever wanted in a daughter, everything she herself longed to be. Not only was she gorgeous and thin, just like Mom, but she seemed to love all the things that mattered to Mom, the things Florence herself hated: outdoors stuff, getting cold and wet and muddy, organizing people and all the rest of it. More importantly, she had a Plan – she knew where she wanted to go to college and what she wanted to be. Florence would give anything to have just some of her drive and confidence.

She put out her arms for balance as she negotiated a large rocky outcrop protruding from the cliff behind her. As far as Mom was concerned, ever since Nell had arrived she might as well not have existed. Dad said Mom just wanted to get to know Nell, same as Zoey wanted to get to know *her*, but Zoey didn't ignore Nell or make her feel like she didn't matter any more. She could see for herself how close the two of them were. Zoey didn't seem at all jealous of Mom, because Nell somehow gave Mom the attention she needed, but at the same time made it clear that Zoey was the most important person in her life, and always would be. How did Nell make it look so *easy*?

She felt a sharp, unwelcome stab of envy. *Everyone* loved Nell. She hadn't even been here a week, and the boys already treated her like she was just as much their sister as she was. Especially Charlie. That hurt almost more than anything. She'd been ten when Charlie was born; Dad used to say she was like a second mother, the way she fussed over him. She bathed him and changed his diapers, stayed up with him all night if he was restless, and even now she let him come into bed with her if he had a nightmare. Now it was all Nell, Nell, Nell. Was it any wonder she hated her?

Except she didn't, of course. She loved Nell as much as everyone else.

She rounded the headland and found herself on a much narrower strip of beach, where the tide was already starting to come in. Dad was there, picking up dry driftwood from the base of the cliff. Zoey was with him, searching for shells.

'Florence!' Dad called, as she came towards him. 'Has your mother come back with the lobster yet?'

'Yes,' she called back.

She took some of Dad's wood, and the three of

them crunched back over the pebbles towards the others. A wave crashed against the shore, further in than its predecessors, splashing them with salt water. Zoey yelped and leaped away. 'I don't think I'm really cut out for all this hardy outdoor stuff,' she confided. 'What's wrong with spending the afternoon in front of a fire reading the papers? I thought the whole point of civilization was that we didn't have to catch and cook our own dinner outside in the cold?'

She giggled. 'Mom believes in fresh air and exercise. She thinks if it doesn't hurt, it doesn't do you any good.'

'Flo-Mo,' Dad reproved. But he was smiling.

'Honestly, what I wouldn't give to sit down on a comfy sofa,' Zoey puffed, red-faced and out of breath.

'There is a sort of café just up the road from where we parked,' she suggested.

'Oh, you angel! You wouldn't come with me for a nice cup of tea, would you? Maybe when we get back those poor lobsters will be all done and the fire will be roaring and then we can all go back to the inn and get warm.'

'Dad? Can we?'

He laughed. 'Go on, the pair of you. And don't get distracted by the antique store hidden up the hill on your right. Be dreadful if you two managed to find it by turning just past the red gate, and missed out on all the *Survivor* festivities on the beach.'

Zoey shot him a grateful look, and the two of them nipped up the cliff path before Mom could see them.

'I'm sure your mother means well and Nell's having a whale of a time,' Zoey panted, 'but it is terribly *tiring* being around her sometimes. Is she always like this?'

'Always,' she said glumly.

'Oh dear. But some of it must be fun?'

'Sure. If you think hiking up a mountain in January when it's minus ten is *fun*. Or having to live in a tent in the woods for a week in the middle of blackfly season. Or getting sent to tennis camp for a month when you can't even hit a ball.'

'Well, I suppose the point is for you to learn how,' Zoey said weakly.

'She always wants me to learn the stuff *she* likes,' Florence said bitterly. 'Last summer, my school organized a trip to Italy, and one of the teachers had actually arranged for six girls to go backstage at a Dolce & Gabbana fashion show. *Dolce & Gabbana*! And Mom said no, it was a waste of time to go to Italy for such a trivial reason. As if fashion is *trivial!*'

'Dolce & Gabbana?' Zoey said reverently. 'What was she *thinking*?'

For a moment, Florence thought she was serious, and then she caught her smile. 'OK, sure, I guess designing dresses isn't as important as bringing about world peace or finding a cure for cancer,' she said, smiling back. 'But creating really amazing clothes is art just as much as painting a ceiling in the Sistine Chapel; at least it is to me. Mom might not agree, but she could at least allow me to have an *opinion*. She still treats me as a child, like I'm just some kind of mini-me she can mould into the daughter she wants. She never seems to care what *I* think.'

'It wouldn't be fair for me to criticize your mother,' Zoey sighed, 'much as I might want to.' They exchanged a conspiratorial grin. 'All I can tell you is that all teenage girls think their mothers don't understand them, and they're probably right. My mother didn't have a clue when it came to me. She wanted me to be something safe and sensible, like a secretary, and marry a nice man who could provide for me. She'd have been *horrified* if she'd known I'd end up a single mother running a second-hand shop.'

'But you understand Nell,' Florence argued.

'Oh, darling, I don't. Not the way you think. Half the time she's a total mystery to me. I know I have to let her make her own mistakes, but it's not always easy to stand back and watch someone you love fail. You want to protect them. Harriet's just trying to do what's best for you. She wants you to be happy, and that's not always the same as giving you what you want. It's much tougher to be a good parent than a bad one, you know.'

They reached the top of the hill and stopped outside the antique store Dad had mentioned. Poor Zoey was puffing again, clearly not used to all this activity. 'Can we go inside?' Florence asked, pushing the door open before Zoey had a chance to answer. 'We might find some more watch pieces and things.'

Trawling round second-hand stores and thrift shops with Zoey yesterday had been really fun. Mom hated those sorts of places; quite apart from her distaste at the very idea of wearing someone else's cast-offs, she loathed the chaos and messiness and crammed rails. She liked spartan shops with white walls and pale wooden floors, neat piles of hand-folded sweaters in monochromatic shades, serried ranks of classic dresses, perfectly aligned rows of kitten-heeled shoes. She refused even to shop during sales, hating the frustration of searching for the right size and the general disorder. Zoey, on the other hand, had been happy to browse the thrift stores for hours, squeezing between the crowded racks, pulling random garments out and holding them against Florence, sifting through boxes of lone earrings and buckles, draping scarves and cinching belts and looping shawls. Florence hadn't had so much fun in ages, and the best bit was that Zoey treated her as if they were equals – friends having a girlie afternoon out. She couldn't remember the last time she and Mom had spent time together like that.

They browsed around the antiques store, picking up and exclaiming over old barometers and Singer sewing machines and knick-knacks they couldn't even begin to identify. Florence was thrilled to find a small cardboard box filled with tiny watch springs and cogs, and bought it immediately for her steampunk collection of jewellery. By the time they tumbled out of the shop and headed for the café, it was spattering with rain.

'Your mother will have to forget about the lobster boil,' Zoey said as they bolted inside the café.'

'Are you kidding? It'd have to be gale-force winds before she'd cancel.'

They sat down at a small table overlooking the beach. The sun was low in the sky, lighting up the black clouds with brilliant flares of gold over the ocean. She ordered a cup of hot chocolate with extra cream, and after a brief hesitation Zoey did the same. 'What about a couple of lemon squares?' she asked conspiratorially. 'Or will it spoil our appetites?'

Florence grinned. 'Be a shame if we didn't have room for any lobster.'

'Wouldn't it,' Zoey agreed.

She pulled her sugar monitor from the small satchel she always carried with her and deftly pricked her finger to check her sugar levels, then did a quick calculation to take account of the hot chocolate and lemon slice before dialling up the correct amount of insulin in her shot pen.

'I can't help feeling a bit guilty about your diabetes,' Zoey said as Florence efficiently attached a needle to the end of the pen and gave herself the shot. 'I know they say it's not hereditary, but my mother had it, and that can't be coincidence, surely?'

'Who knows? The doctors still haven't figured out what causes it. Even if it is hereditary, it's not like you gave it to me on purpose.'

'It's a mother's job to feel guilty,' Zoey teased.

Florence smiled. Zoey had a way of making her feel like she cared, without smothering her. She reminded her a lot of Dad. They were both relaxed and outgoing, just easy to be around. No wonder they'd been getting on so well this week.

'Can I ask you something?' she asked after a moment.

'As long as you don't mind me talking with my mouth full,' Zoey said, spraying crumbs of lemon square onto her T-shirt. 'Goodness, these are delicious!'

'What was my birth father like?'

Zoey put down her cake and looked thoughtfully at her. 'Patrick? Well, in some ways he was actually very like your dad. They certainly looked alike – I can see why everyone says you take after Oliver. And Patrick was very charming, too, and made you feel like you were the only person in the room when he talked to you, just like your dad.' She sighed. 'But he was a bit of a rotter, I'm afraid. Not like your dad at all in that way.'

'How did you meet him?'

'Oh dear. I don't think your mother would approve if I told you.'

'Please,' she said earnestly. 'Nell told me he was married, but I don't care. I won't ask you about him again if you don't want. I'd just like to hear it once. So I know.'

'All right,' Zoey said squarely. 'Just this once.'

By the time they got back to the beach, the rain had stopped. Dad was trying to get the fire going again, cursing the damp wood, while Mom dried off the picnic chairs and unpacked the rugs from their waterproof bags again.

She put a wide berth between herself and all the activity and made her way round a rocky outcrop, ducking down out of sight. She couldn't stop thinking about Patrick, who'd died before he'd even had a chance to meet Nell. Zoey's story was romantic and tragic, but for the first time she actually felt sorry for Nell. She couldn't imagine growing up without a father. How awful never even to meet yours.

She felt so much better with Zoey here. It was nice to have someone listen to her, and in her own flaky way Zoey talked a lot of quiet sense. Maybe Florence should try a bit harder with Mom. By Zoey's own admission she didn't always understand Nell, but Nell didn't punish her for it. She still let Zoey into her life and told her how she was feeling. Florence had been so busy feeling rejected and angry with her mother that she'd never stopped to think how Mom might feel. She'd noticed how often Nell turned to Zoey, including her in the conversation or sharing a private joke. Again, she made it look so easy.

Perhaps if she gave Mom a chance, she might . . . *might* . . . just meet her halfway.

'Hey. Mind if I join you?'

Florence shuffled over on her rock to make room for Nell. 'Be my guest.'

Nell dug around in the pockets of her rain jacket. 'Want a ciggie?'

She looked shocked. 'You *smoke*?'

'One or two won't kill you. Come on. Live a little.'

She hesitated. Her mother would kill her if she knew. But Nell clearly got away with things like this, and everyone still thought she was wonderful. She was fed up with being the square country cousin to Nell's streetwise urban teen. Nell was right: she needed to live a little.

'Sure,' she said bravely.

Nell lit a couple of cigarettes and handed one to her. 'Don't inhale too much,' she warned. 'It'll make you cough.'

She watched as Nell dragged on her cigarette, and then gingerly did the same. Immediately she was overcome by wracking coughs, and bent and rested her hands on her knees till it passed, her eyes watering.

'Nicotine rush,' Nell said as Florence swayed slightly. 'First drag always does that.'

She battled through the cigarette till Nell had finished hers, trying not to throw up. Copying Nell, she stubbed it out on the rock and handed her the butt to return to the half-empty cigarette packet. Her throat burned and she still wasn't entirely sure she was going to make it back home without being sick, but she felt a sudden warm, outlaw sense of exhilaration. She'd broken the rules and the world hadn't come crashing down. She didn't *have* to do everything Mom said.

'Do you talk to your Mom about everything?' she asked suddenly.

Nell shrugged. 'Not everything.'

'Like – boyfriends and stuff?'

'I don't have a boyfriend.'

'Oh. I just figured someone like you would.'

'Someone like me?'

She shrugged, embarrassed. 'Pretty. Trendy. You know.'

'I have a girlfriend,' Nell offered.

Florence smiled nervously, not entirely sure she was joking. 'But you and Zoey are, like, *friends*. She never tells you off or anything.'

'You should see her when I bunk off school,' Nell laughed. 'She takes that shit pretty seriously, trust me. She just doesn't sweat the small stuff, you know?'

'I wish my mom was like that.'

'Your mum's cool. A bit anal, yeah. But sometimes it's kind of nice having someone in charge of stuff. My mum can drive me nuts. She's so disorganized, I worry about how she'll manage when I leave home. I'm so glad she's getting married soon.' She stood up and brushed off the seat of her jeans. 'It's cool that Mum and I are friends, but sometimes I wish she could be a bit more of a *mum*, you know?'

'Do you – ever think what it would have been like if we'd got the right mothers?'

'Yeah, sure. I mean, how can you *not* think about it, right?'

'Does it, like, *bother* you?'

'Finding out, you mean?'

Florence nodded, biting her lip.

Nell looked thoughtful. 'Well, I've got to admit it freaked me out a bit at first. I mean, finding out I had a whole new family I didn't even know about. But it's kind of cool, really. I never thought I'd have brothers, real full-on brothers.'

'Does it upset you at all that Zoey's not your real mom?'

'Not really. What does *real* mean anyway?' She shrugged. 'I mean, I've never had this perfect family. Richard's been my dad since I was seven, and I know he's not my *real* dad, like not my actual biological dad or anything, but to me he's always just been Dad, you know? So who cares if Mum – Zoey – isn't *actually* my mum. She is to me.'

'Zoey's so nice. You're so lucky.'

'So's Harriet.' She held out a hand and pulled Florence to her feet. 'Does it bother you, then?'

'I guess. A bit.'

'But they're still your family. Nothing's going to change. It's not like we've got to swap back or anything.'

185

Florence prodded a rock with her foot. 'I think Mom wishes we could.'

'No way. She loves you, idiot.'

'Maybe. But she likes you better. You're the kind of daughter she always wanted. She might *love* me, but she's never really *liked* me. We're too different.'

'That doesn't mean she doesn't like you. Mum and me are totally different, too, but that's OK. It's probably why we get on as well as we do. If we were both as dippy as she is, nothing would ever get done.' She smiled. 'Look, Harriet's just curious about me, that's all. Same as I was curious about finding my dad's family – I mean Patrick's family. *Your* dad's family I guess it is now. We all want to know where we come from, right? Look at all those TV programmes and websites about ancestry and stuff. But in the end, that's not what makes a family – who's got the same genes as you. It's who you love. And who loves you.'

'I suppose.' She shrugged. 'It's just all so weird.'

'Fucked-up,' Nell agreed.

Florence smiled. Against all her expectations, she was actually enjoying Nell and Zoey's visit. Mom had already started planning a return trip to London in the summer, and to her surprise, she found she was looking forward to it.

Perhaps this might work out after all.

CHAPTER 17

OLIVER

Oliver strode along the shore, hands deep in the pockets of his windcheater, his feet shifting and sliding on the large pebbles. Ahead of him, Zoey was scanning the shore for sea glass, stopping every so often to retrieve a piece and slip it into the pocket of her borrowed anorak. Even in a pair of his old jeans – '*Jeans*?' Zoey had exclaimed in horror when Harriet had given her a list of what to pack for Maine. 'I don't think I've ever *owned* a pair of jeans' – three sizes too big and clumsily gathered at the waist with one of Sam's leather belts, she still managed to look both stylish and unique.

He quickened his pace and caught up with her. 'Find anything interesting?'

'Oh, some of these shells are so pretty!' Zoey exclaimed, the wind whipping her hair round her face as she turned. 'I've even found a couple of fossils. I thought I'd make this one into a necklace or something for Florence. See how there's already a hole in just the right place?'

'She'll love it.'

Zoey smiled and ducked her head, her untidy

blonde hair falling over her face, a gesture so very much like Florence that his breath hitched in his throat. For the first time he found himself looking at her properly. She really was rather pretty, he realized in surprise. More than pretty, in fact. How had he not noticed that before? He'd been distracted by her hippie clothes and dizzy blonde facade, but underneath it all was a very attractive woman. She didn't have Harriet's sharp wit or delicate beauty; she was unfit and disorganized and dressed like a tramp in the dark. But there was an earthy, kittenish sexiness to her of which she was totally unaware, and that only made it more alluring. She didn't take herself or anyone else too seriously, and she had an easy, knockabout sense of humour that chimed with his own. In the past few days he'd seen how kind she was to Florence, how generous she had been to Harriet about Nell. He realized he really *liked* her. With a shock, he had to admit he wasn't sure he could say that about his wife; not any more.

They fell into step as they walked down the beach. 'You looking for something in particular?' he asked.

'Actually, I'm just trying to stay out of the way till all the poor lobsters are dispatched,' she confessed. 'I was hoping the rain would put Harriet off the idea, but now the fire's going again, I think they're doomed. It seems awfully cruel, boiling them alive. Can't you put them to sleep first or something?'

'It's very quick,' Oliver said, struggling to keep a straight face. 'They don't feel anything, I promise.'

'I know it's silly, but the further my food is from looking like it was ever alive, the happier I feel,' she said mournfully. 'I could probably do lobster if it was turned into nuggets. No one would ever guess nuggets were made of anything remotely related to an animal.'

'Try telling Florence that.'

She dropped her voice to a mock-shocked whisper. 'Is it true she's only allowed fast food once a year, on her birthday?'

He grinned. 'Not quite. But pretty close.'

'Well, I'm sure Harriet knows best,' she said doubtfully. 'Though I can't help thinking if something's forbidden, you just want it all the more.'

'Try telling my wife that,' he sighed. 'I've lost count of the times she and Florence have ended up at daggers drawn over nothing because Harriet just won't let something go. It's like this diabetes pump: the more her mother pushes it, the more she'll refuse even to consider it. She'll end up marrying some totally unsuitable boy just to spite her.'

'Like her mother?' Zoey asked slyly.

Oliver guffawed. 'You're probably not that far from the truth!'

'Oh, look at that shell!' Zoey exclaimed, bending to pick up a delicate pale pink clam. She really did have a rather nice rear, he noticed: rounded and voluptuous, like the rest of her. Harriet was a bag of bones, these days. She'd dropped ten pounds since this business had started, and there hadn't been much of her to begin with. He much preferred a few curves. A man liked something to get hold of in bed.

He brought himself up short. What was he *thinking*? He'd never so much as looked at another woman since he'd met Harriet, and here he was giving Zoey the eye like a randy teenager!

He found himself stiffening as she looped her arm affectionately through his, suddenly acutely aware of the soft swell of her breast against his upper arm and the heat of her body as she leaned into him. He didn't know what was wrong with him all of a sudden. He liked Zoey, of course he did, but he didn't – *couldn't* – think of her in that way. She was the birth mother of the child he'd raised, the woman who'd brought up his biological daughter – part of the family, in a way. No more than that. He was confusing affection and the strange familiarity they'd felt towards one another from the very beginning with something else, that's all this was. She was a very attractive woman, of course, and he was responding the way any man would in his position. He just needed to get a grip, that was all.

As casually as possible he freed his arm, ostensibly to zip up his jacket, and dug his hands firmly into the pockets of his jeans. It was just as well she was going home in a couple of days. Not that he was afraid this would get out of hand; he simply didn't need the complication.

A pace ahead of him, Zoey slipped suddenly on a wet rock. Instantly he was there to catch her. For a brief second, she was in his arms.

Behind him, he heard the crunch of feet on pebbles, and quickly released her.

'Oliver, have you got that driftwood yet?' Harriet called. 'The water's boiling and we don't want the fire going out before the lobster are properly cooked. If you could build it up a bit, that'd be useful.'

Useful. There were times he wondered if that's all he was to his wife. Useful. And much of the time not even that.

'I think I might go and see what the girls are up to,' Zoey whispered discreetly. 'They've been thick as thieves all day. I hope Nell's not teaching Florence any bad habits.'

'Where's she going?' Harriet said crossly as she caught up to him. 'I don't want her disappearing just as the lobster are ready. I've gone to a lot of trouble to organize this weekend for her and Nell.'

'Leave her be,' he said tersely.

'What about the lobster?'

'What *about* the damn lobster?'

Harriet pressed her lips into a tight line of irritation. He ignored her, striding over to the campfire and thrusting a large piece of driftwood into it. His nerves were raw and he felt frustrated and angry. For God's sake, couldn't the bloody woman relax and let them all be for five minutes?

Tactfully, Zoey brought the two girls back in

time for the lobster, though he noticed both she and Florence managed to slip all their allocation to the three boys, who cracked claws and picked tails clean with sadistic enthusiasm. Harriet barely spoke on the drive back to where they were staying. Well, let her sulk. If it upset her that Florence preferred to disappear all afternoon to spend it with Zoey and Nell, perhaps she should ask herself *why*.

It was late by the time they got back to the inn. The sea air had tired them all out: Charlie and George had fallen asleep in the car, and Sam was yawning. He and Harriet each carried one sleeping child upstairs with Sam trailing after them, settled them down, and then returned to the small snug for a nightcap.

As he sat down, Nell stood. 'I'm knackered,' she said. 'I think I'll go up to bed too.'

'Off you go, darling,' Zoey smiled. 'I don't think any of us will be far behind you.'

Nell kissed her mother goodnight and then innocently leaned over Oliver's armchair the way she did, no doubt, with Zoey's fiancé Richard. He found himself awkwardly patting her back as her lips brushed his cheek. He knew it was ridiculous; he was Nell's *father*, for Heaven's sake. He still kissed Florence goodnight all the time, and even now she sometimes climbed onto his lap for a cuddle. But Nell wasn't *just* his daughter; she was also a pretty fifteen-year-old girl he barely knew. And there were times, as now, his body in a riot of conflicting emotions, when he was uncomfortably aware of that fact.

His wife threw him a look as she pointedly gave Nell a warm hug, clearly under the impression he was being stand-offish just to annoy her. He sighed inwardly, knowing there was no point trying to explain.

'Night, darling,' Harriet said, releasing her. 'We have to get up early in the morning to drive home, so do try to get some sleep.'

'I will. And thanks again for all the lobster. It was totally amazing.'

'Florence doesn't know what she missed,' Harriet said, smiling tautly at her daughter.

'Florence and I polished off all the baked potatoes, didn't we, darling?' Zoey said quickly, giving her a hug. 'And that marvellous rice salad of yours, Harriet. I know I ate far too much. I'll be the size of a house by the time I get home.'

He smiled gratefully at her intervention. At least someone was in Florence's corner.

'Now, Zoey, have you got everything packed?' his wife asked anxiously.

'Well—'

'So lucky we managed to find a pair of Oliver's jeans that fit,' Harriet added. 'Such a shame if you'd ruined your – uh – London clothes.'

He swallowed his laughter at the expression on Zoey's face. He knew it infuriated his wife, but he rather liked the unconventional way Zoey dressed, with her trailing hems and cannibalized clothes.

She certainly fitted right into Vermont among the lentil-eating, tie-dyed flower children left over from the Seventies.

'Well, then. I think I'll go and finish off upstairs,' Harriet announced. 'Wheels up at eight, remember. We don't want to hit Sunday traffic.'

'Do you think I should go and help her?' Zoey asked after she'd gone.

'Do *you*?'

Zoey giggled. 'I'd probably end up on court-martial for pairing socks the wrong way,' she said mischievously. 'Poor Harriet. I'm sure I must annoy her terribly. She probably thinks I'm an awful mother for letting Nell wear make-up and have her ears pierced. Heaven help us if she finds out she's had her belly button done as well.'

The waitress came into the small sitting room. 'May I get either of you anything to drink? A nightcap, perhaps?'

He shook his head. 'I'm fine.'

'I'd love a Scotch,' Zoey said, surprising him. 'Single malt, if you have it.'

His wife never drank what she disapprovingly termed 'hard liquor'. Wine was her only indulgence; white wine spritzers, at that.

'In that case, I'll join you,' he said, feeling reckless. He stretched his legs out in front of the fire. 'Two Scotches, please.'

'Will Harriet be coming back down to join us?'

He glanced at his watch. 'I shouldn't think so.

It's after nine; she'll probably have gone straight to bed.'

'I suppose we should do the same.' She blushed. 'I mean – not that *we* – obviously, I meant *I* – well, I'm sure you must be tired, what with all the driving yesterday, and having to do it again tomorrow . . .'

'Yes, I suppose we should call it a day,' he agreed.

Neither of them moved. The waitress returned with their drinks, and he swirled the amber liquid in his glass, stealing a sideways glance at Zoey. She'd already half-finished her Scotch and was staring fixedly at her lap, as if the answers to the universe were written on her borrowed jeans. *How like Florence she was*, he thought wistfully. *How different things would have been for his daughter if—*

'How did all this start?' Zoey asked suddenly.

'All this?'

'You know. What made you wonder about Florence? I've been meaning to ask you since we arrived, but the time never seemed right. No one's ever actually told me *why* you asked for those DNA tests.'

He knocked back his Scotch in one swallow and signalled to the waitress for another round. 'It's a long story.'

'I'm not going anywhere.'

Oliver stared into the fire. Where did he begin? Florence's accident, the terrifying phone call he'd received two hundred miles from home, the break-neck journey to the hospital not knowing if she'd

195

be alive or dead when he got there? Or the way his wife of sixteen years had secretly sent off their toothbrushes – their *toothbrushes*, for God's sake! – to find out if her husband was, in fact, the father of her daughter?

Had it all begun when she went behind his back, against his express wishes, and contacted the hospital to try to find her biological child? When she compounded her deceit and betrayal by flying to London to track that child down?

Or had it started long before that? In the end, did it all go back to that night the week before they got married, a night she still claimed she couldn't remember, the night she'd ended up naked in bed with another man?

He'd tried to forgive her. He'd told himself again and again it was just one stupid, drunken mistake more than sixteen years ago; a mistake that hadn't even happened, if this Ben was to be believed.

Perhaps he'd have succeeded if that had been all it was. If she hadn't lied and deceived him again; not once, but repeatedly.

'I should get to bed,' Zoey said, breaking his train of thought.

'Please don't go,' he said softly.

Blindly, he reached out his hand. She took it, like you'd take the palm of a small child.

'Tell me,' she said.

Co-operative Bank
Islington Branch
114 Essex Road
Islington N1 8JS

Ms Zoey Sands
33 Culpepper Road
London N1 4LX

29 May 2013

Dear Ms Sands,

Further to my letters of 5 January, 14 March and 21 April, you will be aware that you have substantially exceeded your agreed overdraft limit with us of £15,000.

The current balance stands at a debit of £19,756.32.

Please telephone my assistant Molly Richardson to arrange a meeting concerning this matter at the earliest opportunity.

Yours sincerely,

Don Green
Manager

CHAPTER 18

ZOEY

Oliver looked so sad that her heart broke. He was just staring blankly into the fire, and for the first time she thought about what all this must have done to him. Until now, her concern had been for Nell, for Florence – and for herself, of course. She'd been terrified she might lose Nell, that somehow everything would change. Her sympathy for Harriet had been tempered by the fact that she was the one setting the pace, pushing them all into this whether they were ready for it or not. But Oliver was as much a victim of his wife's choices as she was.

She'd really come to like and respect him this past week. He'd been so kind to both her and Nell, had gone out of his way to make them feel welcome. He was so gentle with Florence, too, displaying an empathy and tact in stark contrast to his wife's hard-headed pragmatism. And he was so like Nell! It was no wonder Zoey felt so comfortable being with him. It was like she'd known him for ever.

'Please don't go,' he said softly.

His hand sought hers. She took it, feeling that

pull again: that extraordinary charge from him connecting somewhere deep inside her.

She'd realized that afternoon on the beach, as he'd caught her on the slippery rocks, that something was happening between them. She'd only been in his arms a moment, but she knew she hadn't imagined it. Something had passed between them, something powerful and unmistakable. But that was all it was, she told herself firmly now: a moment. No need to confuse it with anything more.

She gave his hand a gentle squeeze of reassurance. 'Tell me,' she said.

The story spilled out of him. As Zoey listened, any remaining sympathy she'd harboured for Harriet evaporated. The woman had been pushing her own agenda since the very beginning, heedless of what anyone else might want or feel. How could she have gone behind Oliver's back, not once but again and again? Never mind waking up naked in bed with your ex-fiancé the week before your wedding! Poor Oliver. Poor, *poor* Oliver.

The fire had died down to a glow of red embers by the time he fell silent. It was only when Oliver brushed her cheek with the back of his hand that she realized she'd been crying.

'I didn't mean to lay all of this on you,' he said regretfully. 'It's just the Scotch talking.'

'Don't be silly. I'm just so sorry you had to learn about it all like this. I wish there was something I could say to make things better.'

'Just talking to you helps.' He looked at his watch again and stood up. 'Jesus, it's past eleven. I've been bending your ear for two hours. You must be exhausted.'

She smiled. 'I'm fine.'

'Let me at least walk you to your room.'

He pushed open the heavy door leading to a small inner courtyard. The children and he and Harriet all had rooms in the main part of the inn, but Zoey had been assigned a beautiful cottage separate from the main house.

She shivered, and he put his arm around her shoulder, pulling her towards him for warmth. She could smell the bonfire tang of his shirt, the salt in his hair.

She fumbled for the old-fashioned door key to her room, her hand shaking slightly as she put it in the lock. She could practically hear the hum of electricity between them. It was just as well she was going home in a couple of days. Not that anything would ever happen, but even so. Life was already complicated enough.

'Well. Goodnight then,' she said, turning in the doorway.

He leaned in to give her a chaste kiss on the cheek. 'Goodnight. And thank you again.'

Her skin burned as his lips brushed the corner of her mouth. Desire, thick and hot, pooled in her belly. Her breath hitched as she tilted her head up towards him and saw the sudden heat darkening his eyes.

And then suddenly Oliver was sweeping her into his arms, kicking the door shut behind them, tangling his hands in her wind-whipped hair as he backed her across the room.

He's married! To the mother of your child! You're engaged to Richard! Nell would never forgive you!

God forgive me, I want him. I want him inside me, right now . . .

Her knees felt weak, literally weak, as the heat from their kiss rippled through her. He broke away only to peel off her sweater and T-shirt, kissing her forehead and eyes and nose and lips as they emerged from the tangle of clothing. She crossed her arms over her belly in embarrassment – *why* couldn't she be wearing sexy lace underwear? Or even matching? She'd settle for *matching* – as he unbuttoned his denim shirt.

'Don't cover yourself,' he whispered, gently moving her arms away. 'You're so beautiful. Let me look at you.'

And then he was pulling her against him again, his hand sweeping the length of her spine, cupping her bottom. She could feel his erection pulse against the thin flowered cotton of her knickers. The heat between her legs bloomed, spreading up into her belly. Her nipples were hard buttons against his chest.

She felt the back of the bed behind her knees, and for a moment she thought he was going to push her onto it, but instead he suddenly released her and sank to his knees. She realized what he was going to do, what she wanted him to do, *oh God, more than anything*. He tugged at her knickers, skimming them down her legs, and she stepped out of them as he buried his face in her pussy. She should've shaved, a bikini wax at least, but how could she have known – *oh, yes, ohh, yes, there, right there . . .*

His tongue darted up and down the length of her pussy, briefly teasing her stiffening clitoris, probing inside her, tasting her wet, sweet warmth, trailing kisses up and down the inside of her thighs. She shivered, twisting her hands in his thick, unruly blond hair, her back arching so that her pussy pressed harder against his mouth.

Finally he eased her back onto the bed. She spread her legs eagerly for him, wanting to draw him further up, further in. He kissed his way from her clitoris up her belly, dipping his tongue into her navel, whispering across her soft, pillowy skin.

Deftly he slipped his index finger into her tired bra, scooping out her breasts, and bent his mouth to her hard nipple. She clawed at the bedspread, feeling the delicious heat sing through her body, pulsating between her legs. *Oh God, she was wet.* His fingers found the other breast and she thought she was going to come from that pleasure alone.

'Please,' she whispered, rocking her hips to position herself beneath his erection, his cock sliding against her wet pussy. '*Oh, please.*'

Oliver thrust his finger inside her and she cried out with pleasure. Gently he eased a second finger inside, and then a third, cupping his hand around her pussy so that his thumb rubbed against her clitoris as his fingers worked within her, stroking the front wall of her pussy. She felt a sudden current run through her, an extraordinary, tense release, and she was wet, *so* wet, it was as if she'd peed herself, but no, that wasn't it . . .

'Oh, that's beautiful,' he whispered, 'you came, you just came all over me.'

'Again,' she panted, 'I'm coming again,' and she did, her body convulsing with utter abandon, her hands twisting the sheets.

Slowly, consciousness returned. He gazed down at her, his blue eyes dark, his expression intense. He leaned forward and rested the palms of his hands on either side of her head, hovering over her, taking his own weight as his body covered hers. She opened her legs again, wider this time, bringing her knees back as he slowly, tantalizingly slowly, eased inside her, the ripples of her fading orgasm curling around his cock.

Her hips moved with his, meeting his thrusts. *He smells so good*, she thought dizzily, the perfect mix of sex and sweat and salt and something else, something that was uniquely Oliver.

Still he didn't take his eyes off hers, even as he picked up speed and pounded into her. It was more erotic than anything she could have imagined, as if he was fucking not just her body but her heart and soul.

Their bodies grew slick. A silver sheen gleamed

on his skin, sweat darkening his thick blond hair. She began to vibrate as her orgasm built inside her again, her breathing harsh and ragged in her own ears. She dug her fingernails into his buttocks – *oh God, so firm, so perfect!* – and pulled him deeper into her, lifting her feet and resting them on his shoulders so that she could take him up to the hilt. Her climax peaked, hot, intense waves radiating out from her pussy.

She fell back against the bed, spent, but he hadn't finished with her yet. Pulling out of her, he stood at the side of the bed, then flipped her onto her stomach, dragging her by her legs towards him until her feet were on the floor and she was bent over the edge of the mattress, her face buried in the covers. One hand slipped between her damp thighs, stroking her clitoris, caressing lightly where his cock had been seconds before. His other hand grasped her hair, tugging gently so that she couldn't squirm away from him, and was held there, at his pleasure.

He brought her to the edge of orgasm with his fingers, and then, as she trembled on the precipice, stopped. And then he teased her again – and stopped. And again. Finally, when she thought she couldn't stand it any more, when she was saying his name over and over, *begging* to have him inside her, he thrust his cock deeply into her and circled his hips, pushing her over the edge, and she called his name again as he came into her, hard and fast and furious.

He collapsed beside her, panting, and the two of them lay in a sweaty tangle on top of the damp covers, breathless and spent.

It was Zoey who broke the silence. 'You should go,' she whispered.

'I know,' he said quietly.

She curled away from him, the full realization of what they'd just done suddenly hitting her. She'd betrayed Richard. Harriet. Florence. Nell. *Oh God, how could she ever live with this?*

He wrapped his arms round her, and she couldn't bring herself to resist. 'Zoey, I'm so sorry. I should never have put you in this position. This is all my fault.'

'Don't say that. We did this together,' she said softly.

'Do you wish we hadn't?'

She closed her eyes. How could she be sorry for what had just happened, when it had made her feel more alive than she had done since she'd lost Patrick? But she'd sworn she'd never repeat the mistake she made with him, never cheat or betray another woman. And it wasn't just Harriet. Richard loved her with his whole heart; this would devastate him if he knew. Not to mention the terrible betrayal of trust they had just committed against Florence and Nell.

He buried his face in her hair. 'I know every man must say it, but I've never done this before,' he murmured. 'You need to know that.'

Tears leaked silently between her lids. She

believed him, which only made her feel more responsible, more guilty.

'Zoey, listen to me. I love Florence with all my heart, you know that. I've watched her grow up, I know her inside and out. And then Nell comes along, a total stranger, but part of me. I barely know her, yet somehow I love her anyway, just as much as I love Florence, though in a totally different way.'

He paused, choosing his words with care. 'I love Harriet,' he said steadily. 'She's my wife, and the mother of my children. We've been married sixteen years. Some good years, and some not so good. But I love her, and I can't imagine life without her.' Gently he turned her in his arms to face him. 'And then you come along,' he whispered. 'A total stranger, but it feels like I've known you for ever. And I find there are different ways to love a woman, as well as a child.'

Her breath caught in her throat. What was he saying? He loved her? Was that the sex talking, or did he mean it? But if he did mean it, what then?

'You should go,' she said, her voice suddenly hoarse. 'She'll be wondering where you are.'

He hesitated, then got out of bed and started to pick his clothes up from the floor. *Was there anything more depressing than watching a man dress when he was leaving you?* Zoey wondered. Turning clothes the right way in. Hunting down missing socks. Picking tell-tale blonde hairs from dark jackets. Restoring order and propriety – as if nothing had ever happened.

She got up and wrapped herself in the hotel bathrobe, suddenly hollowed out and exhausted. How could he have got under her skin so quickly? The thought of not seeing him again was excruciating, but what else was there? Even if they ever overcame the logistics, she couldn't be the other woman again. She wanted more. She wanted it all.

Miserably, he finished buttoning his shirt. 'Are you going to be OK?'

'This never happened,' she said wearily. 'It can never happen again. We can't ever let anyone find out. Promise me, no guilty confessions to make you feel better.'

'I don't want to lose you—'

'You need to go.'

For a moment she thought he was going to argue. He nodded once, then turned and left the room, shutting the door softly behind him.

She sank onto the bed, finally able to let the tears flow. *Oh God, what had she done? How had she ever let this happen?*

She had to keep away from him, that's all there was to it. If she couldn't say no, which she clearly couldn't, she had to make sure he stayed beyond reach.

Even if that meant losing Florence for ever.

CHAPTER 19

HARRIET

'She still says no,' Harriet said, putting down the phone with a bewildered air. 'She won't even *talk* to me now. I had to call Nell on her mobile just to find out what was going on, and she obviously didn't want Zoey to know she was speaking to me.'

Oliver pulled another potato out of the bag and began peeling it. 'What makes you say that?'

'She suddenly started talking about homework in the middle of our conversation. Zoey must've walked in or something.' She frowned anxiously. 'I don't understand. Everything was fine when they went back to England. That's only three weeks ago. What on earth could've happened since then to upset her?'

He shrugged. 'I'm sure it'll sort itself out.'

She watched him drop the potato into a saucepan of cold water on the hob. She hated it when he got helpful in the kitchen: he hadn't dug the eyes out of the potatoes, and peeling them dry meant the earth and grit ended up in the pan too. But she appreciated the gesture; ever since Nell and Zoey had left, he'd gone out of his way to be kind and thoughtful, bringing home her favourite fresh-ground coffee from City Market, popping out to Mirabelle's for a delicious custard tart to cheer her up, doing the laundry without even being asked. She supposed it was his way of trying to make her feel better, and she was grateful for his quiet support, even if it meant she ended up with tie-dyed pink underwear and grit in her teeth.

She reached for a copper pan from the rack and poured in some home-made chicken stock. 'I just don't understand what's changed, Oliver. They both seemed to have a wonderful time when they were here. Nell was in her element. Even Florence perked up by the end of their stay, and she and Zoey obviously got on well. So why the sudden change of heart?'

'Who knows. Maybe Zoey just needs a little time to get her head round things.'

'What things? I thought we'd got past all that before they came out here. Anyway, everything seemed to go so *well* during their stay. We all managed to rub along without too much drama.' She pulled out a wooden board and briskly started to chop some fresh parsley. 'I thought Zoey liked spending time with you and Florence while Nell and I were off doing things. She certainly didn't seem jealous or upset.' She stopped chopping for a moment. 'Though she was a bit tense the last day or two, I suppose, after we got back from Maine. She did seem a bit down, but that's hardly surprising. No one ever likes the end of a holiday.'

She added the parsley to the simmering chicken stock and twisted a bulb of garlic from the string by the stove. Zoey obviously hadn't enjoyed the whole Maine experience, but then she hadn't expected her to. Zoey was a hothouse urban flower, not someone to buck up and take a bit of bad weather or discomfort in her stride. On the contrary, the silly woman couldn't walk more than a few yards without complaining about having a stitch or feeling out of breath.

At least Nell had been a trooper, she thought proudly. Not a word of complaint about anything the entire time she'd been here. She'd hiked Mount Mansfield, mountain-biked thirty miles around the lake, helped Harriet plant forty tomato plants in the back garden; and not once did she say she was tired or fed up or needed a rest. Nor had she got all silly and squeamish over the lobster, ruthlessly tossing them in the pot and then sucking the meat from every leg and claw with relish. *My daughter.*

It pained her to admit it, but somehow Zoey had managed to do a good job with Nell. She didn't approve of the woman on any level: her political views were a ragbag mixture of tie-dyed hippie and hand-me-down liberal, she couldn't seem to keep a thought in her head straight for more than five minutes, and she was clearly an *appalling* business-woman. That flat above their shop barely qualified as a hovel, never mind a home. She'd sent Nell to a sink comprehensive in one of the worst parts of Islington, and until their trip to Vermont, the poor girl hadn't even been abroad as far as Calais. Then there were her morals, which could best be described as elastic. An affair with a married man, an illegitimate baby, and no doubt all sorts of boyfriends paraded in front of Nell over the years. And she was far too lax with Nell. There was that boy she emailed all the time, Terry something, and Harriet hadn't missed the belly-button piercing or the henna tattoos. She was quite sure she'd even smelt cigarette smoke on Nell's clothes a couple of times.

She slammed her pestle against the garlic cloves rather more energetically than was required. Against all the odds, Zoey had achieved something she hadn't been able to do: she'd raised a happy, fearless girl who was totally comfortable in her own skin. Florence had had every advantage: two loving parents, a stable home, the best schools, foreign travel – the perfect childhood, in fact. And look at her: the girl wouldn't say boo to a goose.

Blood will out, she thought crossly. Nell simply had the right genes. She was a perfect combination of Oliver's easygoing charm and her own single-minded will to succeed. Even Zoey couldn't go wrong. Whereas look at what *she'd* had to work with. With that dippy woman's blood in her veins, was it any wonder Florence had turned out the way she had?

And what was wrong with that? She stopped pounding suddenly, brought up short by the thought. Nell wasn't anything like the kind of daughter she'd once imagined having. She was too knowing and streetwise, walking a fine line between independence and teenage truculence. Harriet loathed her edgy, street fashion; she hated the multiple earrings in her lobes and the thick black eyeliner smudged beneath her eyes. And yet, despite all of it, she adored Nell. She was a sweet, smart, funny girl of whom Harriet was already immensely proud.

Florence wasn't the kind of daughter she'd imagined having either. She hated the outdoors, she was too shy and hesitant for Harriet's taste, they had practically nothing in common. But she was sweet and smart and funny too, and wasn't it better that she *hadn't* become a perfect mini-me, that she'd dared to be herself? Didn't she *want* a daughter who knew her own mind?

She should be *proud* of Florence, not resentful of her independence. How had it taken her so long to see that?

She elbowed Oliver crossly out of the way and added the crushed garlic to the bubbling pan. Zoey had told her the same thing, at least in as many words. How irritating that the wretched woman was right.

Try as she might, she hadn't warmed to Zoey. She knew the feeling was mutual; in her own passive-aggressive way, Zoey had made that abundantly clear. All those snide little remarks to justify her own style of parenting, which could at best be described as benign neglect. *You can't wrap them up in cotton wool, can you? Children need to be allowed to make their own mistakes. Learning is about so much more than exam results, don't you think?* She obviously considered Harriet an uptight helicopter parent obsessed with school grades, early nights and plenty of fresh air and exercise. Well, if caring about your children and wanting the best for them were crimes, she'd be the first to plead guilty.

She was only too aware she'd been cast in the role of bad cop. They'd all treated her as if she was some kind of Nazi, including Oliver, just because she'd gone to the effort of organizing things to do and trying to make sure everyone had a good time. The trip to Maine had been about them all bonding as a family; an unusual, hybrid family, yes, but a family of sorts nonetheless. The boys had had a great time, of course, and Nell had been wonderful, but the others had made her feel like a Camp Commandant, chivvying and controlling. It was all very well Zoey and Oliver laughing at her behind her back, but if she hadn't taken charge, who else would've done?

Odd how Oliver had taken to Zoey, she reflected, watching him struggle to work out how to use the new dishwasher. Normally he was the first to complain about women who played the dizzy blonde card.

'Why don't *you* call her?' she asked impulsively. 'You spent much more time with her than I did, and you two seemed to get on. She might listen to you.'

He froze in surprise, the dishwasher soap in his hand.

'Please, Oliver. This isn't just down to me any more. Something's obviously happened to upset her, and we need to sort it out. For all we know, the lawyers at that hospital have told her to keep away from us because of the settlement or something.'

'It's only been three weeks since they got home,' he said, switching the dishwasher on. 'Maybe she just wants things to get back to normal again.'

'We all sat down and agreed when Zoey was still here that we'd go over to London for the summer,' she argued doggedly. 'She even called Richard to cancel their cycling trip to France. Florence is really looking forward to it. The boys can spend time with my parents, who don't see nearly enough of them, and you and I can work on getting the UK end of the business back on track.'

Her husband was now attempting to extricate the black plastic liner from the metal rubbish bin, tearing it in the process so that chicken bones and kitty litter leaked all over the floor. He was like a cat on hot bricks, busying himself with chores so he didn't have to commit to anything. Sometimes he could be such a typical man. She wished he'd just *stop* and talk to her properly. It was like trying to pin down quicksilver.

'Oliver, could you just leave that for a moment?'

He put the bag down awkwardly. 'Look,' he said. 'Maybe it's for the best. I'm not sure I shouldn't stay in Burlington this summer anyway, what with Mark stepping down as VP. Your parents could always come out to stay with us instead . . .'

'My father's just had surgery!' she exclaimed. 'Who knows if he'll feel up to travelling in the summer? Besides, the whole idea was for me to spend time with Nell, and for Zoey to see Florence.'

'Let's just see how things shake down over the next few weeks before we start overreacting. I'm sure it'll all sort itself out if we give it some time—'

'Oh, give me that,' she said crossly, taking the leaking bag from him and depositing it in the wheelie bin outside. She stomped back inside. 'Anyone would think you actually *wanted* this whole thing to fall apart. Nell's depending on us, remember. If we don't look out for her, who do you think's going to? Zoey?'

'She's done a pretty good job so far. Nell's a great girl.'

'Yes, she is. She's quite amazing, given her upbringing. But consider what we could offer her, Oliver.' She moved towards him, resting her palms against his chest as she looked up at him. 'She's only fifteen. The next few years are *so* important. Just think what we could give her: the right intern-ships, the right contacts, interviews at the best universities . . . we could make all the difference to her future. Zoey's done her best, I know that, but she can't give Nell what we could. We can't let her slip through our fingers. We have to do whatever's necessary to give Nell the best future she could have, just as we will for Florence.'

Unexpectedly, he wrapped his arms around her and tucked her head beneath his chin. Pleasantly startled by the sudden display of affection, she relaxed into his embrace. Despite their rapprochement after he'd learned of her trip to London, things hadn't really been right between them for a while. It wasn't just sex, though, that had completely gone out of the window recently – they'd made love only once since Zoey and Nell had left, and that had been perfunctory and unsatisfying, neither of them able to finish – even outside the bedroom, he seemed different. He'd always been such a tactile man, squeezing her shoulder as she cooked, stroking her bottom as she carried a pile of ironing past him, holding her hand across the table in restaurants as if they were a couple of teenagers on a first date. It wasn't that he was being cold towards her now; he was still very attentive in many ways, asking her what she wanted to watch on television, even running her bath for her. He was just . . . *different*.

No, that wasn't quite right, she realized suddenly. He was treating her as if *she* was different. He'd forgiven her for what she'd done, perhaps, but he hadn't forgotten it. She'd lied to him, and no matter how valid her reasons, she knew he would never quite trust her in the same way again.

But she hadn't *wanted* to deceive him, couldn't he see that? She'd never have done it if she hadn't passionately believed she was right. He hadn't wanted to face up to the truth, and she didn't blame him for that, but *some*one had had to. A wound like the one that had been inflicted on their family needed to be exposed to the open air if it was to heal, not left to fester in the dark. Imagine how much worse it would've been for both Florence and Nell if they'd discovered the truth later and found out that their parents had been deliberately hiding it from them?

In time, he'd see she'd had no other choice. He'd let his anger go. He had to.

'Florence really likes Zoey,' she said now, drawing back and scanning his face. 'What's she going to think if she's suddenly dropped for no apparent reason?'

He didn't meet her eye. 'I know. She's already asked me several times why she hasn't heard back from her.'

Harriet was surprised at the sudden pang that information caused her. 'She's been in touch with Zoey? She didn't tell me.'

'Are you surprised? Anyway, it's nothing. She's just sent a couple of emails.'

'But Zoey hasn't replied, has she? We've got to straighten things out, Oliver. If I've been too pushy, I'm sorry. I'll back off. But *you* could still talk to Zoey, couldn't you?'

He hesitated. 'I suppose. I could ask her if you could bring the kids over, anyway. I still think I should stay here, though, to look after the business this end.'

'The business here is fine. And Florence needs you too. We have to go as a *family*. That's the whole point.'

'Let's cross that bridge when we come to it, shall we? Zoey hasn't even said yes to the idea yet.'

Harriet was confused. For the life of her she couldn't see why he was so reluctant to get involved. He'd adored Nell, that had been obvious, and he'd also commented on how much happier Florence seemed after spending time with Zoey. A month ago, he was all for the idea of a spending the summer in London. The boys would love it, the business there needed it, and Florence would give her right arm to actually walk down Carnaby Street. She knew Nell wanted to see Oliver and the boys again, and she was dying to spoil the girl, take her to the Ritz and the National Portrait Gallery and maybe even to Paris via Eurostar for a few days. Admittedly that would mean Oliver would have to hold the fort with Zoey while she was gone, but she could leave the boys with her parents, and maybe Florence would like to come with her and Nell. It was about time the three of them spent some time together. Oliver and Zoey could find something to do together, she was sure.

'Please, Oliver,' she said softly. 'Won't you please try, for me? Don't I deserve that much, at least?'

For the longest time he said nothing, and she wondered what on earth was going on in his head.

'Yes,' he said finally. 'Yes, you deserve that much.'

218

DAILY NEWS, 48 CANARY WHARF, LONDON E14 8RS

COMMISSIONING FORM

Commissioning Editor: Lesley Morgan
Email: lmorgan@dailynews.co.uk
Subject: 'Baby Mix-Up'

This document, when signed by both parties, constitutes our agreement that you are commissioned by DAILY NEWS to provide an interview on the following story: 'Baby Mix-Up'. DAILY NEWS will pay you, upon publication, the fee of £30,000 (thirty thousand pounds sterling). DAILY NEWS will reimburse you for expenses, if agreed in advance. Receipts will be required prior to reimbursement. DAILY NEWS may require revision of the interview and reserves the right to edit the interview. You agree with DAILY NEWS's revision and editing process. In the event that the article is not published, DAILY NEWS will pay you 25% of the agreed fee (plus agreed expenses).

You agree to retain all notes, e-mails and tapes for eighteen months from the date of publication, which you may be required to provide to DAILY NEWS to substantiate all claims made in the interview. In the event that any complaint or claim relating to the article is made by any third party at any time, whether a formal or legal complaint or otherwise, you agree to co-operate fully with DAILY NEWS in responding to and defending such complaints or claims. You will not comment on this work in any media or create any similar work for any other publication or other media without written agreement from DAILY NEWS.

Please sign and return all copies. DAILY NEWS's representative will then sign them and return one copy to you. Only upon DAILY NEWS's receipt of a final, fully signed contract will this commission come into effect.

For *Daily News*:   For the Contributor:

. . . .

Date: . . . .   Date: . . . .

CHAPTER 20

NELL

'So,' Teri said, handing the joint back to Nell, 'your mum finally came round?'

Nell rolled onto her back, tucked her arm behind her head and took a deep drag, exhaling smoke towards the bedroom ceiling. '*Finally*. She'd better not change her mind again. She's doing my head in.'

'What's her problem? I thought she liked your American family?'

'God knows.' She giggled, already a little high. 'Maybe she likes some of them a bit *too* much.'

'What d'you mean?'

'Just that she and Oliver were pretty friendly over there, you know?' She passed Teri the joint. 'I think something happened when we were staying in Maine. Up till then, Mum never minded me going off with Harriet and leaving her with Oliver and Florence, but after that weekend away, she was, like, all hyper about being left alone with him. I just get a feeling something happened there, that's all.'

'You're kidding? Wouldn't that be, like, *incest*?'

'No, you idiot. I'm the one who's related to

Oliver, not her.' She took a final hit from the joint as Teri returned it, and then dropped the roach in the Coke can beside the bed. 'Mind you, it would still be pretty weird. My long-lost biological dad having an affair with my accidental foster mum. Totally Jeremy Kyle.'

'D'you think they did it?'

'Well, if they didn't, they wanted to. I'm telling you, you could've cut the sexual tension with a knife on the drive home. I can't believe Harriet didn't notice. *Some*thing went down.'

'Or some*one*.'

She stroked Nell's bare shoulder and Nell rolled onto her side towards her so that they were facing each other on the tiny single bed. They were naked from the waist up, their long hair spilling loose over their breasts. Teri's were bigger than hers – heavier, paler, their large pink aureole tipped with strawberry-coloured nipples. Nell liked feeling the weight of them in her palm, seeing how those nipples swelled when she bent her mouth to them. Her own breasts were springier – high and firm, her nipples like tiny acorns. So much feeling concentrated in such a small area, she thought hungrily as they grazed against Teri's forearm. Electricity zinged across her body. Even her toes tingled.

Teri leaned closer, her breath warm against Nell's cheek as she ran her hand gently along her collarbone, ski-jumping from her pert brown nipple and then skating back to her shoulder. Nell squirmed with pleasure, twining her bare legs between Teri's, their short skirts riding up around their hips. They hadn't gone this far before − dared to be half-naked, risk being caught. Teri's parents were just downstairs, her sister right in the next room. Nell groaned as she felt a warm thrill shoot through her, its centre the molten dampness at the apex of her thighs.

The two girls froze in alarm as they heard feet on the stairs. 'You two all right in there?'

Teri sat up sharply, holding the pillow against her breasts. 'We're fine, Mum.'

'I thought I heard someone shout?'

'We're just . . . rehearsing,' Teri called through the bedroom door. 'Shakespeare. Alas, poor Yorrick!'

Nell nudged her as Teri's mother clumped back downstairs. 'Well, I call that a rehearsal,' Teri grinned, falling back on the bed. She reached out and lazily tweaked one of Nell's nipples, then dropped her hand lower, sliding between Nell's unresisting thighs. 'An *un*dress rehearsal, in fact.'

Her legs were still rubbery as she turned onto her street, every damp step a delicious reminder of the way she'd spent the afternoon. She could practically wring out her knickers, it had been that amazing. She'd had no idea an orgasm could rip you apart, leave you shattered, and then pull you together in one glorious, incendiary wave again like that. Nothing she'd ever managed alone had even come close.

She felt an erotic clench in her belly. She couldn't wait to see Teri again. She felt dizzy just thinking about warm kisses and cool sheets and Teri, naked in bed . . .

Two shaven-headed men suddenly bundled out of Mum's back door, shoving past her so rudely she was knocked into the dustbins.

'Hey!' she cried furiously.

'Fuck off,' one of them said carelessly without a backward glance.

She dusted herself down, hitching her bag back onto her shoulder and glaring at their retreating backs. They looked like a couple of bouncers from central casting, with their cheap black suits and thick necks. *Morons.*

'Mum?' she called anxiously, slamming the back door behind her and double-locking it, just in case the jerks came back. 'Mum, is everything OK? Who were those men who just left?'

She found her mother in the kitchen, crumpled over a heap of paperwork on the table, sobbing, and cried out in alarm. 'Mum! What's going on? Did they hurt you?'

Her mother shook her head, wiping her nose on the back of her hand. Her eyes were red-rimmed and swollen. Nell hunted fruitlessly for a box of tissues, gave up, and ripped off a piece of kitchen towel. 'Come on. Tell me what happened.'

'Debt collectors,' Mum whispered.

'Debt collectors? You mean, like *bailiffs*?'

Mum nodded.

'What're they doing here? Do we owe them money?'

'We owe *everyone* money,' Mum wailed, the tears starting to flow again. 'Oh Nell, I'm so sorry. I thought if I could just keep the shop going a bit longer, it would pick up again soon, and I could pay everyone back. I didn't realize how bad things had got. And now . . . and now . . .'

Nell pulled the untidy pile of paperwork towards her, ignoring coffee rings and tearstains as she tried to make sense of it. 'You haven't put these through the books – I'd have seen them. How much do we owe?'

'I've paid off most of the credit cards – we don't use them much. They weren't too bad. But we're six months behind on the mortgage, I haven't paid the electricity bill for ages, and then there's the council tax, and America wasn't cheap. I had to take out a small loan for that, that's why those men were here—'

'What sort of small loan?' Nell said sharply.

'Oh, just one of those payday things, but everything was a bit more expensive than I thought it would be, and I couldn't let the Lockwoods keep paying for us, not when we were staying at their house for nothing. Then there was Maine, of course – you shared with Florence but I couldn't allow Oliver to pay for my room. And while I was away, the shop was closed and so we made even *less* money than usual last month.'

Glancing at the final invoices and red bills in front

of her, Nell wondered how that was even possible. 'So how much do we owe?' she asked again.

'Including the overdraft, about thirty thousand pounds,' Mum said, her voice small.

'Thirty *thousand*? Jesus, Mum! What did you plan to do, sell a kidney?'

'It all just mounted up,' she said plaintively. 'This recession just keeps going on and on. I didn't realize how much I owed the bank until we got back from America and I saw their letter. I'd always thought that if I had to, I could sell the shop when Richard and I got married and pay it off that way.'

For the first time, Nell's patience failed her. Mum had always been crap with figures, which was why she'd taken over the books herself a couple of years ago, and she'd never minded. She knew Mum had just been trying to protect her, but in going behind her back like this, she'd put them both in the financial shitter. There was probably just enough equity in the shop to clear their debts, but it would leave them homeless, and Mum without a job. It was lucky they had Richard, or they'd be stuck renting some crappy bedsit in an even worse part of town. She hated to admit it, but she couldn't imagine Harriet ever getting herself in a mess like this.

'So, sell the shop when you move in with Richard. There's no other choice.'

'We can't.'

'Mum, I know you'll miss it, but it's the only thing we can do.'

Her mother picked at her nails, already bitten down to the quick. 'Richard and I are taking a bit of a break.'

'What d'you mean, a *bit of a break*? Since *when*?'

'We just don't want to rush into anything, that's all. We thought maybe September was a bit soon for the wedding. There's no need to make a fuss, darling.'

'You think ten years together is *rushing* things?'

'Eight, darling. But we've only been engaged five minutes.'

'Is it just the wedding, or are you actually breaking up with him?'

'I'm so sorry, darling, but—'

'This is about Oliver, isn't it?' Nell demanded abruptly.

Her mother flushed. 'I don't know what you're talking about.'

'Give me some credit. You fancy the pants off Oliver, it's obvious. You've come home all starry-eyed and decided to dump poor old Richard. How *could* you, Mum? After all he's done for us?'

'It's not like that—'

'I'm not going to let you do it! Richard loves you, he loves *us*! You can't break up with him, you just *can't*!'

Her mother's eyes filled with tears, but for once Nell felt no sympathy for her. The money thing was bad enough. But fucking things up with Richard was a hundred times worse. She liked Oliver, of course, but Richard had been her dad in every way that mattered since she was a little girl. She loved him, she needed him. And Oliver was *married*. That might not mean much to Mum, but it meant something to Nell. You didn't steal another woman's man. It just wasn't right. Men screwed women over enough in this world without women screwing each other over too.

'Mum, he's not leaving Harriet, is he?'

'Of course not.'

'So forget about this,' she pleaded. 'Marry Richard.'

'You don't understand. It's very complicated.'

'You're not kidding,' Nell muttered.

'Why d'you think I didn't want them to come over?' Mum asked tearfully. 'I didn't want to make things worse. I thought if we put a bit of distance between us—'

'Did you sleep with him?' She held up her hand. 'No, forget I asked. I don't want to know. Just promise me you won't screw things up for me, Mum. They're my family. I don't want to lose them.'

'*Your family?*'

Suddenly she wished she could bite out her tongue. 'I didn't mean it like that.'

'I thought *I* was your family,' Mum said quietly.

'You are.' She sighed. 'But so is Richard. And I don't want to lose him, either.'

Mum stood up. 'No,' she said coolly. 'You want to keep all of us, me and Richard and Harriet and

Oliver and the boys, and who knows, Patrick James's family too. I'm sure his son Ryan is a very nice boy. You want to have your cake and eat it. It must be very nice to be you, Nell. Able to pick and choose, pull all the strings and have us where you want us.'

'Mum, that's not fair.'

'No, it isn't,' her mother said bitterly. 'For any of us.'

She couldn't remember ever fighting with Mum like that. She hadn't been able to sleep, and had apologized repeatedly over breakfast, but even though they'd made up, it was as if her mother had put up an invisible wall between them. It wasn't about the money or her accusations about Oliver. It was what she'd said. *They're my family.* The one thing guaranteed to cut her mother to the quick. The fact that she hadn't meant to say it was irrelevant. The damage was done.

'Excuse me?'

A young woman in her mid-to-late twenties stepped forward as Nell locked the back door behind her. She was wearing an inexpensive but neat grey suit, and her blonde hair was twisted up in a tortoiseshell clip. She looked like she belonged in the smart part of Islington, not down here.

'Can I help you?'

'Are you Nell Sands?'

She frowned. 'Why? Who're you?'

The woman extended her hand. Bitten nails, Nell noticed, no rings. 'I'm Lesley Morgan, from the *Daily News*. I wanted to talk to you about Florence Lockwood.'

CHAPTER 21

OLIVER

It was only when he stepped back onto British soil that Oliver realized how many things he missed about England. A lukewarm pint, instead of cold beer – even in high summer. Fat, soggy chips smothered in Worcestershire sauce and vinegar rather than bloody cardboard French fries. Tea the colour of new conkers, slopped into the saucer by a stroppy waitress who would no more dream of telling him to have a nice day than of pole-vaulting over the counter.

Black cabs I can actually fit both my luggage and my damn legs into, he thought as he climbed out of the taxi and paid the joyously surly driver.

'Thanks, mate,' the driver muttered, briefly cheered by the American-sized tip.

Mate, not buddy. Oh, it was good to be home.

Florence dragged at his hand. 'Come on, Dad. We don't want to miss all the good stuff.'

'It's not even ten in the morning,' he said good-naturedly.

'Nell said all the real pickers get here by seven. Come *on*, Dad.'

He followed his daughter into Camden Passage

231

market, careful not to lose sight of her in the crowds already thronging the narrow streets. This wasn't Burlington, where people still left their back doors open and their cars unlocked. Florence had walked home from school by herself since she was ten, and frequently went downtown to Ben & Jerry's for ice cream with her friends after dark. But she had no idea how to survive in an urban jungle like London. Even now, surrounded by crowds and in broad daylight, she was attracting second glances from some dodgy-looking characters, their attention snagged by her youthful prettiness and innocence, not to mention the bag she was swinging casually from her shoulder.

He caught up with her and put his arm around her. 'Why don't you strap your bag across your chest, the way Nell does,' he suggested casually. 'You're less likely to lose something.'

'I can't wait to see her,' Florence enthused, adjusting her bag. 'She said she'd take me to this vintage shop where lots of famous people like Sienna Miller go. I'm so glad Mom agreed to let us spend the summer here after all. It's going to be so cool.'

He winced, thinking how close he'd come to ruining things for everyone, including Florence. Bad enough, Christ knows, that he'd been unfaithful to Harriet; but with *Zoey*? Of all people! As if their situation wasn't complicated enough already. What the hell had he been *thinking*?

He hadn't been thinking, that was the point. It

had been the *smell* of her. The citrus scent of her hair, the wind and salt from the beach, the sweetness that was simply Zoey. It had intoxicated him, blinded him to everything but the need to have her. And then her response when he'd kissed her: as visceral as his own. He hadn't even tried to walk away. He'd wanted her too much. It was as simple and as selfish as that.

He'd never felt shittier as he'd sat on the edge of Zoey's bed and pulled on his clothes. *Was there anything sleazier than dressing to leave while a woman's loving was still wet on you?* Turning your shirt the right way out, hunting down your socks, picking her blonde hair from your jacket so your wife didn't rumble you. He still loved Harriet, no question – she was his soulmate, the mother of his children, his best friend; and yet the pull he'd felt towards Zoey had been like some kind of lethal undertow dragging him out of his depth. If he could love Florence with every fibre of his being, and yet still find room to love Nell, surely it was possibly to love two very different women in two very different ways?

Bullshit. Zoey had known that straightaway, and so had he.

He'd been angry with Harriet, angrier than he'd admitted even to himself, and Zoey had been so sweetly sympathetic, so utterly unlike his wife, listening and not judging. And in return he'd used her and totally taken advantage of her. *A one-night-stand, for Christ's sake.* How could he do it to her?

He'd treated her as shamefully as he'd treated his wife. He was a despicable fucking human being. Even if Harriet never found out – and he prayed to God she didn't – he'd still have to carry the guilt and shame of what he'd done; and it was no less than he fucking deserved.

'Dad? Is everything OK?'

With an effort, he cleared his head. 'Just a bit jet-lagged, Flo-Mo. I'll be fine when I've had another coffee. Where did you say we were meeting them?'

'Outside the Lamb & Flag. Zoey said she'd never met a man who couldn't find his way to the nearest pub.'

Despite himself, Oliver laughed. At least she hadn't lost her sense of humour.

In the aftermath of Maine, Zoey hadn't even been able to look him in the eye, never mind speak to him, and the last two days of their visit had been a nightmare of fear and guilt, the two of them treading on eggshells as they tiptoed around each other. He'd been convinced Harriet would put two and two together, but she'd been so wrapped up in making the most of Nell's last few days that she'd barely noticed he was there. Naturally she'd been hurt and confused by Zoey's sudden volte-face on their summer trip to London, but secretly he'd been relieved. Keeping four thousand miles between them had seemed only prudent under the circumstances.

He'd done everything he could to make it

up to his wife after Nell and Zoey had gone, needing to atone even though she had no idea of his betrayal. He'd done his best to help out around the house, trying to think of small ways to show how much he loved her, doing his best to put aside his previous resentment over Ben and the way she'd gone behind his back and contacted Zoey in the first place. What she'd done wasn't even in the same league as his level of deceit. At least she could plead she'd acted from the best of motives. He'd just behaved like a bastard.

When his wife had begged him to make things right with Zoey, to make their trip to London happen and give him the time with Nell she wanted, how could he say no? *Don't I deserve that much?* After the way he and Zoey had betrayed her, it was the very least she deserved.

Zoey had realized it too. They might not want to come within a continent of one another, but what they wanted no longer came into it. They owed it to Harriet to put things right.

'There they are!' Florence exclaimed.

His heart thumped painfully as the two girls shrieked and threw their arms round each other. He'd forgotten just how strong the pull towards her was.

Zoey gaped at him in shock. 'I was expecting Harriet,' she said faintly.

'Last-minute change of plan. Harriet's father was rushed to hospital. They've found a shadow on his lung and wanted him in for a full MRI.

Harriet's mother's in bits, and she needed Harriet there.'

'That's dreadful! I'm so sorry,' Zoey exclaimed, her own feelings put aside. 'Harriet must be worried sick.'

'She is. It's such a shame. He's only just got over the last bout of surgery, and now this.'

'Does Florence know?'

'Only that he had to go back to hospital for a check-up. No need to worry the children until we have to.'

'Poor Harriet,' Zoey said softly.

Nell linked her arm through Florence's, and the two girls threaded their way through the crowds thronging the Pierrepont Arcade. He and Zoey followed them, tracking them by their laughter as much as the striking contrast they made together: Florence's rude blonde health side-by-side with Nell's slender paleness. Florence had grown up in the past few months, he realized suddenly. Literally: she'd put on a couple of inches and lost some weight, which had sharpened the soft, childish prettiness of her face, bringing her adult beauty into focus. Emotionally, too. He'd never seen her so relaxed, at home in her own skin, as if she had finally discovered who she was; which was ironic, given that was precisely what had been called into question over the past few months. But she no longer seemed eaten up with anxiety around Harriet. It was as if learning the truth about their relationship had let both of them off the hook, releasing them from their mutual guilt. It was still early days, but now they were no longer mother and daughter, they were free to be friends.

He'd been fully prepared for an awkward and uncomfortable afternoon with Zoey, but within minutes they were laughing and talking as if Maine had never happened. He had no idea why, but he felt more at ease with her than with anyone he'd ever met. From the first, Harriet had been a challenge – and he'd relished it; they'd matched wits and will, and he wouldn't have had it any other way. It was what had sustained their marriage over sixteen years. He couldn't imagine being married to Zoey for that length of time without getting bored, sweet thought she was; and yet it would be so much easier to tamp down his desire for her if he didn't *like* her so much.

Two hours later, weighed down with trinkets Florence had begged him to buy and then to carry for her – including a pair of art deco silver earrings for her mother – he declared retail defeat. 'I've travelled four thousand miles for a pint,' he said firmly. 'The only amber I'm interested in now comes in a glass.'

'But Dad, Nell said she'd take me to that really cool vintage clothing shop—'

'It's only at the end of the Passage,' Zoey put in. 'They can meet us later when they're done. They'll be quite safe.'

He hesitated. He hadn't anticipated being alone with her.

'Dad? Please?'

He was being ridiculous. This had to happen sometime. They were adults. Friends. They could do this.

'Do you have your phone on you?' he asked Florence.

She rolled her eyes. 'Yes. Honestly, Dad. We won't be long.'

'We're going to the Narrow Boat on the canal. Remember where it is?' Zoey asked Nell.

'Yeah. Have fun,' Nell said, throwing her mother a look. 'Don't do anything I wouldn't.'

They reached Regent's Canal, and turned left along the leafy towpath, grateful for the shade from the beating midday sun. 'So, how have you been?' he asked quietly.

'I'm selling the shop,' Zoey said abruptly.

He halted in the middle of the path. 'Selling the shop? But you love that place!'

'Love doesn't pay the mortgage,' Zoey sighed. 'Or the electricity, or the council tax. The shop hasn't made money in years, but I always earned enough from my designs to keep things going. But these days, no one wants to spend the money on clothes, even my recycled budget couture.' She smiled ruefully. 'Most of my regulars have drastically cut back. I barely made enough to pay the phone bill last month.'

'But things will pick up. Once the economy starts to recover—'

'We won't survive that long. If I don't sell in the

next few months, the shop will be repossessed. I've already had the bailiffs round.'

'Why didn't you tell me? You know I'd have helped.'

'That's why I didn't tell you.' They started walking again. 'It's not your problem, Oliver. I've never been very good with money. And without Richard—'

'What do you mean, without Richard?'

'We split up.'

He digested this for a moment, unsettled. 'Because of what happened with us?'

'I'd be lying if I said no,' she admitted. 'But not in the way you think. It just made me realize I wasn't being fair to Richard. "Good enough" isn't good enough, if you see what I mean.'

'How has Nell taken it?'

'Not well.'

'Does she know? About us, I mean?'

'Your daughter doesn't miss much.'

'Christ. No wonder she was off with me earlier.'

'It's not you. It's me she's upset with. She loves Richard. And she's hopping mad I won't marry him anyway and just have an affair with you.'

He laughed shortly. 'She doesn't pull any punches, does she?'

'She has her own idea of loyalty,' Zoey said.

They reached the Narrow Boat pub, and Zoey settled herself at a picnic table by the water, puffing slightly from the exertion of walking so far in the heat, while he went inside to order drinks. By the time he returned five minutes later, she had several ducks quacking in the water at her feet and pigeons on the table.

'You look like Snow White,' he grinned as a butterfly landed on her shoulder. 'All we need now are a couple of bluebirds.'

She giggled and crumbled some more bread into the canal. 'I always carry a bit of stale loaf in my bag in the summer for the ducks.'

He took a gulp of beer and sat down astride the picnic bench next to her. Zoey brushed her hands clean of crumbs and picked up her glass of wine. Her bare shoulders were already freckling and turning pink in the sun. He could see tiny dewdrops of sweat beading between her breasts. He brushed a damp curl of hair from the back of her neck where it had escaped from her plastic clip.

She closed her eyes and turned her face up to the sun, like a flower. 'God, you don't get many days like this in London. Makes me want to kick off my shoes and paddle.'

'You could always take a dip in the canal,' he teased.

She shuddered, grimacing at the green water. 'Don't. I can't even swim.'

'Seriously?'

'Terrified of water. I used to lock myself in the equipment room during games in the summer so I didn't have to go in the school pool.'

He put down his glass and rested his arm on the table so that their shoulders touched. The heat from her sun-kissed skin burned through the thin fabric of his linen shirt. He shifted slightly; the movement brought their bodies closer together. With a soft sigh she leaned back against him, and, unable to stop himself, he stroked his thumb against the inside of her arm, lightly brushing the outer swell of her breast. He felt her tremble slightly, and his cock leaped instantly to attention. She must have been able to feel his erection against her, when she leaned back against him, but she didn't try to pull away.

His hand drifted down across the curve of her breast, and he heard her breath catch. Gently, he brushed his palm back and forth across her nipple, feeling it leap to attention beneath his touch. Her knees parted, and he leaned forward and scooped the skirt of her sundress away from her knees. Concealed by the table, his hand slid beneath the hem of her skirt, inching up the soft warmth of her inner thighs.

She opened her legs further, granting him access, and his erection pressed painfully against the zip of his jeans. *This was a public place, for God's sake. He couldn't just – here, in broad daylight. There were people on the towpath, anyone could see . . .*

The apex between her thighs was damp with sweat. He eased his hand under the edge of her knickers, pushing them to the side. His cock throbbed. *Christ, she was wet.*

He worked his fingers through the silkiness of her pubic hair. She turned her head into his chest to stifle a moan as he teased her clit with his middle finger, moistening it with her own juices. Her breathing was loud and fast in his ear.

'Come on,' he murmured softly. 'I've got you. I've got you.'

She arched against him, and he wrapped his left arm around her, holding her against him, his right hand working between her legs. There was a sudden gush of slippery wetness against his fingers, and she shuddered and then sagged against him, her eyes closed.

He straightened her dress, and enfolded her in his arms, kissing the back of her neck. Slowly, their breathing returned to normal.

She twisted in his arms so she could see his face. 'That was . . .'

'Yes. It was.'

So, not just friends, then, he thought as his mouth found hers. *Not just friends at all.*

Neither of them even noticed the camera lens pointed in their direction from the other side of the canal.

Subject: BABY MIX-UP
Date: 09/08/2013 16:43:44 P.M.
From: c.wood@dailynews.co.uk
To: l.morgan@dailynews.co.uk

Sent from the Internet (details)

Annie confirms quote from hospital's lawyers, and legal have signed off on the story as long as we don't use pix of the kids. Run the piece tomorrow with the photo of Lockwood and Zoey Sands, and send Ben to see if he can get a quote from the wife. Once the story breaks, we may be able to get interviews. Tell the girl to invoice you.

   Chris

Chris Wood
Deputy Editor, Daily News
020 7322 1149

CHAPTER 22

FLORENCE

Florence adjusted the waistband of her cropped jeans so that they sat comfortably below her navel, and pulled her sleeveless ribbed T-shirt over her head. In the mirror, her new belly-button piercing glittered against her tanned stomach. There was no way Mom was going to miss it, though Dad hadn't even noticed she'd had it done after she and Nell had sneaked off the other day when he'd been at the pub with Zoey. Mom'd flip out when she saw it – which was precisely why she'd done it.

Except she didn't really want Mom to flip out about it, not any more.

It wasn't that she worried about getting into trouble. She was fifteen; the worst they could do was ground her. It was just that, all of a sudden, it seemed childish and . . . well, a bit *mean* to wind Mom up simply to prove she could.

She yanked the bottom of her T-shirt down so that it covered the tiny aquamarine and silver piercing. Gramps was in hospital, and although no one had actually spelt it out for her, she knew the prognosis wasn't good. Gran spent most of

244

the time crying, or looking like she was about to, and of course the boys were picking up on the tension in the house and using it as an excuse to act up. It didn't help that they were all crammed in here together like sardines. Her grandparents' townhouse in Kensington was pretty big by English standards, as Mom kept reminding them, but back home they were all used to having not just their own bedrooms but separate bathrooms, too, and here everyone had to share two between them. At least she got the attic box room to herself, even if she did have to sleep on an inflatable mattress. If she'd had to stay in the same room as her three brothers, she'd have probably died of the plague by now.

She perched on the edge of the window sill and laced up her Converse. Mom and Dad weren't getting on at the moment, either, and for the first time ever she found herself in the weird position of taking Mom's side.

Dad had been in an odd mood since they'd arrived in London. She knew he hadn't wanted to come from the get-go, though she had no idea why. He liked Zoey and Nell, she knew he did; he'd got on really well with them when they'd come to stay in Vermont. They'd all had a great time last week, too, at the Camden Passage market. So why was he giving Mom such a hard time? Every time she walked into a room these days, he walked out. Mom seemed as confused by his attitude as she was, though she was doing her best to hold it together for Gran's sake. Which was why, for once, Florence didn't want to add to her problems.

'Are you ready, darling?' Mom called.

She grabbed her phone and ran downstairs, gathering her long blonde hair into a loose plait over her left shoulder and twisting a pink elastic band around the end. 'Sorry. Didn't realize it was nearly nine already. Where's Gran?'

'She got back quite late from visiting Gramps last night, so she's having a bit of a lie-in. Aunt Lucy's going to pick her up later and bring her along to the hospital.'

'What about Dad? Isn't he coming?'

Mom picked up her purse and keys from the hall table. 'Not today. He wants to take the boys to the Chelsea match in Fulham later. He says they need to experience *proper* football while they're in England.'

She rolled her eyes. 'Dad *hates* soccer.'

'Just because he's got two left feet it doesn't mean he can't hold forth for hours about the intricacies of the offside rule,' Mom said dryly. 'And you might want to tuck your T-shirt in before we see Grandpa, darling. I'm not sure his heart is strong enough to cope with belly-button piercings just now.'

Florence stared down at the silver ring in her stomach as if she'd never seen it before. 'Aren't you mad?'

'Not as long as you had it done somewhere

decent with a clean needle,' Mom sighed. 'Nell doesn't seem any the worse for three earrings in each ear and a ring through her navel, so why should you? Just promise me, darling, no tattoos. At least not where I'll ever have to see them.'

'I thought you'd hate it.'

'Well, I'm not thrilled about it – though I have to admit it does seem quite a pretty one, darling – but it's your body. I know you all think I'm a prudish old battleaxe, but I'm just trying to get you and your brothers to adulthood in one piece.' She smiled. 'We all make mistakes, Florence, but it's my job as your mother to make sure none of yours are irrevocable.'

'Like getting pregnant or being killed on the back of a boy's motorbike?'

Mom laughed. 'I guess I am a bit of a broken record.'

Florence gave her a sudden, impulsive hug. 'I don't mind. At least I know you still care.'

'Of course I do! Why on earth wouldn't I?'

She shrugged, her gaze on her pink Converse.

'Oh, darling. I've handled this so badly, haven't I? Your father kept telling me, but I wouldn't listen.' She pulled back from their hug so that Florence could see her eyes. 'Look at me, Florence. I love you more than life itself. Nothing, *nothing* will ever change that. When you're a mother your-self, you'll understand that the human heart is infinitely elastic. When George was born, did you love Sam any less? Or George, when Charlie came along? Of course not.' She framed her daughter's face in her hands. 'Sweetheart, it was no different when I found out about Nell. Loving her hasn't taken away a single jot of what I feel for you. If anything, I love you *more*.'

'More?'

'It's made me appreciate everything that *you* are. You, *Florence*. Not you, a mini-Harriet. I kept trying to make you like me, instead of letting you be yourself. Look at Nell: she couldn't be more different from the kind of daughter I'd ever have imagined having, but she's turned out to be a wonderful, amazing girl. And so have you. You're your own person, and I love you for it.'

Florence suddenly found it hard to swallow. 'Come on, Mom,' she mumbled. 'Gramps'll be waiting.'

She opened the front door. There was a sudden loud hum as she stepped outside, like the roar of a thousand angry bees, and she let out a small scream. Instantly, Mom grabbed her shoulder, and pulled her back inside the house, slamming the front door shut.

'Who're all those people?' Florence gasped. 'Why're they taking pictures of me?'

Mom pulled her away from the window. 'They're journalists.'

'Journalists?'

'Photographers.'

'What, like *paparazzi*? Why on earth would they want photos of *me*?'

'At a wild guess, I'd say it has something to do with you and Nell,' Mom said grimly. 'I can't think of any other reason they'd be here. Go upstairs and get your father. And try not to wake Gran. This is the last thing she needs.'

Florence found Dad in the shower. By the time he'd grabbed a towel and followed her downstairs, Mom had already flipped open her laptop and was furiously surfing various news sources. 'I can't find anything online,' she said tersely. 'It's not in the *Mail* or any of the broadsheets.'

'What the hell is going on?' Dad demanded.

'Someone's leaked the story about the girls,' Mom said shortly.

He leaned over her shoulder, dripping water onto the screen. 'Are you sure?

'Take a look outside,' Mom snapped. 'Why else would we have snappers camped on the doorstep? Someone's broken the story, and now half of Fleet Street's chasing it.'

'Mrs Lockwood?' a voice called suddenly, echoing down the hall. 'Mrs Lockwood, this is Lesley Morgan from the *Daily News*. Can I talk to you a minute?'

Mom stalked towards the front door, Florence close behind her. She could see a pair of heavily made-up eyes peering through the mailbox. 'What do you want?' Mom demanded.

'Please, Mrs Lockwood, if you'd just open the door—'

'I said *what do you want*?'

'Have you seen our story today, Mrs Lockwood?'

Mom turned to Dad, hovering out of sight in his towel. 'It's the *Daily News*. See if you can find it online.'

The woman crammed a folded newspaper through the mailbox. 'It's our lead story. Look, Mrs Lockwood, I'm here to help. I'd like to hear your side of things. If you could just open the door—'

'Don't hold your breath,' Mom snapped, grabbing the paper and turning on her heel.

Florence caught a glimpse of the headline above the fold. *Teen Girls Switched At Birth. Newborn daughters who were accidentally mixed up in a maternity hospital and grew up with wrong parents have been reunited – with devastating consequences. Florence Lockwood and Nell Sands . . .*

Mom tossed the newspaper into the empty fireplace. 'How did they get hold of this?' she demanded.

Dad shrugged. 'How the hell should I know? The hospital, I should think. Someone in the admin office probably leaked it. I'm surprised it's taken this long to come out, given the stink you made there.'

'So this is *my* fault?'

'That's not what I said.'

'How did they find us?' Florence asked.

'The same way I found Zoey and Nell,' Mom sighed. 'As soon as you have a name, you just have to look online.'

'No, I mean, how did they know we were *in London*?'

There was a long silence. Mom sank onto the sofa. 'She's right,' she said tiredly. 'How would any of the papers know that? Nell and Zoey would be easy to track down, but surely the first port of call for anyone looking for us would be Vermont? Even if they knew we were in London, how would they guess where to look? Morgan's a very common surname – there must thousands in London. They'd never have found my parents this easily. Someone must've tipped them off. Someone we *know*.'

Dad raked his hand through his wet hair. '*Who*? Only our families know we're here, and none of them know the truth about the girls, because we were waiting for your father to be well enough before we broke the news. No one else knows.'

'Zoey does,' Florence said uncertainly.

They both stared at her. '*Zoey*?' Dad exclaimed. 'She'd never talk to the papers! She's wanted to keep this quiet even more than we have!'

'Newspapers pay a lot of money for this kind of story,' Mom said slowly. 'And Zoey needs a lot of money very much.'

'Sell out her own *daughter*? Come on, what kind of person d'you think she is?'

'A desperate one, trying to keep a roof over her head.'

'She'd never do that,' Dad repeated. 'No matter how desperate she was.'

'Why don't we call her and ask?'

'Are you *serious*? You actually think it was her?'

'So what if it was?' Florence said unexpectedly. 'I'd rather she and Nell got the money than anyone else. They're the ones who need it. They'll lose their shop and their apartment otherwise. Like you said, the story was bound to come out sooner or later. At least this way Zoey and Nell get something out of it.'

'Either way, she's probably got photographers on her doorstep too,' Mom added. 'I'm surprised she hasn't phoned us already. At the very least we need to talk to her to discuss how we're going to handle this.'

'She won't be at home,' Florence said. 'She told me last week she was going down to Bath for some special antiques market this weekend. I remember because she said she was getting the early train, and she hates getting up early.'

'What about Nell?' Mom asked.

'She's spending the weekend at her friend's house.'

'In that case, we'd better try Zoey's mobile,' Mom said tersely. 'And before you start, Oliver, even if she wasn't behind this story, she still needs to know what's going on. Florence, you should call Nell and warn her too. Tell her to stay at her friend's house for the time being, out of sight.'

Dad gripped the damp towel at his waist. 'You're overreacting. It's not the end of the world. We just need to release a statement and move on. It'll be yesterday's fish-and-chip paper by next weekend.'

'Really?' Mom snapped. 'I didn't realize you were such a PR expert. There's no such thing as yesterday's news any more. The Internet has seen to that. This story will still be out there in the ether when Florence and Nell have teenagers themselves.'

'Does that really matter?'

'Yes, it *matters*! Apart from anything else, my father's in no state to deal with this right now, and nor is Mum, to be honest. And what about the rest of our families, having to read about this over the breakfast table instead of hearing it from us? You can be sure the American networks will pick this up once they discover the US connection. Florence is going to have to deal with this all over again when we get back home. Think what that's going to be like for her.'

'It's OK,' Florence said staunchly. 'I don't care. You're still my mom and dad, and that's what I'll tell everyone.'

'Good girl,' Dad smiled, giving her a hug.

'Oh, Oliver. You're not even dressed,' Mom said illogically. 'Florence, darling, you don't understand. I worked in PR for years. I know what the press can be like. They'll follow you everywhere, trying to take pictures, talking to your friends . . .'

'But what if we give them an interview?' Florence suggested. 'Me *and* Nell. Let them take all the

253

photos they want. It'll be over and done with, then.'

Mom hesitated. 'It would put a stop to this circus, certainly,' she said thoughtfully. 'We could do an interview with one of the better papers – the *Mail* or *Express* would be our best bet. The supermarket magazines will pick it up, but they're not going to chase you down the street. Maybe a slot on one of the daytime shows. If we pull this all out in the open now, it'll be chaos for a week or two, but then the story will run out of steam.'

'So let's do that, then,' Florence said.

'Hang on a minute,' Dad protested. 'She's got no idea what that means. Live television, for God's sake! She's only fifteen!'

'Do you have a better idea?'

'Yes! We sit this out and wait for them to go away! Call the police if necessary! I could take Florence to visit your aunt in Montreal—'

'I think we should ask Florence,' Mom said firmly, turning towards her. 'What do *you* want to do, darling?'

Florence felt a sudden glow of pleasure. Regardless of the circumstances, it was the first time Mom had treated her like an adult and actually considered her opinion. Maybe things really *had* changed.

She peered through the bamboo blinds at the photographers on the front steps and around the railings. There were at least four or five of them, plus a dozen or so curious bystanders who'd gathered to see what was going on. It was like that scene in *Notting Hill* when Hugh Grant opened the door to see the world's paparazzi waiting for Julia Roberts. Well, maybe not quite that many people, but loads, anyway. It was actually kind of exciting. If she ended up on TV, her friends would be able to see it on YouTube; she'd be almost famous. And all she had to do was talk about how it felt to be her. How hard could that be?

'I want to do it,' she said.

'In that case, I suppose we'd better see what they've got so far,' Mom sighed. 'Florence, can you hand me the newspaper?'

Florence picked it up from the empty fireplace, unfolding it as she did so. She stared at the colour photograph beneath the headline, struggling to make sense of what she was seeing. Suddenly, she felt sick.

'Dad,' she said, her whole body trembling as she turned to her father. 'Dad, why were you kissing Zoey?'

CHAPTER 23

ZOEY

Zoey was on the train down to Bath when she saw the newspaper. Another passenger had left it behind on his seat when he got out at Swindon. He'd been halfway through the sports section; it was only when she flipped the paper back to the front page that she saw the headline.

And the photograph.

Her first panicked thought was not for Oliver, or Harriet, or even Nell, but for Florence. How could they ever make this up to her, how could they *ever* put it right? She felt physically sick just thinking about what the child must be feeling. She'd told Florence she could *trust* her. How could she have let her down like this? *How?*

She'd lose her for ever now. Even if by some miracle her daughter forgave her, Harriet certainly wouldn't. She'd never let her anywhere near Florence again.

Oh God. Harriet. What a terrible thing to do to a woman who, whether she liked her or not, had never been anything but her friend. She'd felt guilty enough when she'd been having the affair with Patrick, but she'd been so *young* then – she'd had no idea what it was like to be a wife. She hadn't really stopped to think how it must feel to be the heartsick woman sitting alone at home, night after night, wondering where her husband was, what he was doing – and with whom. She'd never met Patrick's wife, didn't even know her name. She'd just been a faceless shadow, an *obstacle*, not a real person with feelings; a woman who, after all, had had a prior claim on Patrick. Zoey filled with hot shame now to think how careless she had been with another woman's heart, how cavalierly she'd excused everything because of *love*.

But what she had done to Harriet was a thousand times worse. Harriet had welcomed her into her home, into her *family*. She'd met her children, sat down and eaten with them, leafed through family photograph albums filled with Harriet and Oliver, Oliver and the boys, Florence and her parents. She'd known exactly, intimately, what this affair had been jeopardizing.

The train pulled into Bath and she grabbed her old-fashioned Lady Bracknell carpet bag and got out, crossing straight to the platform on the other side. The display board told her there was a train back to London in thirty-five minutes. She had to go home and face the music. She couldn't leave Nell to deal with this on her own.

She sank onto a bench and buried her head in her hands. She'd never meant any of this to happen.

That night in Maine had been a mistake – a dreadful, unforgiveable, unrepeatable mistake. She'd struggled through the next two crucifying days only by clinging to the knowledge that there would soon be four thousand miles between her and Oliver. Four thousand precious, safe, unbreachable miles.

She'd done everything she could to stop the Lockwoods coming to London. It had broken her heart to think of never seeing Florence again, and knowing how keenly the poor child would feel the rejection had rubbed salt into the wound. But she'd told herself it was for the best. She'd absorbed Nell's anger, Harriet's frustration, Florence's hurt, sticking resolutely to her guns to protect them all. It had been Oliver who'd talked her round, who'd persuaded her that the only way they could atone for what they'd done was to make Harriet happy, which meant giving her the big family summer reunion she'd wanted. She *never* should've listened to him.

She raised her head and blew her nose loudly on a grubby tissue culled from her coat pocket. No point denying how much she'd wanted to be persuaded. She was just as responsible for this mess as Oliver. She'd let him talk her into agreeing to the London visit, knowing how dangerous it was, because she'd wanted to see him again more than anything. She hadn't expected him to appear out of the crowd at the market with Florence, but the moment he had, her world had exploded from grey into technicolour. Her knickers had practically hummed. She'd seen the way he'd looked at her, too. As if she were naked. And *she* was the one who'd sent Nell and Florence off together, leaving the two of them alone. She'd let the afternoon by the canal happen. She'd *wanted* it to happen.

She could tell Harriet it had just been a kiss. One snatched kiss, the heat of the moment, too much wine and sunshine – and maybe Harriet would even believe her. But the damage hadn't been caused by the kiss itself. It was the *intimacy*: erotic, undeniable, captured on camera for the entire world to see. How could any wife forgive that?

Somewhere in her bag, her phone rang. She started, tempted for a moment to ignore it, and then realized it might be Nell and frantically groped through cough sweets and sunglasses and spare umbrellas and folded magazines and charity flyers – she could never say no to those poor people standing on pavements, desperate to get rid of their bundle for the day – until she found it.

Unknown number. She answered it anyway.

'It's me,' Oliver said tersely. 'I don't have long before Harriet comes back. Where are you?'

'At the station in Bath, waiting for a train to London. I just saw the newspaper. Oliver, I'm so, *so* sorry.'

'Where's Nell?'

'Staying at her friend's. Oliver, what's happening?

How's Harriet? And Florence, please, tell me, how's Florence?'

'How d'you think they are?'

She deserved that. 'What have you told them?'

'I told them it was just a kiss. What else could I tell them? I don't know if Florence believed me, but Harriet certainly doesn't. That photograph was pretty fucking damning. She's barely talking to me right now. I don't even know if I have a marriage left.'

'I'm sure once she calms down—'

'How did the photographer know where to find us?'

She straightened, taken aback by his tone. 'I don't know. They're journalists, I suppose. Tracking down people is what they do.'

'It probably helps when someone tells them where to start looking.'

'But who would *do* that?'

'You tell me.'

Her stomach plunged. 'What's that supposed to mean?'

'Just tell me the truth,' he said wearily. 'I'm sure they paid a lot of money for this story, and we both know you need it. Did you talk to the paper? Did you set me up?'

'You really think I could *do* something like that?' she demanded incredulously. 'You think I'm so desperate for money that I'd actually blow all our lives apart?'

'Look, I know what these bastards are like. Once

you let the genie out of the bottle, it's very hard to put it back in. You probably didn't mean for it to go this far—'

'I didn't mean for it to go *any*where! I haven't spoken to anyone, I swear! Oliver, you have to believe me! I would never, *never* do anything so underhand, so *vicious*!'

There was a long silence. For a moment she wondered if he'd hung up on her.

'Yes. Yes, I believe you,' he said finally. 'I'm sorry, Zoey, of course I believe you. I'm just – this is such a fucking shit-storm, sweetheart. I don't know what I'm going to do. Harriet's threatening to rain seven kinds of hell on my head, Florence can't even look at me, I'm worried frantic about you and Nell, and to be honest I just want to crawl under a rock and hide till it all blows over.'

Despite her grief and panic, Zoey glowed. *He'd called her sweetheart. He was worried about her.* He still cared, then.

'Is there – is there anything I can do to help?' she asked hesitantly.

'We need to talk about this properly and make sure we're on the same page. You can't go back to your flat – it's probably staked out by bloody journalists. You'll have to stay at a hotel until this dies down.'

'I can't afford a hotel!'

'Yes, I know that. I've already booked you a room at the St George; it's a nice, quiet hotel not far from me in Kensington. No one will bother you there. It's all paid for, so please don't argue. You can call Nell and tell her to stay with her friend, or have her join you at the hotel.'

'What are you going to do?'

He sighed heavily. 'Harriet's working on a press release to get the vultures off our backs. We need to get some kind of story out there and see if we can put a lid on this. Text me when you get to London.'

'Oliver—'

'Sorry. I have to go.'

She dropped the phone back in her bag, shaken and unnerved by the conversation. How could he have thought, even for a moment, that she could do something like that? She'd *never* sell out her own daughter – or anyone else for that matter. She despised what her mother used to call 'yellow journalism': sensational, sex-driven stories that had nothing to do with news or information, and everything to do with a prying, sleazy interest in other people's lives. She didn't mind a bit of celebrity gossip, of course – that was fair enough; celebrities invaded their own privacy to make a living, and they knew the score. But *this*? She shoved the newspaper deep into her carpet bag. How could a story like this do anything to make the world a better place?

She hadn't sold the *Daily News* the story, but clearly someone had. Oliver was right: it had to be someone who knew they'd be at the market that day, who'd picked them up there and followed them to the pub beside the canal. They must have thought all their Christmases had come at once when they'd seen the two of them making out like a couple of horny teenagers. What on earth had they been *thinking*?

And the details in the story – they went beyond anything an employee of the hospital would know. The trip to Vermont, the lobster on the beach in Maine – who would know that sort of thing but someone who'd been there?

She knew the answer before she'd even formed the question in her mind. *How much do we owe? Thirty thousand? Jesus, Mum! What did you plan to do, sell a kidney?*

Oh Nell. My darling, what have you done?

The London train pulled into the station. She climbed aboard, her body aching all over as if she had flu. Nell must have thought she was doing the right thing, the only thing to save the shop and bail her mother out. She was only fifteen. She'd have had no idea what happened when you let the genie out of the bottle, as Oliver had put it. Once a story was out there, you had no control over it. Nell was as much a victim of these jackals as they were. She'd never have done this on purpose. No matter how much money they were paying her.

She tried calling Nell's mobile for the umpteenth time, but yet again it went straight to voicemail. This time, she left a message. 'Darling, it's Mum. I know about the *Daily News* story, and you're not to worry. I know you didn't mean for all this to happen. We'll sort it out. But please don't talk to any more journalists. Call me as soon as you can. Love you, darling.'

She leaned back against the headrest and closed her eyes. Regardless of what she'd just told Nell, she had no idea how they were going to fix this.

She couldn't help feeling guilty as she stepped out of the shower and wrapped herself in a huge, fluffy white bathrobe. She was only here because she'd done an awful, horrible thing; she was effectively a pariah, cast out and unable to go home. But it had been fifteen years since she'd set foot in a hotel as luxurious as this, during her affair with Patrick; she couldn't help delighting in the chocolates on her pillow, the complimentary massage when she arrived – a *massage*! – the bottle of champagne on ice beside her bed, even the little bottles of shampoo and conditioner which she'd already squirrelled away in her carpet bag. Ever since she'd had Nell, she'd been robbing Peter to pay Paul; she'd got so used to cutting her own hair and squinting because she couldn't afford a trip to the optician's, she'd forgotten what it was like to be pampered. Richard had tried, of course, but she hated being beholden, and besides, there were so many more important things to spend money on than facials and manicures. Like the electricity bill, for one.

She didn't want to think about Richard. When they'd agreed to take a break, she hadn't breathed a word about Oliver. He'd accepted her excuses about needing time before taking such a big step as marriage with his usual stoicism. It would break his heart when he read about this. *Oh, Richard. Why couldn't you have fought for me a bit harder? Maybe then none of this would ever have happened.*

She padded over to the mini-fridge and took out a bottle of still water. Goodness knew how much this would cost. She picked up the list of prices and nearly dropped the bottle in shock. *Four pounds fifty!* For a bottle of *water!*

Hastily she shoved the bottle of water back into the fridge and filled a toothbrush glass from the tap in the bathroom. Even if she wasn't the one paying, she couldn't in all conscience drink a bottle of water that cost nearly five pounds.

The phone beside her bed rang suddenly, and she jumped, spilling her water.

'Ms Sands?' the receptionist said. 'You have a visitor. A Mr Lockwood?'

'Oh,' Zoey gasped. Oliver had said he'd come round that afternoon, but she hadn't expected him so early. She wasn't even *dressed*.

'Ms Sands? Is it OK if he comes up?'

'Yes, yes — of course.'

No point trying to change now. She raked a brush through her damp hair and pulled it into a scrunchie, then picked up her clothes from the floor, bundling them into a drawer. She just had time to slick some Vaseline onto her lips before there was a knock at the door.

She opened it. Standing behind Oliver, looking like an avenging Valkyrie, was Harriet.

'May we come in?' Harriet inquired icily.

She nodded dumbly and backed away from the doorway, tightening the belt of her bathrobe. Being confronted by your lover's wife was bad enough, but did it have to happen when she was barefoot and make-up free in her *dressing gown*?

'I see you've made yourself comfortable,' Harriet said coolly, taking in the champagne, the 800-thread white Egyptian cotton sheets, the chocolates. 'Easy to do on someone else's dime, of course. Or did you pay for it yourself with thirty pieces of silver from the *Daily News*?'

'Of course not!' she exclaimed indignantly. 'I told Oliver, it wasn't me who talked to them!'

He shot her a warning look. She realized he didn't want his wife to know they'd had a chance to compare notes and get their stories straight.

'I'm sure this all seems very amusing to you,' Harriet said bitterly. 'Screwing up my life, screwing up my daughter, *screwing* my husband. You must've been laughing all the way to the bank.'

'Harriet,' Oliver said wearily.

'Oh, I'm sorry, Oliver, we agreed to stick to the facts, didn't we?' She turned to Zoey. 'It was the only condition under which he'd lead me to your little love-nest, you see. No *unpleasantness*, just the facts.'

'What facts?' she asked faintly.

'The *fact* that you were photographed kissing my

266

husband,' Harriet spat. 'The *fact* that my private life has now been splashed across the front page of the tabloids, thanks to you. The *fact* that yours was the first face my father saw when he woke up from surgery in hospital and a helpful nurse gave him the newspaper he asked for. The *fact* that my children are asking why Daddy is kissing Florence's mommy – her *real* mommy – in front of everyone. Those facts might be a good place to start.'

'It was . . . just . . . a kiss,' Zoey managed.

'Is that really what this looks like to you?' Harriet thrust a copy of the newspaper in her face. 'My husband conveniently also tells me it was just a spur-of-the-moment embrace. The happy result of a joyful reunion between friends, in the sunshine, with a glass of wine.'

She pushed the paper away. 'Yes, that's all it was.'

'It was broad daylight,' Oliver sighed. 'For God's sake, Harriet, we were sitting in a pub garden in full view of anyone walking past. What the hell d'you *think* we were doing?'

Harriet glared at him. 'Well, you weren't playing tiddlywinks, were you?'

'Why are you doing this?' he demanded. 'You said you wanted to come and talk things through so we could decide how to handle this, for the girls' sake. Why are you turning this into some kind of witch-hunt?'

His wife ignored him and threw the paper on the bed. 'Did you sleep with my husband?'

Zoey squirmed. Answer yes, and she'd hurt

Harriet, lose Florence, and condemn Oliver as a liar and a cheat. Answer no, and she'd betray Harriet yet again, compounding her own deceit with yet more lies.

She refused to look at Oliver. This was between her and Harriet. Either way, she lost.

LAW OFFICES
TOPOLESKI, WILLIAMS & OUIMETTE, P.L.L.C.
100 MAIN STREET
P.O. BOX 1100
BURLINGTON, VERMONT 05402-1100

JERROLD M. TOPOLESKI

KAREN A. WILLIAMS

MICHEL OUIMETTE

JENNIFER HARRIS, PARALEGAL

BENJAMIN GREEN, PARALEGAL

TELEPHONE: (802) 881 6768

FACSIMILE: (802) 881 6769

OF COUNSEL:
TERESA P. FLETCHER (802) 881 6767

August 12, 2013

Harriet Lockwood
c/o Mr & Mrs M. Morgan
55 Cheyne Avenue
Kensington SW7 5AF
United Kingdom

Dear Mrs Lockwood,

Enclosed please find confirmation of the transfer of funds

in the amount of $150,000 to our family law office in London as requested.

I regret to inform you that Mr Lyon has declined to represent you in this matter. Our London office has, however, engaged Mr Neil Hatfield, who is highly recommended in this field. We believe he will pursue your custody action with the determination and proactive energy you require.

Sincerely,

Jerry Topoleski

Enclosure

CHAPTER 24

OLIVER

'Did you sleep with my husband?' Harriet demanded.

He tried to catch Zoey's eye, but she was staring at his wife like a rabbit caught in the headlights. *Dear Christ, don't say yes,* he pleaded inwardly. *We may get away with the photo if that's all she thinks this is. Don't throw me under the bus. For God's sake, keep your mouth shut.*

'Yes,' Zoey said.

Christ almighty. Christ al-fucking-mighty.

His wife stalked towards the door, and he felt physically sick. How in God's name was he going to make this right? She'd kill him the moment they got out of here. She'd have his balls for breakfast.

Except he never got that far.

'Don't think you're coming home now, Oliver. You can have him.' She added, shrugging at Zoey. 'It's up to you if you want him or not.' Harriet slammed out of the room. For a moment, he was too stunned to react. What had just happened? What the *hell* had just happened? Was she serious? Had his wife just *left* him?

Zoey touched his arm. 'Oliver—'

He shook her off, suddenly spurred into life. Wrenching the door open, he ran the length of the corridor and pummelled the lift button. *Still four floors away, damn it!* Impatiently, he shoved open the fire door and started down the stairs, taking them two and three at a time, landing hard on each turn. His chest was tight and his legs aching by the time he reached the ground floor and rushed out into the foyer.

No sign of Harriet. He turned, panting, to the doorman, hands on his knees as he fought for breath. 'Have you seen a woman . . . jeans and . . . pink sweater?'

'She just got into that cab, sir,' the man said, nodding towards the street.

He pushed past him into the street, but the cab was already a hundred metres away. He'd missed his moment. There was no point chasing after her now.

Zoey was still sitting on the bed, wrapped in her bathrobe, when he returned wearily to her room. She leaped to her feet when she saw him. 'Did you speak to her?'

He shook his head.

'Oliver, I'm so sorry.'

'It's my fault. If you can't do the time, don't do the crime, right?'

She winced.

'I'm sorry,' he sighed. 'I didn't mean it like that.'

'Is that really how you think of us?'

'You know I don't. But it's been a fuck of a day, Zoey. And you haven't exactly helped.'

'She asked me directly,' Zoey said tearfully. 'I didn't know how to lie to her. I'm so sorry, I didn't want to cause trouble. I swear I wasn't trying to make things worse, but she asked me, and . . .'

He closed his eyes and pinched the bridge of his nose. 'You did what you thought was right. It's my fault. I should never have let her come upstairs with me. Seeing you practically naked, in a hotel bedroom – talk about rubbing salt in the wound. Christ. I don't know what I was thinking. I should never have let it happen.'

'What must she have thought when she saw me?' Zoey cried. 'In a *dressing gown*?'

'I'm sorry. I honestly had no idea she was going to pull a stunt like this. I thought she was going to wait for you to come downstairs. She said she just wanted to talk things through with you in person, so we could clear up any misunderstandings. She seemed so bloody *calm*.'

He remembered a friend once commenting that the definition of an adulterer was a man who made two women unhappy instead of one. Well, he was certainly proving that in spades.

'What are you going to do now?' Zoey asked.

'God knows.' He sank onto the edge of the bed, his head in his hands. 'There's no point going home, not tonight. I don't want a scene in front of the kids. I need to give her some time to calm down so we can sort this out properly, without an audience.'

'Are you – do you want to stay here tonight? Not like that,' she added hastily. 'I just meant . . . oh, Oliver, it's all so horrible. Nell's really upset with me; she won't answer my calls, and all I've had from her is a text saying she's staying at Teri's. I can't go home because of all the journalists, and I probably won't have any friends left after all this. I know what we did was terrible, but if it wasn't for the girls getting mixed up in the first place, none of the newspapers would care.' She started to cry in earnest. 'Please don't leave me alone. Not tonight.'

He hesitated. She looked so miserable, and so *young*; she reminded him achingly of Florence when she'd had a really bad day at school. Zoey hadn't asked for this. Maine had happened at a vulnerable time, when she was confused and emotionally wrung out. He should've known better. He was the one who was married.

He put his arm round her, sighing as she leaned against him. Where else was he going to go? He could book a different hotel room, but what was the point, really? They'd already been caught with their trousers down. It would be like locking the stable door after the horse had bolted.

And Zoey *needed* him. Something it seemed Harriet hadn't done for a very long time.

He woke first, as daylight streamed through the open window. Zoey was still pillowed on his shoulder, as she had been for most of the night.

Carefully, he eased his arm from beneath her head, gently replacing it with his pillow, wincing as pins and needles shot through his deadened muscles.

He tiptoed softly into the bathroom to take a piss, then turned on the shower. He could still smell Zoey on his skin. Sleeping with her had definitely *not* been part of the plan. All he'd done was make an impossible situation worse.

He'd known from the second he'd agreed to stay it was a mistake. She was in love with him; he could see it, feel it, as she dropped her robe and pulled him into her pliant arms. She'd opened not just her body, but her heart to him. And when she touched him, when she wrapped her arms around him and he breathed in the citrus scent of her skin, when she bit down on her lip and smiled up at him, he couldn't say no.

Dammit, he should have done! She was the one who'd seduced him this time, he knew that, but he still should have had more self-control. For her sake, as much as anyone's. He loved being with her. She was easy company, she made him laugh, she made him feel strong and masculine and protective. But he didn't love her the way he loved Harriet – he never would – and it was unfair of him to lead her on like this, even if she was the one doing the running. She deserved better than a man in love with another woman. Harriet was complicated. She was so consumed with doing the right thing – being a good wife, a good mother, a good manager at work – she often forgot to simply have fun. Living with her was complex and frequently frustrating. But even after sixteen years, she challenged and fascinated and intrigued him in so many ways. He simply couldn't imagine not being married to her.

He left before Zoey awoke, leaving her a note telling her he'd gone into the office. He knew it was cowardly, but he couldn't face another emotional scene, not this early in the day. He needed some time and space to get his head straight, to figure out a way to break free without causing any more damage. And right now, he simply didn't trust himself to be around her.

The moment he was outside the hotel, he called Harriet's mobile. He wasn't surprised when it went straight to voicemail. 'It's me,' he said. 'Please don't just delete this. We need to talk. You have to let me explain. Please, Harry. For the kids, if not for me. Call me any time.' He paused. 'I love you.'

She didn't return his call, and he didn't expect her to. She wasn't going to lower the drawbridge right away. She was going to make him work for it, and he didn't blame her after what he'd done.

The office was deserted on a Sunday. For the first time in his life, he felt grateful to the Inland Revenue. Such was the cluster-fuck his now-ex-manager had created, he found his hands too full with work to dwell on his domestic drama. The company was behind with both their tax and VAT payments, and the Manchester office – which serviced the entire

North of England – was in an even worse mess. They owed the taxman tens of thousands of pounds – money he hadn't budgeted for and, right now, had no idea how they would find.

It took him the rest of the day simply to sort out what needed to be done, and he was surprised when he leaned back in his chair and stretched out his aching muscles to find it was already after five. He needed to get back to the hotel, sort things out with Zoey. It wasn't a conversation he was looking forward to, but he couldn't hope to mend things with Harriet until he drew a line under the past.

To his surprise, Zoey had already checked out. 'She left this for you, sir,' the receptionist said, handing him an envelope.

Darling Oliver, she'd written in a looping, untidy scrawl on the back of his own note from that morning. *I don't want you to be with me because you have nowhere else to go. I'm going to collect Nell and take her back home. If you choose me, you know where I'll be. Love, Zoey. xoxo*

Not quite sure whether he was sad or relieved she'd gone without saying goodbye, he requested a new room and handed the receptionist his credit card.

'Excuse me, sir? I'm afraid your credit card has been declined.'

'Run it again,' Oliver said impatiently.

He watched as the receptionist swiped his card through the machine. 'Afraid not, sir.'

'Oh, for God's sake. It was fine yesterday.' He handed the man another card. 'Try this one.'

The receptionist's attitude was a little more frosty this time. 'Not having any luck with this one either, sir.'

'Are you sure it's not your machine?'

They were interrupted by another guest wanting to check out. Oliver waved for him to go ahead, watching with mounting frustration as the other man's credit card went through instantly. God knows what the problem was. All his credit cards were American; no doubt some officious jobsworth had noticed the UK activity on his account and flagged it up as suspicious. And since it was Sunday, there was bugger all he could do about it till tomorrow.

'Does sir have cash, perhaps?' the receptionist asked tightly as his fourth and last card was declined.

'Not enough for the prices you charge,' he retorted.

The receptionist smiled coldly. 'I'm sorry, sir. I'm sure it's just a computer glitch. We'll be happy to accommodate you as soon as it's resolved.'

He checked his wallet as he walked back out onto the street. Seventy pounds sterling, and about eighty dollars and some change. Not going to get him far. He supposed he could borrow some money from the petty cash at the office, but with the taxman crawling all over him, he was a little wary of being caught with his hand in the till.

He had no idea where on earth he could spend the night. He couldn't afford the fare to Hampshire, where his brother lived, and he didn't want to risk photographers following him if he went to his parents. They were too frail to deal with this kind of shabby situation.

He'd have to go to Zoey. Go to her and tell her the truth, and hope she'd at least give him a place to say till he got all this sorted out.

CHAPTER 25

FLORENCE

Florence peered out of the window at her father as he pressed the doorbell for about the fifteenth time. How could you love someone so badly and hate them so much at the same time? Half of her wanted to run out and hug him to pieces, and the other half of her – the half that was winning right now – never wanted to speak to him again.

'Please, Harriet,' her father shouted through the letterbox. He backed down the front steps and glanced up at the sitting-room window. 'I know you're in there, I can see you. Please, can't we at least *talk*?'

She ducked away from the window, her heart thumping. She was the only person in the house; her mother had gone with Gran to the hospital, and the boys were at the ice rink with their cousins. Dad looked so miserable. She knew it was his own fault, but she couldn't help feeling a bit sorry for him. She supposed she could let him in for a few minutes, just to say hi. It wasn't like Mom had forbidden her to talk to him. Anyway, she wasn't here, so she didn't need to know. And if Dad kept on ringing the bell and hammering on the door like he was doing now, one of the neighbours would end up calling the police, it would be all over the newspapers again, and Mom would totally *flip*.

Quickly, before she could change her mind, she ran into the hall and opened the front door.

'Florence!' Dad exclaimed.

'You don't have to sound so surprised,' she said crossly. 'I am staying here too.'

'Yes, of course.' He shifted uncomfortably on the front step. 'I just hadn't expected to see you. Is your mother in?'

'No. She really isn't,' she added, taking pity. 'She and Gran have gone to see Gramps at the hospital, and then she's got stuff to do. They've only just left, so they won't be back for ages.'

'What about the boys?'

'Aunt Lucy took them to Streatham ice rink with Ben and David.'

Dad hesitated. 'Can I come in?'

She shrugged and walked back down the hall. Her father followed her into the kitchen, where she perched on a stool and started flicking carelessly through a celebrity magazine.

'So, how've you been?' he asked awkwardly.

'Well, let's see,' she said without looking up from the Kardashians. 'In the last three days, my father's run off with my birth mother, my *actual* mother is losing her shit and surfing the net for lawyers, Gran is in floods of tears twenty-four seven and

281

practically measuring Gramps for his coffin, Sam fell out of a tree yesterday and had to go to the ER for three stitches in his chin, George dropped Mom's iPhone in the toilet and trashed it, and Charlie won't talk to anyone and refuses to wear anything but his Spiderman costume, even in bed. So life is peachy, all in all. Thanks for asking.'

'Is Sam all right?' Dad exclaimed. 'Why didn't anyone call me?'

'Why should anyone think you care?'

'Florence—'

'Yes, he's fine,' she said impatiently. 'Proud he'll have a macho scar. Was there something in particular you wanted, or is this just a social call?'

'Watch your tone, Florence. I'm still your father.'

She smiled coolly. 'Ah, well that's just it, isn't it? You're *not*.'

Dad snatched the magazine away from her and threw it across the kitchen. 'Don't you dare, young lady! Don't you even *think* about going there! I have been your father for fifteen years! I have changed your nappies, wiped up your puke, cuddled you when you've had nightmares, worked my arse off on your science projects, and taken your side a thousand times when your mother was actually the one in the right. Don't you *dare* tell me now I'm not your father!'

'If you're my dad, how come you left?' she cried, leaping from the stool. Her entire body was shaking with rage. 'How could you leave us? How could you *do* that?'

'I didn't leave *you*,' he protested. 'I would *never* leave you.'

She clenched her fists against her thighs. 'You slept with Zoey! I heard Mom telling Aunt Lucy. You *fucked* her!'

'Florence, please!'

'You *fucked* her, you *fucked* her, you *fucked* her!' she yelled. Hot tears spilled down her cheeks. 'The moment you did that, you left us! How could you do it, Dad? You ruined our family! You ruined *everything*!'

She saw he was fighting back his own tears as he pulled her roughly into his arms and held her tightly against him, even when she struggled to escape. For a moment she went as rigid as a board, and then suddenly she fell against him, gripping him for support, giving in to her grief and pain and fury. He held her as violent sobs wracked her body and let her cry it out, softly stroking her hair and murmuring her name.

Finally, she raised her head. Tears and snot soaked his shirt-front. She dashed the back of her hand across her nose, hiccoughing and barely able to speak.

'I didn't leave you,' Dad repeated quietly when she'd finally calmed down. 'I made a mistake. A huge, terrible, God-awful mistake. I never meant to hurt you, or Mom, or the boys. I swear to God, if I could take it back, I would.'

'So are you' – she hiccoughed – 'are you going to get divorced?'

He sighed heavily. 'I don't know. That's for Mom and me to decide. At the moment, she won't even talk to me.'

'I told you, George dropped her cell phone in the toilet.'

'You don't need to make excuses for her, Florence. I know your mother, she wouldn't last twelve hours without that phone. She'll have bought a new one as soon as the shops opened. And I've left messages on the house phone. She knows I'm trying to reach her. She just doesn't want to talk to me, and right now, I can't blame her.'

She wanted to stamp her foot in frustration. How could men be so stupid? Reason and logic weren't going to sort this out! He was the one in the wrong! He should fall on his knees and *beg* her to take him back, if that's what it took.

'You can't just quit!' she exclaimed. 'You have to keep trying!'

'Why d'you think I'm here?'

'Yes, three days later!'

'Well, it's a little difficult to arrange to meet her when she refuses to speak to me,' he said tersely. 'And I was giving her time to calm down so we could have a proper conversation. Look, Florence, we shouldn't even be having this discussion. You don't need to be part of this; it's between me and Mom. I just want you to know that whatever happens between us, we both love you, and nothing's going to change that. Somehow, we're going to work this out.'

She narrowed her eyes. 'What about Zoey?'

He hesitated. 'None of this has anything to do with you, sweetheart. Don't take it out on her.'

She wasn't going to let him off that easily. 'Are you living with her?'

'Not the way you think,' Dad said uncomfortably. 'Your mother stopped all my credit cards, which didn't leave me many choices.'

'So you and Zoey are, like, an item now?'

'Florence, please. This isn't a gossip column in one of your celebrity magazines. This is real life. None of it's straightforward.'

'You're married to Mom. You should be *with* her. That seems pretty "straightforward",' she said, sardonically making quotation marks in the air with her fingers.

'And Nell's our biological child. Is that "straightforward"?' he said, mimicking her gesture. 'Should we be *with* her, too? Or should we be *with* the child we've loved and raised for fifteen years?'

Her cheeks burned. He was treating her like a kid, using smart-ass answers to dodge the real question. She turned away, angrily shrugging him off when he tried to stop her.

'Florence, all I'm saying is that sometimes life's confusing. Relationships are confusing. Doing the *right* thing isn't always the same as doing the *best* thing.'

She didn't turn round. 'Do you love Mom?'

'Of course. With all my heart.'

'And Zoey?'

285

'I don't know how to answer that.'

Suddenly she was too tired to argue any more. She faced him, feeling about a hundred years old. 'Just tell me the truth, Dad. It's not like you can make things any worse.'

'Look, Florence, I can't talk about this with you. I should go. I'll come back tomorrow.'

'Mom won't be here. Gramps has to have some big procedure at the hospital. She's going to be there most of the day with Gran.'

'Shit. She did tell me.' He rubbed his hands over his face. 'I have to go to Manchester for the day on Thursday. I'd cancel if I could, but it's the Inland Revenue. Friday, then. Tell her I'll be here Friday afternoon. Three o'clock. Please tell her to call me any time before that if she wants to. Will you do that for me?'

She nodded.

'Love you, Flo-Mo. You know that, don't you?'

She shrugged, and then nodded again, quickly, unable to help herself.

He kissed her on the top of her head and gave her a brief, hard hug. She watched him from the window again as he walked down the street, his shoulders bowed as if the weight of the world was on them. She was still angry with him; but she was sorry for him as well. She couldn't tell Mom she'd let Dad in the house; it would feel like she was taking his side. She'd just have to tell her he'd phoned or something and pass on the message about Friday.

She suddenly felt light-headed and sat down

quickly on the arm of the sofa. All the emotion of the past half-hour had taken its toll. Adrenalin affected her sugar levels just as effectively as exercise. Her vision started to blur, and she felt clammy and hot. *Oh no, not now.*

Juice, or some glucose tabs. She had to boost her sugar again.

She was halfway to the kitchen when she passed out.

'If I'd got home twenty minutes later, you'd have ended up in the ER,' Mom scolded, tucking her into bed as if she was Charlie's age. 'How could you let yourself get so low? You're normally so responsible about your sugar.'

'It was just so *quick*,' she protested. 'I didn't get any warning. One minute I felt fine, and the next, it was too late.'

'Did you get your insulin wrong at breakfast?'

'No, I just had a bagel and gave myself three units to cover it, same as always.'

'Did you do anything to set it off? Have you been running or something? No crazy diets? Please tell me, Florence.'

'I didn't *do* anything,' she said guiltily. It was almost true. Talking to her father didn't really count as *doing* anything.

'Well, it's lucky I had your glucagon pen in my bag,' Mom sighed, standing up. 'You gave me the fright of my life when I walked in and saw you on the floor.'

'I know. I'm sorry.'

'No harm done. After the last few days, I suppose I was almost waiting for something like this to happen. Try to get some sleep, and come and find me if you feel low in the night. Don't let it get this far again.'

She definitely couldn't tell Mom about Dad coming over now, she thought bleakly as her mother shut the bedroom door. Mom would find some way of blaming him for what had happened. She was paranoid enough about her diabetes – she'd freak if she thought he'd set off a sugar low, even though it really wasn't his fault. She'd just have to wait and tell Mom his message about Friday tomorrow. One day wouldn't make any difference.

Except that by the time Mom got home from the hospital well after ten, tired and fraught from a day of supporting Gran and worrying about Gramps, Florence had already fallen asleep. And on Thursday morning, Mom had again gone out before she'd got up, and she was so grumpy and sad when she got home that Florence knew it was the worst time to give her Dad's message. Maybe it would be better if he surprised Mom, she decided finally. That way, she wouldn't have a chance to refuse to see him. She knew Mom would be at home on Friday afternoon because she was collecting Gramps – who was doing so well now, the doctors could hardly believe it – from hospital on Friday morning, and no way would she leave him on his first day home. Dad had promised he'd

288

come and talk to Mom. He'd promised he'd sort it all out. She just had to trust him.

She didn't sleep much on Thursday night, worrying that the hospital would keep Gramps in another day or something else would go wrong, but Mom was safely home by noon on Friday, curled up with a book in Gran's conservatory, and she was still home at three, and at four, and five.

And Dad never came.

CHAPTER 26

HARRIET

Harriet had no time for pain or grieving. That could come later. Right now, all she had room for was anger. It was what sustained her, giving her the strength to do what needed to be done.

She tapped her foot impatiently, glaring round the empty waiting room. It looked more like the office of a trendy advertising firm or dot.com company than that of a family lawyer − all black leather, chrome fixtures and white walls covered with garish red and black modern art. She'd loathed it on sight.

Nor did she like being kept waiting. This *Mr* Neil Hatfield had better be all Jerry Topoleski had cracked him up to be. She wasn't happy Nicholas Lyon had declined her case; he was among the best family lawyers in London, and she knew his refusal had nothing to do with his workload, as his paralegal had tried to suggest when she'd phoned to beg him to reconsider that morning. Nick Lyon was famous for only taking on divorce and child custody cases he felt he could ethically stand behind; gold-digging trophy wives and abusive ex-husbands need not apply. Merely having him represent you effectively gave you the moral high ground in court. His refusal to take on her case underlined the grey nature of the ethics that underpinned it.

Hatfield, on the other hand, had a reputation as a ruthless, amoral shark who'd out his own grandmother as a crack-dealing whore if it would help him win his case. And right now, as far as she was concerned, winning was all that mattered.

A platinum blonde in a tight charcoal pencil skirt and clingy satin blouse sashayed out of his office and nodded curtly at Harriet. 'Mr Hatfield is ready for you now.'

She stood up, smoothing her own conservative trouser suit. 'Thank you so much for the coffee.'

The girl looked puzzled. Unsurprisingly, since she hadn't bothered to offer Harriet any.

Hatfield came out from behind the vast slab of green glass that served as his desk and extended a hand. His grip was cool and firm, she noted with relief. She couldn't abide men with damp haddock handshakes.

He wasn't what she'd expected, given his reputation. Far more Establishment, for a start: his grey suit was neither sharp nor shiny, his tie discreet. No showy Rolex or flashy gold cufflinks. In his mid-fifties, he had a heavy, leonine head with a distinguished shock of thick salt-and-pepper hair, and his blue gaze was coolly appraising. Mentally she chastised herself for buying into stereotypes. She was better than that.

She sat down on the uncomfortable armless black leather chair on her side of his desk. Its eye-line meant she was looking up at him – Psych 101.

'I assume Jerry Topoleski has briefed you,' she said crisply.

'And arranged the transfer of funds to our corporate account,' Hatfield replied, taking his own seat. 'I should inform you that ten thousand pounds will be withdrawn immediately as a retainer. Should you decide not to pursue your case, it will be non-refundable.'

She frowned. 'Even if I walk out now?'

'Mrs Lockwood. People bring me unwinnable cases because they know I can win them. To do that, I may resort to methods and tactics that, whilst perfectly legal, they often find distasteful. I find it irksome in the extreme when they change their minds. My time is valuable. I don't like it being wasted.'

'So regardless of its outcome, this meeting has already cost me ten thousand pounds?'

'It has.'

'Good,' Harriet said grimly. 'A ruthless bastard is precisely what I need.'

The lawyer laughed and flipped open the manila folder on his desk. She'd researched Hatfield online as soon as her American attorney had emailed his letter. She knew he'd been happily married for twenty-four years and was a father of three, but there wasn't a single family photo or personal memento on his desk or in his spartan office.

'Now then, Mrs Lockwood. Let's talk about your case. You realize you haven't got a hope in hell, don't you?'

She didn't rise to the bait. 'I believe that's why you've just made ten thousand pounds for ten minutes' work.'

'Indeed. You want to divorce your husband on the grounds of adultery – yes, yes, so far, so dull.' He looked up. 'Far more interesting to me is the fact that you want custody not just of your own four children, including a daughter who, it transpires, is not your biological child, but also of the biological daughter with whom she was switched, and whose foster-mother – for want of a better word – has just run off with your husband.'

'I see you read the *Daily News*.'

'Once it becomes known that we are suing for custody of *both* girls, the phone will be ringing off the hook with researchers for *Jeremy Kyle*,' Hatfield shot back. 'You must realize the level of media interest in this case will be intense. Your children will be subject to public scrutiny, and your lives will be picked over until you have no secrets left. The world will know what you eat for breakfast, your brand of toothpaste, the date of your last menstrual period. You will have no privacy, and, frankly, no right to expect it.'

'I'm aware of that,' she said coolly.

'I hope so.' He tossed the folder aside and leaned forward, skewering her with that sharp blue gaze. 'I hope you have no skeletons in your cupboard,

Mrs Lockwood, since our only hope of winning custody of your biological daughter is to go after Zoey Sands for what is still quaintly called "moral turpitude" in legal circles. Our case would be significantly undermined if you are seen to be anything but whiter than white.'

'I'm not claiming to be a saint,' she snapped. 'But Zoey Sands had an affair with a married man and then gave birth to his baby. She slept with my husband while she was a guest in *my home*. Who knows how many men have passed through her bedroom in the interim. I can't allow Nell to spend a minute longer than necessary in that woman's house.'

'She'll fight you, of course.'

'And I'm paying you to beat her.'

The lawyer nodded, relaxing back in his chair. 'I hate to ask the obvious, Mrs Lockwood, but have you considered what Nell wants?'

For the first time, she hesitated. Of course Nell would want to stay with Zoey. But how could she trust the woman to look after her daughter properly now? Yes, she was angry with Zoey; she wanted to hurt her as much as she'd been hurt herself. But more than anything, she wanted to protect Nell from ever being let down by Zoey again.

'I'm her mother,' she said tightly. 'I have to do what's best for her, even if she doesn't see it that way now.'

'By exposing her to the jackals of the Fourth Estate?'

'Since when were you paid to pass judgement?'

Hatfield shrugged. 'I don't give a damn about the rights and wrongs of the case, Mrs Lockwood. You pay me to enter the ring, I'll fight till I'm red in tooth and claw. I just want you to know exactly what that is going to entail. As I said, I don't like wasting my time.'

'I want my daughters,' Harriet said. '*Both* of them.'

'Please don't do this,' Nell begged as soon as Harriet answered the front door a couple of days later.

She stepped aside, beckoning the girl in. 'Go through to the kitchen. My mother's taken the boys out; we won't be disturbed.'

'You can't mean it,' Nell cried as soon as the door shut behind her. 'I know what Mum did was total crap, and I don't blame you for being mad at her, but you don't want to do this. I *know* you don't.'

Harriet ignored her outburst, leading the way into the kitchen and pulling out a stool. 'Sit down, Nell.'

The girl folded her arms, stubbornly remaining standing.

'Have it your way.' *God, she was like her father.* 'Tell me, do you *really* want to stay with Zoey and Oliver, after everything that's happened?'

Nell shrugged.

'Think about Richard,' she said softly. 'He's

practically raised you for the last eight years, and she dumped him without a second thought. She's broken Florence's heart. Not to mention selling the whole sordid story to the newspapers and washing our dirty linen in public—'

'It wasn't Mum who sold that story,' Nell interrupted, her eyes suddenly bright with tears. 'It's all my fault. I told my friend Teri. I thought I could trust her! I told her everything, and she went and sold it to the papers! How could she do that to me? We were supposed to be *friends*!'

Harriet stared helplessly. She ached to wrap her arms around Nell, but didn't dare. 'Just because she let you down, it doesn't mean she didn't care about you,' she said gently. 'We often hurt the people we love the most. She must have had her reasons.'

'Money,' she said bitterly. 'Like, thirty grand. Thirty pieces of silver, more like.'

The same words she'd used to Zoey.

Nell grabbed a tissue from her pocket. 'We need the money just as much as she does, but *I* didn't sell the story when that woman tried to talk to me.'

'What woman?' Harriet said sharply.

'The journalist who wrote that story. She came to our flat a few weeks ago and asked me about Florence, but I just told her to fuck off – sorry – and she left. She never came back, so I thought that was it.' Noisily, she blew her nose. 'I told Teri about it, but I didn't mention anything to Mum

– I didn't want her to freak. Teri must've called the woman later and spilled her guts. I didn't know it would end up in the papers, I swear!'

Harried sighed. 'Neither of you could've known what would happen. Teri probably thought the story would just be about you and Florence. Maybe she even thought you'd like being a bit famous for five minutes. She couldn't have guessed it would get so out of hand.'

'That's what *she* said.'

'So let it go, sweetheart. I'm sure she didn't mean to hurt you.'

'I can't trust her again,' Nell said simply.

How could she argue with that?

'Now you know it wasn't Mum, you'll stop all this legal stuff, right?' Nell added eagerly. 'You can't punish her for something she didn't do. It's not fair.'

'Nor was stealing my husband,' Harriet snapped before she could stop herself.

'So this is *revenge*?'

She flinched, stung by the sudden contempt in Nell's voice. 'No! I admit I'm angry with the pair of them, so angry and hurt I can't breathe some-times, but I'm doing this for *you*. I'm not trying to punish Zoey! Whatever you may think of me, I wouldn't do something that low.' She hesitated, choosing her words with care. 'But what d'you think will happen if you stay with her? How is that going to work, now Oliver's part of the picture? And if he leaves, you'll end up looking

297

after her for the rest of her life, just like you have so far.'

'I'm not just going to *abandon* her!'

'I know you love her, Nell. But soon you're going to want your own life, and what happens then? I could give you so much,' she said earnestly. 'A proper family life and the chance to really get to know Florence and your brothers, the best education, travel, everything you need or want. You could still see Zoey as often as you wished. I'd never try to stop that. But you wouldn't be responsible for her any more. You could have your own space and freedom. Isn't that what you want?'

'She needs me! I can't go off and leave her on her own!'

'You'll be going to college in three years. Or do you plan to study in London and stay with her then, too? It's not like your mother will be alone,' she added painfully. 'She'll still have Oliver.'

'He only went back to her because you froze his credit cards,' Nell said scornfully. 'He couldn't afford to stay in the hotel. If you'd just stop all this legal stuff, he'd come home to you, I know he would. And then we could all go back to normal.'

He'd come home to you. Her heart twisted longingly. Nell made it sound so easy: all she had to do was drop the lawsuit, call off the dogs, and she could have her husband back. Was she throwing her marriage away out of pride?

No. Nell was wrong. Oliver could have gone to

stay with his brother if he was that desperate for a bed; shit, he could've slept on a park bench.

He could have come to her and begged her to take him back – but he hadn't even tried.

Rainville • Hayes • Lavoie

Our Ref: SCP/1568-2/er   16 August 2013
Client ltr 2

Your Ref: Secretary email: ellie@RHLlaw.co.uk
                             Secretary direct line: 020 7663 9042

Without Prejudice

Ms Zoey Sands
33 Culpepper Road
London N1 4LX

Strictly Private and Personal

Dear Ms Sands,

   We act on behalf of the Princess Eugenie Hospital, and have been instructed by our clients to make an offer in the sum of £1,000,000 (one million pounds sterling) in full and final settlement of your claim with regard to the incident, on or around February 3rd 1998, in which your biological child, now known as Florence Lockwood, was switched with the biological child of Harriet and Oliver Lockwood, now known as Eleanor (Nell) Sands.

Should this offer prove acceptable to you, we will draw up the appropriate documents for signature.

With kind regards,

Yours sincerely,

Edward Rainville

Regulated by the Law Society

8–15 St David Street, London EC4A 5BF · Tel 020 7663 9000 · Fax 020 7663 9001

email: RHL@RHLlaw.co.uk

Edward Rainville · Stephen Hayes · Jenifer Lavoie

Susan Roberts Consultant

CHAPTER 27

ZOEY

Zoey had seen it all before, sixteen years ago, in another man's face. Surprise, delight, pride even; and then, as reality sank in, the surprise turning to shock, delight to horror, pride to fear. And after that, the careful distancing; the gentle, but firm and implacable, rejection.

It was happening all over again, and she was powerless to stop it.

Checking out of the hotel alone had been a calculated gamble. She'd realized she ran the very high risk he'd go straight back to Harriet. She knew how much he loved his family, including – *especially* – his wife; no matter how much he may have liked going to bed with Zoey (and she knew, without vanity, that he did, very much), he'd never have walked out on them for her. But Harriet had made the cardinal mistake of letting her pride rule her heart, and had handed Zoey an unexpected gift, effectively pushing her husband into her arms. Harriet had left *him*. Or left him behind in her hotel bedroom, which had amounted to pretty much the same thing.

Zoey had seen immediately that it was her one

chance, a chance she'd neither expected nor sought but had no intention of wasting, so she'd deliberately appealed to his masculine, primitive need to protect, knowing it was his greatest weakness. And as he'd put a consoling arm around her shoulders, she'd allowed him to see a tantalizing glimpse of her breasts. She'd let her robe slip open. She'd unfastened her belt and lain back on the bed, spreading her legs and waiting for him to make love to her – and it *was* making love, for her, at least, not just sex – determinedly refusing to think about Harriet, or Florence, savouring instead the sweetness of his kisses, the fullness of him inside her, the salty smell of his sweat on her slick skin. She gave herself to him without reservation, revelling in her own greedy, animal hunger, binding him to her with her body. He poured himself into her and as she came around him, again and again, her legs pretzelled around his hips, fingernails digging into his back, she'd known he was hers, completely hers, for this one night at least.

But the next morning, she'd woken to find him gone, leaving just his scent on the pillow and a note saying he'd had to go into the office – on a Sunday! – and she'd realized winning him by default wasn't winning him at all. A friend of hers who'd had a passionate four-year affair with a married man had once explained why the relationship had swiftly turned to ashes when the long-suffering wife had finally left *him*. 'He never *chose* me,' she'd told Zoey sadly. 'He only came to me because he couldn't bear to be alone. He never picked *me*. I was always second best.'

She didn't want to be second best. She had to be sure Oliver *wanted* to be with her. She had to know.

And so, in the biggest gamble of her life, she'd written that note to him and checked out of the hotel. *I don't want you to be with me because you have nowhere else to go. If you choose me, you know where I'll be.*

When he'd turned up on her doorstep just hours later, she'd been dizzy with gratitude and joy. *I didn't steal him!* she told the nagging voice of her conscience. *Oliver came to me of his own accord. He could have gone back to Harriet. But he didn't. He came to me. He chose me!*

Except he hadn't, of course.

'I can't,' he'd said painfully as she'd thrown herself into his arms. Gently, he'd unwound her from his neck. 'I'm so sorry, Zoey. That's not why I'm here.'

'I don't understand . . .'

'Zoey, please. Let me explain.'

And he had. It wasn't her fault, of course, it was his. He'd been wrong to give in to temptation, wrong to make love to her, wrong to let her believe he was responding to her note when the truth, the depressing, prosaic truth, was that he really *did* have nowhere else to go. He cared about her deeply, would always care about her, and there was Nell, and Florence, of course, but more than that, he had genuine feelings for her, Zoey, and he hoped they could always be friends. But he loved his wife, there was no getting around that. He loved Harriet and even if she refused – as seemed increasingly likely – to take him back, he couldn't short-change Zoey like that. She deserved better than to be second best.

'It's all right,' she said, and 'I understand,' because she did, and he was right – she *did* deserve better, even though it hurt like hell, and she wondered despairingly how she was ever going to scrape up enough courage and energy to put her life back together a second time.

He'd spent the night in Nell's empty room, and the next morning he'd left before she awoke. He'd gone to see Harriet, no doubt, to beg her for a second chance; and despite his gloomy prognostications of the night before, she was quite certain his wife would take him back. Harriet loved him; she could see that. After all, it took one to know one.

She'd felt sick with grief and misery. It was as if time had stood still: she was twenty-two again, pregnant and deserted, curled up on her bed and listening to Patrick quietly let himself out of the house for the very last time.

It was Nell who'd pulled her out of her mire of self-pity and tears. Nell, crashing into the house, slamming the front door and pounding up the stairs to her bedroom, throwing herself on her bed in a violent fit of sobbing audible through the thin walls, who had Zoey up in a moment, dry-eyed and ready to fight like a tigress for her child.

She'd run into her daughter's room, knotting the belt of her threadbare dressing gown – nothing like as luxurious as the one from the hotel – around her waist. 'Darling! What is it? What's happened?'

'Mnnnff! Drmmmnt msss pmprss!' Nell wept into her pillow.

'Sweetheart, calm down and tell me what's happened. Has someone hurt you?'

Violent shaking of the head.

'Upset you, then?'

A nod.

'Is it – is it about me and Oliver?'

A terse shake of the head.

'Is it a boy?'

More violent shaking.

'Oh dear,' Zoey had sighed. 'I've never been very good at these games. Couldn't you just *tell* me?'

Nell had rolled over on the bed, lifting a red, tear-stained face to her mother. '*Teri* was the one who sold the story to the newspapers. They gave her thirty thousand pounds for it. I thought she loved me!'

Zoey scooped her into her arms. 'Oh darling. I'm so sorry.'

'How could I have been so *wrong* about her?' Nell wailed. 'That's the worst bit. I thought she was special and she wasn't. She was just . . . just *banal*!'

She'd sighed. 'Life *is* banal, darling. Except when it's happening to you.'

'Mum,' Nell had said as her hiccoughing slowed. 'About Oliver.'

'It's OK. I know how you must feel—'

'It's not that I don't like him,' she'd said in a rush as if Zoey hadn't spoken. 'I *do*. He's cool, most of the time. But he's *married*, Mum. He's not yours. It's . . . it's like wearing a pair of shoes that don't belong to you. You've always said that's the one thing you can't recycle. They're never going to fit, because someone else has worn them and made them shaped like their own foot.'

'Yes,' she'd said sadly.

'Can't you try again with Richard? He loves you so much. He'd take care of you. You wouldn't have to sell the shop – you could settle down and relax. Maybe even have another baby . . .'

'Nell!'

'What? You're only thirty-nine. It's not like you're past it. Lots of middle-aged women have babies these days.'

'Have you been talking to Richard?'

'He keeps calling,' Nell said defensively. 'He saw the piece in the paper and he said he understood. It only happened because of Florence and me and all that stuff. He says he doesn't care, he still loves you.'

'I don't love him,' she'd said softly. 'Not the way he deserves.'

Nell had looked down at her hands. 'The way you love Oliver? Even though he doesn't love you?'

307

'Yes. I'm so sorry, Nell.'

'It's OK,' she'd said sadly. 'I love him too.'

The letter from Harriet's lawyer hadn't upset her the way Harriet had probably hoped it would. She'd quickly thrust it back in the envelope so Nell couldn't read it upside down across the breakfast table as she did everything else, and shoved it into the kitchen drawer where she kept all the bills and bank statements and everything else she couldn't quite bring herself to deal with.

The lawyer's threats had been so preposterous she didn't take them seriously. Either he was some kind of monstrous Victorian throwback who still thought unwed mothers should be institutionalized, or he was an unscrupulous bastard taking easy money from a woman too emotionally overwrought to think straight. Probably both. Not even the most reactionary judge could possibly believe, in the twenty-first century, that having an affair was reason enough to take a fifteen-year-old girl from her mother and her school and her friends and her home and transplant her four thousand miles across the Atlantic to live with a family she barely knew. For heaven's sake, *Prince Charles* had had an affair! Adultery practically came with a royal warrant these days!

The other reason she hadn't cared about the letter, of course, was that she'd had too much else to worry about.

It had been something Nell had said the morning

she'd come home that had planted the first seed in her mind. She hadn't quite been able to believe she hadn't thought of it before, *considered* it even, but she'd got so used to thinking of herself as Nell's mother, the parent of a teenager, middle-aged and, yes, *past it*, that it had never occurred to her that actually she might *not* be. And as Nell had pointed out, thirty-nine wasn't old these days at all.

She'd called Oliver. 'I need to see you,' she'd said without preamble.

'Zoey, I'm in Manchester. Working.'

'When will you be back?'

'Friday. Tomorrow morning.'

'Then I need to see you tomorrow afternoon.'

A long, static-filled silence. 'Zoey, I don't think that's a good idea.'

'Oliver, I'm not asking you to meet me to reminisce about the old days,' she'd said sharply. 'This is important. I wouldn't ask if it wasn't.'

'I can't do tomorrow afternoon. I'm meeting – I have a meeting at three.'

Harriet, Zoey thought, trying not to feel bitter. 'What time do you get back to London?'

Another silence. 'I could meet you around one. The Bluebird Café on the King's Road. If it's really important.'

She'd agreed and put the phone down with a firmness she hadn't really felt. Perhaps, if Harriet's lawyers hadn't sent that letter, if Harriet hadn't threatened to take her child – however empty those threats might have been – she wouldn't have called Oliver at all. Perhaps she'd have let events take their course, shouldered this on her own, dealt with it alone as she'd dealt with everything for the past twenty years.

But Harriet *had* threatened to take Nell. And she was tired of being the only one who ever had to face the consequences. So now here she was, sitting opposite Oliver in the Bluebird Café, telling him she was pregnant with his child, watching that painfully familiar play of emotions sweep across his face: surprise, delight, pride even; and then, as reality sank in, the surprise turning to shock, delight to horror, pride to fear.

She waited wearily for him to tell her he had a family to think of, other children to consider, to promise to make sure she 'didn't suffer financially' and to know he was 'always there for' her, as Patrick had.

But, to her surprise, there was no careful distancing, no rejection. He didn't brush her off with meaningless platitudes and empty promises.

Instead, he reached across the table and took both her hands in both of his.

'It's going to be OK,' he told her. 'I'm not going anywhere.'

CHAPTER 28

OLIVER

For a brief, hallucinatory moment, Oliver fantasized that everything would be OK. They'd go back to Vermont and form a flower-power commune, all of them: he and Harriet and Zoey, their mixed-up, switched-up daughters, the boys, and a new baby who would somehow connect them all, bind them together as a *family* . . .

Of course it wasn't going to be OK. Nothing was ever going to be OK again.

Zoey's big grey eyes filled with hope as he took her hands across the café table. 'You'll *stay*?' she said incredulously.

'This isn't just your problem,' he said, trying to keep the despair from his voice. 'We both got ourselves into this. I'm here if you need me.'

'Need you?' she gasped. 'Of course I *need* you!'

Of course she did, he thought dully. It was what he'd found so attractive about her, a lifetime ago.

Harriet had never needed him, not in the helpless, damsel-in-distress way Zoey did. Not in a way that aroused his primitive, masculine impulse to *protect*. His wife had always been so capable and competent. Running their business, running their home. For most of their marriage it hadn't bothered him because, deep down, he'd known she *did* need him, in her own way: as a husband, a father, a business partner. Between them they'd created a perfect balance that was the core of their family. She was conscientious, intense, a setter-of-bedtimes and enforcer-of-homework; by tacit agreement, he was the easy-going one, indulgent, the breaker of rules. At work, his creativity and headlong passion was tempered by her grounded practicality. For sixteen years, they'd each brought something different but equally necessary to the table, balancing one another, yin and yang.

But then, six months ago, they'd faced the single most significant crisis of their marriage, and he'd been shut out. Instead of listening to him, taking him seriously, she'd simply pursued her own agenda, seeking out Nell and Zoey on her own, as if he no longer mattered. She hadn't needed *him*. She hadn't needed anyone.

He didn't want to think about how much his affair with Zoey had been prompted by his hurt pride and an unconscious desire to pay Harriet back. To deceive and hurt her as much as she'd deceived and hurt him.

'What about Harriet?' Zoey asked suddenly.

He released her hands and rubbed his palms over his face. 'I'll have to tell her.'

She looked alarmed. 'You can't! She's already *so* angry. She'll set the hounds of hell on me when she hears this, never mind the lawyers.'

'Zoey, I can't *not* tell her. I assume you intend to keep the baby?'

'You want me to *get rid* of it?'

'No, of course not,' he said sharply. No matter what the circumstances, or the consequences, he would never for a moment wish a child of his unborn. 'I just mean that Harriet will need to know sooner or later. I'd rather that it was sooner, and from me.'

She nodded. 'I'm so sorry, Oliver. You know I didn't plan this, don't you? What happened in Maine – I never expected it. Any of it.'

He suppressed a sudden flare of anger at her pure *carelessness*. He didn't think for a moment she'd got pregnant on purpose, but Harriet would never have got caught out like this, no matter how unexpected the situation might be. Zoey's entire life was a fucking train wreck, and now he was trapped in the middle of it with her.

Your choice, he thought grimly. *No one forced you into bed with her.*

'It's my fault as much as yours,' he said wearily. 'I never even considered the possibility. So bloody irresponsible. Like a couple of teenagers.'

'Teenagers these days are much too savvy to get caught out unless they want to be.' She hesitated. 'I know this couldn't come at a worse time. I wish there was something else I could say.'

Tell me to go back to Harriet, Oliver pleaded inwardly. *Tell me you* don't *need me. Love me enough to let me go.*

'I know,' he sighed. 'I told you, I'm not going to leave you on your own to cope with this. I'll support you financially, and I'll stay in England as long as you need me.'

'But.'

'But?'

'There is one, isn't there? A "but" I'm not going to like.'

He fiddled with a packet of sugar, turning it end over end between his fingers.

'Oliver, please. Are you going to *stay* stay? With me, I mean? I'm not talking about giving me money or coming along to scans. I'm not even talking about being a good father later. I'm talking about me. Are you going to stay with *me*?'

He met her gaze head-on. 'No,' he said steadily.

'I didn't think you'd come,' Oliver said.

Harriet slid into the booth opposite him. '*I* didn't think I'd come.'

'I'm glad you did. Thank you.'

'Don't thank me. Thank Nell.'

'Nell?'

'She came to see me two days ago,' Harriet said evenly, reaching for the laminated menu pinioned between the salt and pepper shakers. 'Didn't she tell you? Came to plead your case. Well, not yours. Zoey's.'

Her voice stuck on the name as if was covered in burrs.

'I didn't realize,' he said. 'I've been in Manchester all week. I only got back yesterday morning.'

He watched the fact that he hadn't been with Zoey register.

'Well, she was very persuasive,' Harriet said after a moment. 'And tough. Frighteningly so, in fact.'

'She's your daughter,' Oliver observed.

He signalled to the waitress. The two of them ordered a pot of tea, deferring to each other politely over the blend – they settled on English Breakfast – as if they were on a first date. He leaned back in his chair, watching his wife as the waitress fussed with spoons and saucers. Harriet seemed the same as ever: her hair in its neat brown bob, no make-up beyond a slick of lipsalve, the pearl earrings her mother had given her on her twenty-first. Yet she looked different. It was in her eyes. Nothing had changed; and everything had changed.

There were two types of fury, he thought: hot and cold. The latter was far more terrifying and effective.

'I know I promised I'd come and see you yesterday afternoon, but something happened. Something I had to deal with before I could talk to you,' he said carefully as the waitress placed their teapot on its cast-iron stand. 'I hope Florence wasn't too upset I couldn't make it. She'd promised to make sure you'd be there at three—'

'You saw Florence? When?'

'Tuesday, before I went to Manchester. She didn't tell you?'

Harriet shook her head. 'It's been a difficult few days.'

'Christ. Of course. I should've asked before. How's your father? Florence said the poor old bugger had to have another procedure—'

She smiled for the first time since she'd arrived. 'He's doing much better. The surgery went well, and they actually let him come home yesterday. He's not out of the woods yet, but they think they got all of it this time. He's still got to go through chemo, but the odds are looking so much better than they were.'

'Thank God,' Oliver said feelingly. 'Send him my best, won't you?'

'He'd like to see you,' Harriet said. 'If you've got time.'

'He would?'

'For Heaven's sake, Oliver. Regardless of what's happened between us, you know how much he loves you. The son he never had and all that nonsense. You owe him more than to run away and hide.'

'Does he . . . has he . . .'

'Of course he knows. That story was impossible to miss,' she said dryly. 'Dad's an urban fox, Oliver, not a country mouse. He's also seventy-six and the father of four daughters. He doesn't judge. I'd stay out of Mummy's way, though,' she added.

'She'll have your balls on a plate if she catches you.'

'Appreciate the heads-up,' Oliver mumbled.

He knew better than to think the apparent détente between them meant anything. Just because Harriet had finally returned his umpteen phone calls, just because she'd agreed to meet him and sat conversing pleasantly with him now, didn't mean anything had changed. He knew his wife. She did anger as efficiently and coolly as she did everything else.

The two of them sipped their tea, looking no doubt like any other happily married couple enjoying a Saturday morning brunch without the kids. *If only that were true,* he thought desperately. He felt like a tethered lamb being circled by a wolf, waiting for it to pounce.

'I'm taking the children back home to Vermont next week,' Harriet said abruptly. 'School starts in less than a fortnight. I need to get them settled after . . . after this summer.'

There it was. Straight for the jugular, too. He'd known somewhere in the back of his mind that this would happen. The kids couldn't stay in London for ever, but he still felt sucker-punched at being told the news casually, as if he were an outsider. He'd only been gone a week! Christ, there was so much they had to sort out, so much he wanted not to think about.

Briefly, he closed his eyes. 'Harriet, if there was something I could say that would make any difference, believe me, I'd say it—'

'Try,' Harriet said.

It took him a moment to realize she was serious. For the first time in his life, he was speechless. He'd spent the last seven days imagining what he'd tell her if she'd just give him a chance to explain, apologize, plead his case – and now that he had it, he didn't know where the fuck to begin.

Suddenly he was scrambling frantically to make up ground. 'Oh God, Harriet, you have to know how sorry I am. If I could take it back, I would. I'd give everything I own to have things back the way they were.'

Her expression was unreadable. He had no idea if he was getting through to her or just making things worse.

'I love you so fucking much. I'd take a bullet for you, you know that.' His eyes stung suddenly, but he didn't care. 'I've been so damn stupid, but I never stopped loving you, Harry, not for a moment. I know how much I've hurt you. I know you're going to find it hard to trust me again, but I swear to you, I swear to God on our kids' lives, if you give me a second chance I will never, ever let you down again.'

She swallowed. 'And Zoey?'

'Zoey was a stupid, idiotic mistake! You know that! I love you. Please, Harriet. If you believe nothing else, believe that.'

'Oh, shit, Oliver. Shit.'

He waited, his heart pounding.

'It would be so much easier if you were a

philandering bastard,' she said painfully. 'I've spent the past week trying my best to hate you, and I just can't. I'm so fucking angry I could spit tacks, but I can't hate you. It's just . . . I thought we were above all this kind of thing – cheating, affairs, all the rest of it. The *lying*. I'm not saying I haven't made mistakes too. I should have told you about that stupid night with Ben a long time ago. I should never have gone behind your back to find Nell. But I didn't deserve this!'

'No,' he said hoarsely. 'No, you didn't deserve this.'

'How did we end up like this, Oliver? I thought this kind of thing happened to other couples, not to us. Not to *Oliver and Harriet*.'

'It was me, it was all my fault.'

'The affair, yes. But it didn't happen in a vacuum.'

'None of this was down to you.'

'Oliver,' she said, regarding him squarely, 'if we're to have any chance of putting this back together, we both have to be honest. I have to own my part in this too.'

'Do we?' he asked. 'Have a chance?'

For a long moment, she said nothing. He could feel the blood rushing in his ears as if he had vertigo, as if he was standing on the edge of a cliff, looking down at the rocks below. She was his life. It was as simple as that. He loved her now more than he'd ever have thought possible; more than he had the day he married her, more even than the day she made him a father. He loved her with every fibre of his being. Whether she needed him or not suddenly no longer mattered. He needed *her* just to breathe.

'Can I trust you?' she said finally.

His heart contracted. He had to tell her. He didn't want to – oh Christ, he didn't want to tell her – but how could he ask her to trust him unless he did? Lying to her by omission would destroy any chance they might ever have to rebuild their marriage – if not now, then later. But if he told her, he risked losing her anyway. She might forgive him the affair, but a *baby*? How could any wife be asked to forgive that?

'Zoey's pregnant,' he said quietly.

He could see her withdraw from him, close down, frost over. She didn't move, but suddenly she seemed a thousand miles away.

'Then she's won,' Harriet said.

'No! She hasn't *won*! Of course she hasn't won! This makes no difference to *us*, to how I feel about you!'

Harriet gave him a cool, measured look. 'Oh, Oliver. Of course it makes a difference. It makes all the difference in the world. Zoey won't survive on her own, not again. She can't. She doesn't have it in her. She'll cling to Nell like a drowning man. You know it as well as I do. If you don't go back, Nell won't have a chance. And you won't forgive yourself for doing that to her, and nor will I.'

He knew, the moment she said it, that she was

right. Had known, deep down, ever since Zoey had told him she was pregnant.

She'd won.

He missed his stop on the tube and had to double back, sitting in the sour, stifling air hundreds of feet below the ground, wondering if there was any point in ever returning to the surface again.

He had no idea where he'd go after he collected his things from Zoey's. He couldn't keep up this pretence any longer. No matter what Harriet said, he didn't belong with Zoey. He could never love her, not in the way she needed and deserved. He'd do everything he could to help her and the baby – he'd stay in London, give her all the emotional and financial support she needed. But that was all.

She didn't answer the door when he knocked. He knew she must be in; he could hear music playing in the kitchen. He knocked again, harder this time, and when she still didn't answer, he cupped his hands and peered through the window.

Suddenly he was hammering on the back door. 'Zoey! Zoey!'

The door didn't yield. He flipped over the mat, and grabbed the spare key. *Who'd burgle me?* Zoey had said, laughing, when he'd pointed out the singular lack of originality in her hiding place. *They'd take one look at this place and probably leave me a fiver.*

Shoving the door open, he forced his way through

cardboard boxes and plastic bags into the kitchen, where Zoey lay sprawled on the floor. She was still breathing – shallow, hoarse gasps that filled him with a mortal fear. Her skin was waxy and clammy to the touch, her lips blue.

'Zoey! Oh, dear Christ, Zoey!' He groped in his pocket for his phone as he pulled her into his arms. 'Come on, sweetheart, hang in there. It's going to be OK. Christ, somebody answer!'

Seconds later, the operator picked up. 'Emergency, which service do you require? Fire, Police or Ambulance?'

'Ambulance!' he cried, rapidly barking directions into the phone. 'Please, hurry! I'm losing her!'

Zoey's grey eyes focused on his face. 'Nell,' she said clearly.

He dropped the phone, cradling her against him. 'I'll find her,' he promised desperately. 'Don't worry, I'll look after her. You just have to hold on, Zoey. Help's coming. Just hold on a little bit longer.'

Her eyes fluttered shut. And for the first time in years, Oliver prayed.

BABY-SWITCH MOTHER DIES

The mother at the centre of a baby-switch scandal died yesterday from a suspected heart attack.

Zoey Sands, 39, collapsed at home on Saturday. Emergency services tried for an hour to revive her, but she was declared dead on arrival at the Princess Eugenie Hospital.

Ironically, the same hospital was at the centre of controversy two weeks ago, when it was revealed that two baby girls had been accidentally switched at birth fifteen years ago.

The two families were reunited with their biological offspring earlier this year. It was later revealed that Ms Sands, the mother of one of the children involved in the scandal, had an affair with Oliver Lockwood, 40, the father of the other girl.

Doctors say preliminary autopsy results revealed Ms Sands had a benign tumour which had been pressing on her lungs and heart, restricting blood flow and eventually leading to cardiac arrest.

'These tumours are slow-growing and can be very hard to detect,' a hospital spokesman said. 'Lung capacity would have gradually been reduced as the tumour grew, leading to breathlessness and fatigue, but other than that, there would have been few symptoms.'

Last night, Ms Sands' 15-year-old daughter was being cared for by relatives.

CHAPTER 29

HARRIET

It was Richard who'd taken it hardest, Harriet thought as she watched him file into an empty pew across the aisle with his mother. The poor man looked like he'd been hit by a bus. Zoey had cuckolded him, publicly humiliated him, destroyed his dreams of a wife and family, taken away the child he'd raised as his own for nearly a decade; and yet here he was at her funeral, utterly broken and lost without her.

Nell turned to her. 'I think I should go and sit with him.'

'Of course,' she said, trying not to mind.

Nell slipped out of their pew and into Richard's. She put her hand on his shoulder as if she were the adult and he the child. He turned to her, stricken, resting his head lightly against hers, his shoulders shaking with suppressed sobs. On his other side, his mother put her thin arm round him, and the three of them clung together like shipwrecked souls.

The organist began to play 'The Lord Is My Shepherd', and everyone in the small church stood. It seemed Zoey hadn't been one for religion;

according to Nell, she'd believed god – 'with a small g' – was in everything, from daisies to people, which probably made her spiritually closer to Buddhism than anything else. But she'd been baptized a Catholic, and Harriet was a firm believer in the necessity of ritual to mark the important milestones of life and death. So Oliver had spoken to the Catholic priest in Zoey's parish, a kind and empathetic missionary from the Ivory Coast, who'd promised to remember the tiny unborn soul of Zoey's lost baby in his private prayers, hadn't asked once about the regularity of her attendance at church, and had incorporated Nell's request for the funeral service to be 'something Mum wouldn't mind being seen dead at' into the more conventional framework of the Catholic Requiem Mass.

Which meant that after the first reading from Luke's Gospel, Nell stood up and read Auden's anguished lament for all the clocks to be stopped in a clear, unwavering voice. She didn't cry, though she left few in the small congregation with dry eyes. Many of those who had turned out were friends of hers as well as Zoey's; among them was a young boy of about seventeen who bore such an uncanny resemblance to Florence, Harriet dropped her hymnbook when she saw him. *That must be Ryan James*, she thought in astonishment, watching him slip into the church and hide self-consciously behind a pillar. The son of Zoey's first love, Patrick, and therefore Florence's half-brother. How strangely they were all linked.

Richard read the eulogy. He broke down several times, especially when he talked about Zoey's zest for life, and how it was now up to Nell to keep her memory alive.

And then the organist played 'Jerusalem', and six pall-bearers, led by Oliver and Richard, picked up Zoey's coffin – recycled cardboard, as Nell had insisted – and led the way outside to where the hearse was waiting. Zoey had wanted to be cremated, Nell said, her ashes scattered 'everywhere I was ever happy', but Nell didn't want anyone to go to the crematorium. 'We'll say goodbye to her in church, and then we'll all go home and remember her alive, not stuck in a cardboard box disappearing behind a curtain like something from *The Wizard of Oz*.'

Harriet had offered to host the wake at her parents' house, but Nell insisted everyone should come back to Zoey's cramped flat in Islington. 'Of course there'll be room,' she'd said in the face of Harriet's practical objections. 'We can all spill out on the streets if we have to, like we did for the Royal Wedding and the Jubilee.'

There was something desperately sad about Nell's bravery. She was so determined not to go to pieces for Zoey's sake, not to let her mother down. Even when Oliver had broken the news to her at the hospital – in another of those dreadful beige rooms that seemed to resonate with past griefs and pain – she hadn't cried. She'd insisted on seeing Zoey's body: 'I need to *know*,' she'd explained, pressing her hands against her stomach. 'I need to *feel* it. I need to understand she's really gone.' And then she'd returned to Harriet's parents' house with Oliver and gone upstairs with that same eerie calmness to play computer games with Charlie and the boys, while she and Oliver had sat silently at the kitchen table, frozen with shock.

All those times she'd privately sneered at Zoey's lack of fitness, her inability to walk more than a few yards without getting out of breath. She felt awful about it now. There was so much she wished she could take back.

Florence had walked into the house from a day out with friends and seen her parents sitting in the kitchen, seen their white stricken faces, and immediately assumed it was her grandfather. When they'd told her about Zoey, for one agonizing moment she'd started to laugh; and then she'd begun to howl, a terrible high-pitched wail that went on and on and on, her grief ragged and desperate and all-consuming. 'It's my fault!' she'd cried. 'I wouldn't talk to her. She kept leaving messages on my phone and I was so angry about her and Daddy, I wouldn't talk to her, and now she's *dead*, she's dead because of me!'

Harriet had held her while she cried, had stroked her hair and absorbed her fury and told her it wasn't her fault, of *course* it wasn't her fault, it was an accident, just one of those dreadful things that happened – no one could possibly have known. But it was Nell her daughter had turned to as she'd come running down the stairs in response to her cries. The two girls had gone out into the tiny walled garden at the back of the house, arms wrapped around each other, heads pressed together, and talked for over an hour. When they'd finally come back inside, both faces were tear-stained and swollen from crying, but Harriet had known that for Nell as well as for Florence, the first dreadful, shocking wave of the storm had passed.

She didn't know how either girl would have coped if they hadn't had each other. They spent every moment of the next ten days closeted together, sharing Florence's tiny box room and talking well into the small hours every night. Harriet could hear them through the thin wall of her bedroom, their voices low and murmuring, occasionally broken by a sob or a brief, glorious moment of laughter. 'Those girls are looking after each other,' Oliver had said when she'd worried she should be doing more. 'We're just the parents now. We can't expect them to tell us what they're thinking any more.'

Until the funeral, she hadn't seen him since the day Zoey had died. It had simply been too much. Too much regret, and pain, and guilt, and loss. Florence still hadn't forgiven her father for the affair, even if Nell had, and Harriet wasn't about to put her through any more emotional anguish. More to the point, she still didn't know how *she* felt, now that Zoey was gone.

She'd never thought she could ever forgive an affair.

How could you love someone when respect and trust were gone? But that day in the café, she'd realized it wasn't nearly so black and white. She hadn't forgiven Oliver, but she had believed him when he'd said he loved her. She'd believed him when he'd sworn it had been one stupid, idiotic mistake, that he didn't love Zoey, that if he could turn the clock back, he would. But was it enough? She still loved him, yes. But could she trust him again?

He'd told her about the baby. Even as she'd wanted to strangle him for being so bloody *careless*, she couldn't help a grudging respect that he'd owned it upfront, knowing it could cost him everything.

She'd had no choice but to send him back to Zoey then, for Nell's sake. And now Zoey and the baby were gone.

Her heart twisted. *It didn't change things*. He'd betrayed her and Florence and the boys, and she loved him, but she couldn't forgive him. She wanted to, but she couldn't find it in her. She thought she hated him for that most of all.

She readied herself now as Oliver walked over to talk to her. Around them, mourners stood chatting quietly on the paved terrace outside Zoey's kitchen door, helping themselves to sandwiches and vols-au-vent the boys were offering round.

'I was hoping for a quiet moment,' he murmured. 'Have you spoken to Nell yet? About what happens next?'

'I thought it would be better to wait until the funeral was over.'

'We can't leave it much longer.'

She sighed. 'Oliver, we both know she needs to come back with me. You know how much she needs Florence. She needs a family. She needs a *mother.*'

'London's her home,' he said sharply. 'She may not want to leave. She's just lost the one constant in her life. You can't expect her to abandon her friends and her school and everything she knows just because it'll tie everything up neatly for you.'

'Are you suggesting she should stay here with *you?*'

He'd looked at her then, his eyes dark with emotion. 'It's up to her,' he said finally. 'We have to let her choose.'

You could both come back, she thought suddenly. *You could come home to me, and everything would be, if not quite as it was, as it should be. My husband, my daughters, my family under one roof.*

But there would still be Zoey, a ghost between them.

They waited until all the guests from the funeral had left. Florence and Nell collected paper plates and cups from the street where they'd been left on walls and tucked behind lamp posts. The boys had found a football from somewhere – a little deflated, but serviceable – and were kicking it around the paved-over gardens whose lawns had long since been sacrificed for parking spaces. Richard sat on the low wall outside Zoey's terrace watching them. She knew he was only in his mid-forties, but he could have passed for a man fifteen years older.

'Could you keep an eye?' she asked. 'We want to talk to Nell for a bit on her own.'

Richard nodded. He seemed such a *nice* man. For a brief second, anger flared that Zoey had rejected him for a man who wasn't even hers to take, and then she remembered the poor woman was dead and pushed the thought away.

They found the two girls cleaning up in the kitchen. Something Florence would never have voluntarily thought to do before she'd met Nell, Harriet thought with chagrin.

Oliver tried to give Florence a hug, but she stiffened in his arms, and after a moment he painfully let them drop. It was strange: Harriet had always wanted to be the favoured parent, the one her daughter turned to, but it cut her to the quick to see the two of them like this. She had no idea how long it would take Florence to forgive him, if she ever did. Either way, their relationship would never be the same again. *Was it worth it, Oliver? Was Zoey worth paying a price this high?*

'Could you give us a moment with Nell?' Oliver asked his daughter tightly.

Florence looked as if she was about to protest, then she glanced at Nell, whose face was suddenly shuttered, composed. 'Let me know if you need me,' she said to Nell.

Nell calmly led the way into the sitting room. Dust motes danced in a large square of sunlight on the worn faux-Persian carpet. She sat down on an armchair, smoothing her long black skirt over her knees. She looked far older than fifteen. Older than any girl her age had the right to look.

'I know what you want to talk about,' she said evenly as they took the sofa opposite her. 'You want to ask me to come and live with you in America.'

Harriet glanced briefly at Oliver. 'We want to give you some choices and see what you think of them,' she said carefully.

'Do I want to go to Vermont with you and Florence and the boys? Or do I want to stay here in London, with Oliver?'

She could have been talking about which film to see that evening at the local cinema.

'You don't have to decide right away,' Harriet answered. 'It doesn't have to be one or the other, either. You can spend the school term with one of us, and the holidays with the other. Whatever you choose. We won't mind. You're not choosing between *us*. We're both your parents now. We want what's best for you.'

'I know you do,' Nell said softly. 'And I appreciate the offer, really.' She looked squarely at Oliver. 'None of this was your fault, I know that. You'd have saved her if you could. You were there when she died, and that means a lot.' She hesitated, clearly struggling to find the right words. 'But I'm sorry – I don't want to live with you. If you and Mum hadn't had an affair, maybe it would be different. But you broke her heart. I'm not angry with you any more, not the way Florence is. I guess I never had you on such a pedestal in the first place. People make mistakes, I get that. But right now, I want to be with someone who loved Mum as much as I did. Someone who really *knew* her. Do you know what I mean?'

Oliver flushed in the face of Nell's blunt honesty. Harriet realized there was nothing she could do that would punish him more than his two daughters were already.

Suddenly she understood what Nell was getting at. 'You mean Richard, don't you?'

'*Richard*?' Oliver exclaimed. 'But Zoey broke it off with him. What does Richard have to do with anything?'

'Mum made a will,' Nell said, talking to Harriet. 'Richard nagged and nagged at her, and she finally made one, a couple of years ago. I found it in the kitchen drawer, with all the other bills and stuff. Typical Mum.' She smiled briefly. 'She left everything to me – the shop and the flat and everything. I guess that includes the money the hospital gave her, since that's part of her estate now. And she made Richard my guardian.'

'You can't *possibly* be considering—'

'Oliver,' Harriet said warningly.

'Richard's been my dad for as long as I can remember,' Nell said staunchly. 'Mum never got round to changing her will, and I'm glad. He really needs me right now. And I need him. I love him, and I *trust* him.'

'Does he know about the money?' Oliver demanded.

'Oliver!'

'It's OK.' Nell shrugged. 'It doesn't make any difference. She left everything to me, not him. He doesn't care about money – he never has. He's not like that. Anyway, I won't be able to get it till I'm eighteen. The lawyers told me. So you don't have to worry about that.'

'Harriet, say something,' Oliver protested. 'Tell her *we're* her family. She should be with *us*.'

Harriet thought of the lawsuit she'd threatened, trying to force Nell to come and live with them, and felt nothing but shame. She was infinitely glad she'd withdrawn it before Zoey had died; that she'd called Neil Hatfield the morning after Nell's impassioned visit and told him she didn't care about losing the ten thousand pounds, she just wanted it to be over.

'Oliver, you of all people know family has nothing to do with being related,' she said quietly. 'Your family is made up of the people you love. Richard's her family now.'

'I'd like to come to Vermont in the summer holidays, if that's OK,' Nell added tentatively. 'To see you and Florence and the boys. And maybe, in a couple of years, when I'm done with school, we could talk about colleges in America. I'll have enough money – I'll be able to do what I want. But right now, I need to stay in London. I need to be close to Mum. Richard's going to look after me.' She smiled ruefully. 'Well, we'll look after each other. As best we can.'

'And Richard's agreed?' Oliver demanded.

'It's all sorted.' She stood up and crouched down in front of him, taking his hands in hers. 'Please, can you try to understand? I don't want to hurt you, but I know where I am with Richard. He's been my father for eight years. I can't just leave him now.'

Harriet watched as Oliver took in the full consequences of that brief night in Maine with Zoey. He hadn't just destroyed his marriage – he'd alienated Nell; he'd lost Florence, at least for now. *He doesn't deserve this*, a voice inside her whispered. *Not for one mistake.*

The kitchen door slammed suddenly. Florence appeared in the doorway, her youngest brother in her arms. 'Dad, I think you'd better come and sort out Sam and George. Sam kicked the ball into someone's garden, and they won't stop arguing about it.'

'Can't Richard take care of it?' Oliver said irritably. 'We haven't finished our conversation with Nell.'

'We have,' Harriet smiled, standing up and giving Nell a hug. 'Richard needs you, of course he does, and you need to be with him. We'll only be a phone call away. And we'd love to have you over to visit, both of you, at Christmas or in the summer or whenever you want. And if things change later, you only have to ask. You know that.'

They went outside and stood on the pavement. Nell walked over to sit beside Richard on the wall, holding his hand, while Florence ran off to chivvy Sam and George, with Charlie bouncing excitedly up and down in her arms.

'Let me hail you a cab,' Oliver said stiffly, raising his hand. 'You don't need to be hauling the kids halfway across London on the Tube.'

'What are you going to do now?'

He shrugged. 'Don't worry about me. I'll figure it out.'

He was just going to let her go, Harriet thought, irrationally angry at the notion. But wasn't that what she wanted? Wasn't that what she'd asked for? She'd made it plain to him at every turn that he was no longer part of her future. *She'd* been the one to offer Nell a bald choice: come to Vermont with me, or stay in London with Oliver. He was the one who hadn't given up on them. *Harriet, say something. Tell her* we're *her family. She should be with* us.

He'd fight for Nell. But not for her.

'Fine,' she snapped, turning to scan the street for taxis. 'If that's what you want.'

He grabbed her arm, jerking her round to face him. 'Of course it's not what I *want*!' he cried. 'What I want to do is get in that cab with you, take the kids home, and know I still have a marriage and a life to get up for! You think I wanted *any* of this? Zoey's dead, Nell doesn't want me, you don't want me – what am I supposed

336

to do? Throw myself into my work? Live for alternate weekends when I can see the kids in a McDonald's halfway between my place and yours? Jesus, Harriet! You've broken my fucking heart!'

Her chest tightened painfully. 'What makes you think I don't want you?'

A taxi glided to the kerb beside them. 'Just a minute,' Oliver said to the cabbie.

'What makes you think I don't want you?' Harriet repeated.

His expression was suddenly wary. 'I think you've made that pretty damn clear.'

'I'm angry, Oliver! You had an *affair*!'

'And how do you know you *didn't*?'

'*Ben*? Really, that's your defence? Something I may or may not have done sixteen years ago, before we were even married! For God's sake, Oliver, even if I did, I didn't mean to!'

He laughed hollowly. 'Jesus, Harriet. Nor did I!'

The cabbie leaned on his horn. 'You want to go anywhere, mate, or not?'

'Can you just wait?' Oliver said impatiently. 'Start the meter. I'll pay.'

Harriet searched his face. She couldn't deny she loved this man, for everything he had ever been to her and everything he still could be. She understood the difference between love and sex. She knew it was deceit and betrayal that broke a marriage, not a brief coupling between the sheets, however passionate. And hadn't she been just as guilty of that as Oliver? Not just because of Ben,

337

whatever had or hadn't happened that night, but because she had lied and gone behind his back, telling herself it was for the best of reasons. She'd broken the trust between them just as much as he had.

Part of her had gone looking for Nell because she'd had an atavistic need to know the child she'd carried inside her for nine months was safe and happy. She'd realized that until she did, there'd be an invisible wall between her and Florence, the lie driving an ever broader wedge between them. But if she was truly honest with herself, it had been more than that. Oliver was right: she'd been looking to start over. To find the perfect daughter, to have another chance to be the perfect mother. Instead, she'd fallen in love with Nell, flawed as she was, the kind of daughter she'd never imagined having. And she'd understood that the daughter she'd wanted all along had been right there at home with her.

She acknowledged as she stood there that she'd wronged Oliver just as much as he'd wronged her. He'd been in the right as much as she had. So why was she finding it so hard to forgive him?

It wasn't anger or hurt pride that was holding her back from giving him a second chance. It was *fear*. Fear that he'd let her down again, of course, and hurt her a second time; but more than that, she was terrified of her own feelings. If she opened the door to him and finally allowed herself to be vulnerable, there'd be no going back.

'I love you, Oliver,' she said suddenly, her voice

shaking. 'You're my best friend. I can't picture a world without you. I can't be happy without you. Life without you wouldn't be living, but surviving. And the thought of that scares me fucking shitless.'

'Christ, Harriet,' he said, choking, pulling her into his arms. 'Christ. Of course. Of course it scares you fucking shitless. That's what love *does*.'

She pressed her head against the crisp white linen of his new shirt, bought especially for the funeral of his mistress, and breathed in the scent of laundered cotton and tea-tree shampoo and coffee, and something else that was uniquely Oliver. His arms tightened around her, and she fought the overwhelming urge to simply yield. How could she risk having him break her heart again? Yet how could she bear to give him up? How could she live without *this*?

'I don't know,' she whispered. 'I don't know if I can trust you again. I want to, Oliver. You have no idea how much I want to. I'm just not sure we can fix this now.'

'Can't we at least *try*?'

She pulled back, holding him at arm's length as she searched his face for answers. His sincerity was evident, but was it enough? The road to hell was paved with good intentions. He'd never *meant* to cheat on her with Zoey, but it'd happened. How could she be sure it wouldn't happen again? If she forgave him, wasn't she tacitly condoning his affair? Having got away with it once, would he think he could do it again?

Surely he couldn't be that stupid – or that cruel. He loved her, she knew he did. He wouldn't risk losing her again.

He risked it before, a voice whispered in her head. *You can't be sure he won't do it again.*

No. There were no guarantees. She had two choices. She could play it safe, walk away from him, raise the drawbridge, drop the portcullis. Or she could take a chance on the man she loved.

She gave him his answer.

'Yes,' she said. 'We can try.'